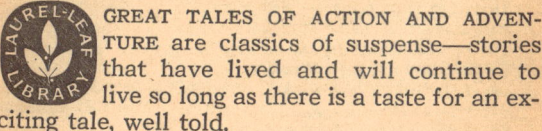 GREAT TALES OF ACTION AND ADVENTURE are classics of suspense—stories that have lived and will continue to live so long as there is a taste for an exciting tale, well told.

GEORGE BENNETT taught English at Phillips Exeter Academy for over thirty years and was chairman of the English Department 1959–1964. He also edited TURNING POINT: 14 Great Tales of Daring and Decision for Laurel-Leaf.

THE LAUREL-LEAF LIBRARY brings together under a single imprint outstanding works of fiction and nonfiction particularly suitable for young adult readers, both in and out of the classroom. This new series, under the editorship of M. Jerry Weiss, should also prove of great value to the general reader in search of knowledge, instruction and pleasure.

OTHER ANTHOLOGIES AVAILABLE IN THE LAUREL-LEAF LIBRARY:

AMERICANS ALL: *The Story of Our Latin American Neighbors,*
  edited by Benjamin Keen
ANIMAL STORIES, edited by Nell Murphy
CHUCKLEBAIT, edited by Margaret Scoggin
THE CRIME-SOLVERS: *13 Classic Detective Stories,*
  edited by Stewart H. Benedict
GREAT SCIENCE FICTION STORIES, edited by Cordelia Smith
GREAT TALES OF ACTION AND ADVENTURE, edited by George Bennett
INCREDIBLE TALES BY SAKI, edited by
  Richard Corbin and Ned E. Hoopes
A JESSE STUART HARVEST, by Jesse Stuart
A JOURNEY OF POEMS, edited by Richard Niebling
MAN AND WAR, edited by Jerry Weiss
PIONEERS WEST, edited by Don Ward
TALES OF TERROR AND SUSPENSE, edited by Stewart H. Benedict
TEN SHORT PLAYS, edited by M. Jerry Weiss
THREE ENGLISH COMEDIES: *She Stoops to Conquer, The Rivals,*
  and *School for Scandal,* edited by John Bettenbender
TURNING POINT: *14 Great Tales of Daring and Decision,*
  edited by George Bennett
THE WONDERFUL WORLD OF HORSES: *15 Superb Stories,*
  edited by Ned E. Hoopes

GREAT TALES OF ACTION AND ADVENTURE

Edited by George Bennett

Published by
DELL PUBLISHING CO., INC.
750 Third Avenue, New York, N.Y. 10017
Copyright © 1959, by George Bennett
Laurel ® TM 766734, Dell Publishing Co., Inc.
Cover painting by Richard Powers

First Dell printing—June, 1958	Sixth Dell printing—Jan., 1965
Second Dell printing—December, 1960	Seventh Dell printing—Nov., 1965
Third Dell printing—September, 1962	Eighth Dell printing—Sept., 1966
Fourth Dell printing—May, 1963	Ninth Dell printing—Dec., 1966
Fifth Dell printing—February, 1964	Tenth Dell printing—April, 1967

Eleventh Dell printing—November, 1967

Printed in U.S.A.

ACKNOWLEDGMENTS: The following selections in this anthology are reproduced by permission of the authors, their publishers or their agents:

"Action" by C. E. Montague, from *Action and Other Stories* by C. E. Montague, published by Chatto & Windus, Ltd., London. Reprinted by permission of Chatto & Windus, Ltd., and Mrs. C. E. Montague.

"The Adventure of the Dancing Men" by Arthur Conan Doyle, from *The Return of Sherlock Holmes* by Arthur Conan Doyle. Reprinted by permission of the Estate of the late Sir Arthur Conan Doyle.

"August Heat" by William Fryer Harvey, from the book *The Beast with Five Fingers* by William Fryer Harvey. Copyright, 1947, by E. P. Dutton & Co., Inc. Reprinted by permission of the publishers, E. P. Dutton & Co., Inc., and by J. M. Dent & Sons Ltd., London.

"The Bamboo Trap" by Robert S. Lemmon, from *Short Stories*, Vol. 103, No. 2, April 25, 1923. Copyright, 1923, by Doubleday, Page and Co. Copyright, 1950, by Short Stories, Inc. Reprinted by permission of the author.

"The Blue Cross" by G. K. Chesterton. Reprinted by permission of Dodd, Mead & Company from *The Innocence of Father Brown* by G. K. Chesterton. Copyright 1911 by Dodd, Mead & Company. Renewal copyright 1938 by Frances Chesterton. Also reprinted by permission of Miss D. E. Collins, of Cassell & Co. Ltd., London, and of A. P. Watt & Son, London.

"To Build a Fire" by Jack London, from *Lost Face* by Jack London. Copyright, 1910, by The Macmillan Company. Reprinted by permission of Irving Shepard.

"The Fourth Man" by John Russell. Copyright 1917 by P. F. Collier & Son. Reprinted by permission of Brandt & Brandt.

"The Interlopers" from *The Short Stories of Saki* by H. H. Munro. Copyright 1930 by The Viking Press, Inc. Reprinted by permission of The Viking Press, Inc., and Max Reinhardt Ltd., London.

"Leiningen versus the Ants" by Carl Stephenson. Copyright, 1938, by Carl Stephenson. Reprinted by arrangement with Ann Elmo.

"The Most Dangerous Game" by Richard Connell. Copyright 1924 by Richard Connell. Copyright renewed 1952 by Louise Fox Connell. Reprinted by permission of Brandt & Brandt.

"Rescue Party" by Arthur C. Clarke, from *Astounding Science Fiction*, copyright, 1946, by Smith and Smith Publications. Reprinted by permission of the author and the author's agents, Scott Meredith Literary Agency, Inc.

Contents

Introduction 6

The Bamboo Trap by Robert S. Lemmon 7

   Leiningen versus the Ants
      by Carl Stephenson 23

The Blue Cross by G. K. Chesterton 49

   The Most Dangerous Game
      by Richard Connell 71

The Fourth Man by John Russell 95

The Interlopers by "Saki" (H. H. Munro) 117

   The Adventure of the Dancing Men
      by Sir Arthur Conan Doyle 124

   The Pit and the Pendulum
      by Edgar Allan Poe 153

Rescue Party by Arthur C. Clarke 171

August Heat by William Fryer Harvey 203

To Build a Fire by Jack London 209

Action by C. E. Montague 228

Introduction

A surprising amount of literature appeals equally to young and old: from books like *Gulliver's Travels* to poems like Walter de la Mare's *The Listeners* and Robert Frost's *Stopping by Woods on a Snowy Evening*. To appeal to both young and old a story must have a special quality. Perhaps it is the quality of wonder, or of delight. It is as if we were in another dimension, as if we were looking at another world, a world both like and unlike our own, a world of surprise.

This is a collection of stories for readers of all ages. The older reader may experience the strangeness of reading again what he read a world ago, or he may find stories that he has missed. If you are a younger reader, begin with any one of the stories: a title may intrigue you or an opening catch your attention. You will probably like all the stories, for they were chosen by persons your own age. But though they were chosen by the young, they were not written just for the young. The stories in this collection are famous ones, and many are by writers whose work you will go on reading through the years.

This collection is only partly mine; it belongs also to countless students at Exeter and to my colleagues Paul Molloy, John Heath, William Bates, and Thomas Ragle.

GEORGE BENNETT

Phillips Exeter Academy
Exeter, New Hampshire

The Bamboo Trap

by Robert S. Lemmon

"A letter, *patrón*."

One corner of the mosquito bar that made of the tent fly an airy, four-walled room was lifted and a brown hand thrust in the envelope with its array of foreign postmarks and smudgy thumb-prints, all but concealing the familiar American stamp. Outside, the steady roar of the Chanchan River, softened by distance as it charged down the last pitches of the Andes on its way to the Gulf of Guayaquil and the Pacific, blended into a musical background for the messenger's guttural voice.

John Mather laid down the birdskin on which he was working and reached eagerly for the missive. Any word from the outside world was a godsend here in the jungle—doubly so when it came in the form of a letter whose bulk proclaimed several pages of home news. He ripped open the flap with dexterous, capable fingers and flattened the folded sheets on the camp table before him among the litter of skinning tools, cotton, and specimen labels.

For a space he read absorbedly, sensing behind the cold impersonality of the typewritten words the analytical mind of the man who had dictated them. Not until he came to the last page did his expression change and a half frown pucker the corners of his eyes.

"Hell!" he growled. "Isn't that the way of things? Just when I'm finishing up my collections here, too, and planning to catch the next steamer north. No Christmas at home this year! Let's see—how many of the damn things does he say he wants?" He re-read the final paragraphs of the letter, mumbling them half aloud in the manner of one in whom many years of living alone in the back of the world's beyond have bred the habit of self-conversation:

"The Department of Entomology is extremely desirous of securing several specimens of the Cuabandan spider, to complete their habitat group of insects* from the high Andes. It seems that the ones they intended to use proved to be rather poorly prepared and could not be mounted satisfactorily.

"Also, I am in receipt of a letter from the International Museum in Chicago offering to exchange a valuable collection of humming-bird skins from Guatemala for a complete series of these same spiders. You know how incomplete our Guatemalan material is, and therefore how anxious I am to secure these specimens from Dr. Huston. He asks that we furnish him with at least a dozen Cuabandans of both sexes, and perhaps twice that number of immature ones.

"You will find the spiders inhabiting the slopes of the mountain Chuquipata, probably between the 9,000- and 12,000-foot levels, although reliable data on this point is impossible for me to secure. The species is decidedly rare, and I can give you little information to help you in your search. Beyond their appearance and great size, with which you are perhaps familiar, and the fact that they are carnivorous and often prey upon small birds, nothing is really known of them. I shall depend upon you to remain in the region long enough to gain at least an outline of their life habits.

"I am sorry to have to give you this new assignment, Mather, because I judge from your last letter that you have about finished your field work on the west side of the mountains and are looking forward to your re-

* Probably an error by the author since spiders are not true insects. Editor's Note.

turn to New York. But I know that you will appreciate my position and postpone sailing for the few additional weeks which the Chuquipata expedition will entail.

All good wishes to you from myself and the Staff.

"Sincerely yours,
"ELIOT A. RODGERS,
"*Curator of Ornithology.*"

Mather folded the letter thoughtfully and thrust it into the pocket of his flannel shirt. With the buttoning down of the flap he seemed to dismiss his irritation and become again the seasoned museum collector, taking each task as it comes and subjugating all personal desires to the duties of his calling. As he turned again to the half-skinned bird before him he summoned his Indian guide and general assistant in the terse Spanish fashion, "Pedro—*ven aquí!*"

"*Ahora sí, patrón,*" sing-songed the Quichua from the cooking lean-to near by. "*Yo no más!*" In a moment he stood before the white man, a squat, stolid figure with the humble eyes of a whipped dog.

Mather snipped the wing bones of the bird close to the body and stripped the skin down the neck and over the skull to the eyes, turning it inside out skilfully. A few crunching clips with his scissors separated head from neck and exposed the base of the brain. He set the raw body aside and commenced scooping out the clotted, grayish matter from the interior of the skull.

As he worked he spoke pointedly. "You know Chuquipata, Pedro?"

A grunt and nod signified the Indian's assent. In the presence of the American his words were customarily few, a reticence inspired not so much by awe of his employer as by inherited fear of the whites handed down from the days of the first enslaving of his race by the Spanish *conquistadores* four centuries ago.

"Rough country, isn't it? *Muchas quebradas—no?*"

Another affirmative, more vehement this time. Then, "You not go there, *patrón?*"

Mather finished cleaning the birdskin, dusted its inner surface with arsenic and alum powder to cure and preserve it, and turned it right side out again.

"Yes, we go to Chuquipata in three days," he answered as he shook the ruffled feathers into place and began filling out the skin with cotton. "You will go to the village to-morrow and get *cargadores* to carry the outfit. Four good men I will need, Pedro. Or, if you can find them, two mules instead; pack animals are better than men, but there are not many to be had. See what you can do."

He dismissed the man with a wave of the hand, and tied an identifying label to the crossed feet of his specimen. As carefully as if it were of the most fragile and costly porcelain he wrapped the tiny green and yellow effigy of the bird in cotton to hold it in shape until feathers and skin should dry, and added it to the rows of similar mummies in the tray of his collector's trunk.

"That makes eight hundred from this region," he commented as he made the entry in a record book. "Not bad for three months' work, considering the weather I've had. It brings the total up to nearly two thousand for the whole trip, and several of the species are new to science, too. Well, I suppose I'll have to let it go at that and begin to get ready for this Chuquipata hike. It'll take nearly a day just to pick up my small mammal traps in the jungle around here."

Toward the southward end of that semi-arid plateau which stretches for three hundred rolling miles between the East and West Cordillera of the Ecuadorian Andes lies a land that God forgot. High in the air it is, as men measure such things—a matter of two vertical miles above the slow lift of the Pacific out beyond the sunset. Tumbled and stark too, a dumping ground of the Titans, a scrap heap from the furnaces in which the world was made. For in ages far beyond the memory of man, volcanic peaks whose summits have long been smoothed by the erosion of the centuries belched forth their hot lava and ash and laid a blight upon the land. Ravine, hillock, mountain, wind-swept, gaunt, and all but uninhabited, magnificent in the splendour of their distances—such is the setting of Chuquipata to-day, and such will it remain until Vulcan kindles his forge anew.

Up into this sky-top world John Mather rode on a day as glittering and telescopically clear overhead as it was harsh and dusty underfoot—up out of the green rankness of the coast jungles into a land of illimitable space. To the condor swinging a thousand feet in air, his pack-train seemed like ants crawling in single file across a rugged boulder.

Where a ravine gashed the side of Chuquipata he pitched camp on a little grassy flat protected on three sides by the crumbly walls of the cut, and braced his tent pegs with rocks against the tugging of a wind that pounced down in unexpected gusts. Scrubby brush and the stunted, gnarly trees of the high altitudes straggled here and there, promising firewood in limited and smoky quantities. A score of feet from the tent door a brooklet tinkled under overhanging wire grass, ice-cold and diamond-clear. And above it all, stupendous in miles of waving, yellowish *páramo,* dwarfing men and camp to pigmy size, the mountain swept up and up into a cap of clouds.

When the equipment was unloaded, Mather dismissed his packers and their two mules, for he had no way of telling how long his search for the giant spiders might last, and there was no point in feeding idle mouths week after week. Only Pedro he retained, to do the camp chores and leave him entirely free for his collecting work. Besides, the Indian would be useful when, at the end of the stay, new carriers would have to be secured from one of the villages a day's march away.

It was mid-afternoon before the camp was fully arranged and Mather set out for his first survey of the area he might have to cover as with a fine tooth comb. Hopeless enough it seemed, as he looked up at it from the ravine head, an appallingly vast and rugged haystack in which to search for one small needle. Were his quarry a bird that flew or an animal that ran, the task would not have looked so hopeless. But a spider, a crawling creature of the grass and brush, probably never coming into fair view—that was different.

He set to work methodically, covering every type of ground that lay between the points which his aneroid told him were eight and twelve thousand feet above the sea. Bunch grass, scrub, rocks, volcanic ash—he went over them all with keen and patient thoroughness but no success. Inquiries of Pedro and the occasional mountain Quichuas whom he met elicited no information of value; either his attempts to describe the creatures he sought were not understood, or the spiders were so rare that even the natives were unfamiliar with them. Evening after evening he returned wearily to camp, empty-handed save for a brace of mountain partridges or a few wild pigeons which he had shot for food, or the half-dozen smaller birds of which his collection stood in need.

"If I had only had some line on the habits of the beasts it would be easier," he mused as he ate his cornbread lunch one day beside a stream that plunged down the mountain far to the north of where his camp lay. "As a matter of fact, I don't know even whether they're day or night feeders. About the only thing I'm sure of is that they're not to be found on the south slope where I've been working. Pedro and I will have to move the outfit around to this side, I guess; the vegetation is quite different here—thicker and not so dried, as though it got more rain. I'll take a look down this spur and then work back around the base. There may be a good camp site down that way."

He picked up his gun and started to descend the ridge that dropped sharply toward a valley so far below that its brush and trees blended to a uniform sage-green carpet of marvellous softness. Rocks and beds of loose pumice that broke and slid treacherously as he crossed them covered the slope. He edged his way down cautiously, grasping the rare handholds of bush or tough grass, above him the blue spaces of the sky, the patchwork quilt of the world far-flung below.

A half-hour of this, and then the knife edge fanned out into a broader, easier descent across which trailing bamboo had spread an unbroken mat. As far as Mather could see on either side, and forward to the last steep pitch that dropped to the valley floor, that tangle of interlacing stems and off-shoots extended, three feet or so above the ground and in some places strong enough to support a man's full weight. Had a leafy cloth been woven to cover the mountain's bareness it could not have more perfectly concealed what lay beneath.

"I'm not very keen to tackle that," Mather muttered, halting at the edge of the tangle. "Too tough to smash through, and not quite tough enough to walk on—I've tried ground cane before."

He looked back at the pitch he had just descended and shook his head.

"About six of one and half a dozen of the other, I guess. Damned if I'll shin up that ridge again. Can't work around the edge of this bamboo, either—those cliffs block me off. Well, here goes for a bad two hours' work."

He took the shells out of his gun, slung the weapon on his back so as to leave both hands free, and started down, choosing what appeared to be the least rugged part of the slope.

It was rough going. On hands and knees he would crawl along for a few yards over the bamboo, then strike a weak spot and smash through to the ground in a smother of leaves and hampering tendrils, scramble out and go on. By the time he was half way to the bottom of the valley he was soaked with perspiration and nearly fagged out. Only his indomitable will and the knowledge that to turn back now would be doubly impossible kept him going.

It was nearly sunset when he reached a comparatively level stretch beyond which the mountain dropped away suddenly as though to make up for lost time. Across this place the cane was unusually thick, and he was getting along quite well, when, a few yards short of the steep slope the supporting mat broke with a ripping, tearing noise and he slithered down sickeningly into hot, pitchy darkness. Then a crunching jar, red lights flickering before his eyes, and unconsciousness.

How long he lay insensible he could not tell. It must have been many hours, for when he came to he was stiff and sore and the blood from a long scratch across his wrist had dried. A thousand tiny hammers seemed beating on his brain, each stroke an ache that quivered through a nerve. Dazedly he tried to sit up, failed, and lay flat on his back, hands clutching at the ground as he fought for control of his twitching eyes.

Gradually things steadied, and he saw that he was in a sort of pear-shaped cave perhaps a dozen yards in diameter and half as high. Daylight filtered through a ragged hole at its apex, pitifully weak, but enough to disclose the mingled rocks and earth that formed the walls of the enclosure and the whitish, diseased-looking vines that twined up them to the opening.

"That's where I fell through—that hole," Mather croaked. "Yes—that hole—fell through—yes, *fell through*. I've got to—get out—up there."

He wavered to his knees and waited grimly for the whirling in his head to abate.

"Now, let's—see," he whispered hoarsely, creeping toward the wall.

Twice he made the circuit of the cave, groping his way over boulders and loose débris that gave out a dank, nauseous odour. His hands pawed uncertainly at the walls, seeking firm holds, but finding nothing except the mass of vine stems, clammy and breaking at the first hard pull.

"Fool!" he growled at last. "I couldn't get up there anyway. It slopes in. A man can't climb on a ceiling. God!"

He slumped back and tried to think rationally.

"Let's see, now. I was coming down the mountain, headed west. The steepest part was just ahead of me when I fell—forty-five-degree slope, about. Not more than twenty feet or so away. This hole, now—yes, it's close to forty feet wide at the bottom—maybe five feet through to the face of the slant—"

He started up eagerly, the realization that he could burrow his way out clearing his brain and putting new life in his racked body. He reached for the sheath knife at his belt, the only digging tool he had. As he stood there with it in his hand a thought flashed over him that drove all the zest from his face.

"I don't know where to begin," he muttered. *"Which is the west side?"*

He looked about helplessly at the prison that hemmed him in. Somewhere, to right or left, ahead or behind, that mass of earth and rock must be comparatively thin, hardly more than a shell separating him from freedom and the broad reaches of the sky. If he could find that spot, strike that downhill side, he might be able to dig through to the outer world in a few hours. If he missed it, started work on the wrong side, his burrowing would only lead him deeper into the mountain, wasting his strength and the precious element of time. And between those two extremes, the heart-warming right and the hopelessly wrong, was no faintest clue to guide him to a decision. Yes, there was one—his compass, of course! Stupid not to have thought of that before; the surest possible proof. Everything was all right now.

He fumbled in the side pocket of his coat and drew out the instrument, a watchlike affair in a heavy nickel case. His first glance showed the needle bent crazily beneath the shattered glass, twisted and utterly ruined by the crash of his fall.

Mather's face went hard as he tilted the broken thing in his hand, testing its uselessness with a sort of grim irony.

"So-o," he said bitterly. "You're about as much good

to me as a piece of cheese, aren't you? Or a chunk of lead—because I could eat the cheese. Well, I guess I'll have to depend on Old Lady Luck to help me out. I may as well pick out a place that looks like easy digging, anyhow."

He stumbled across the cave and began to pick away at the wall where the earth was crumbly and yielded readily to knife and hands. A few inches in he struck rock. Working along it, he came finally to loose rubble, but the mass was too large for him to dislodge without starting a disastrous cave-in from above. He would have to try another place. And an hour had been wasted.

A second location was even less promising, but the third gave him hope. He burrowed on stubbornly, his fingers torn and bleeding from the sharp fragments of rock embedded in the soil like chips of glass, his muscles aching from their exertions in the cramped space which his progress created. Two feet, a yard—at this rate he ought to break through in a few more hours, unless he were working in the wrong direction. At thought of that contingency he redoubled his efforts, determined to end the uncertainty as soon as possible. And a few inches farther on he came squarely up against another boulder that defied every attempt to move it.

Exhausted and reeking with perspiration, he backed out of the hole and stretched full length on the floor of the cave. In a little while, when the cramps had left his back and shoulders, he would start in again. Yes, just a few minutes rest, and then—then he was roused from uneasy half-sleep by a slow, insistent rustling like a snake crawling through grass. He listened tensely, eyes closed in concentration, striving to locate its direction. The sound came closer, louder, on all sides of him, filling the cave with eerie whispers. Then suddenly it seemed to reach a focus close by, and a creeping hairy body brushed against his neck. With a leap he gained his feet, his eyes wide with horror.

The light in the cave had dimmed, but he could see

that the walls were alive with huge spiders, thick-legged and hideous, their bodies as large as a sparrow's and covered with straggly fuzz. Some were blackish in colour, others were a sort of cherry red. They were crawling sluggishly, as though gorged with food, down the vines that reached the opening above his head. A dozen had gained the floor, others were nearly there. Hundreds more were creeping in at the hole and groping for convenient stems down which to clamber.

With a shudder Mather knew—knew that here, in this dark prison, was the night shelter, the universal rendezvous, of the beasts he had come so far to catch. By day they hunted through the cane tangle that covered the mountainside, perfectly concealed and safe from all detection, and as night approached they convened here from all directions to take refuge from the rains which each night spilled across the land. They were gathering now, crawling, crawling with that infernal rustling sound—

"God!" he muttered. "And he said they were rare!" Full darkness came, bringing to John Mather the torture of eternal nightmare. With hands, coat, hat, he beat and crushed the furry hordes that swarmed over him. But for every one killed two more were ready to take its place; there seemed no end to their numbers. Their curved jaws clipped into him wherever his skin was exposed. Though he could see nothing in the pitchy darkness, an odour of decay told him that shreds of flesh from their victims of days before still clung to them, and the dread of blood-poisoning obsessed him. In a quiver of loathing and fear he fought on bitterly hour after hour, dropping into snatches of exhausted sleep only to struggle up again when the writhing burden on his face threatened to choke off his breath.

At last the blackness began to gray. Dawn was coming up over the mountains, and as the light strengthened, the spiders scattered, climbing the vines again to the open air and the sunshine. Singly and in battalions they went rank after rank up the stems of their living ladders. And as the last stragglers disappeared through the opening above him Mather sat with head sunk between his hands, fighting to retain a sanity that hung on the very edge of destruction.

It must have been midday before he pulled himself together enough to eat some of the emergency rations which were as much a part of his collecting outfit as his gun or butterfly net. The food helped to steady him, and presently he began moving about under the hole at the cave's peak, trying to determine the points of the compass by the appearance of the scraps of sky he could see through the openings in the bamboo. A few minutes' study convinced him of the hopelessness of this, for leaden clouds had blotted out the sun. So uniform was their mass that he could not even detect their own direction of movement, which, if he could have ascertained, would have served as a fairly accurate indication here in this land where the prevailing wind at the higher levels blows from the east.

"I'd better get back to my digging," he told himself finally. "It's the only chance, for Pedro would never find me among all those acres of cane, even if he knew enough to come this way to look. I didn't tell him which way I was going, when I left camp."

He groped his way into the tunnel he had started the day before and renewed his struggle with the rocks that blocked its end. He felt stronger now, and the physical work helped to shove into the background of his mind the horror that he knew the night would bring again. Perhaps he could break his way through before dark—a mere chance, but enough to add incentive to his labour.

By superhuman effort he worked out the largest rock at last, backed into the cave with it, and wriggled in again to the attack. Prying and digging with his knife, he burrowed on through earth that gave way more readily as he progressed. Sweat streamed from

The Bamboo Trap 19

him unheeded; with each foot that he advanced the air in the tunnel grew warmer. A nauseating, steamy odour crept into it, so faint at first as to defy analysis, but increasing momentarily.

Presently Mather drew his hand back with an exclamation of surprise. His fingers had touched a rock so hot that it almost burned them.

"What the hell?" he growled, then lay still, thinking, his chest heaving as he gasped for breath.

Crushingly the explanation came to him: The burrow was leading into the mountain, straight forward toward those infernal caverns of molten lava and steam which underlie that whole mighty continental backbone from Cape Horn to Panama. Already he had dug far enough through the mountain's outer shell to reach the heat that radiated from them.

Mather's heart sank with the realization that all his work had gone for nothing. Then a great wave of hope swept over him as the thought came that out of this very failure sprang success, for since he had been digging toward the mountain's centre, the opposite way must lead to light and life and freedom.

He wormed his way backward, gulping with relief as he reached the cooler air near the tunnel's mouth. A few more wriggles, and his knee struck something that crushed flabbily under the pressure. Across one hand dragged a fat, rough body, paused and sent a tingle of pain up his forearm as he shook it off with a jerk. The spider army had returned.

Through the endless hours of that second night of horror John Mather clung to two things with the desperation of a wave-buffeted man whose arm is crooked across a slippery, floating spar: the knowledge that daylight would bring relief from his tormentors, and the hope that before another evening drove them scurrying back to shelter he would have won his way through the cave wall. Every atom of will power, every drop of that fine essence of determination which some men call upon to carry them against impossible odds he threw into the mental struggle, knowing that to lose sight of his goal would mean gibbering madness.

And in the end he won. Taut and quivering as a plucked string, he sensed rather than saw that the crawling hosts were gone.

"Now!" he rasped, the sound of his own voice grating across his nerves. "Now you dig."

He hurled himself savagely into the work, slashing and tugging at the hard-packed earth and stone opposite the mass of débris he had scooped out the day before. His knife wedged between two rocks and the blade snapped short off as he tried to extricate it. He cursed chokingly and hacked away with the haft, pitifully futile by comparison.

"Got to make it!" he muttered. "Got to make it today! I'll go crazy—*crazy*, I tell you!"

Inch by inch, a foot, two feet, three, he won ahead through the darkness, driving his battered hands without mercy. Out there somewhere beyond that stubborn, unseen barrier against which he pressed were fresh air and the sane, unhampered sweep of God's world. Behind, unspeakable gloom and torture more horrible than death. He must, he must keep going!

It was nearly noon when he stopped from sheer inability to do more and slithered back into the cave for a few minutes' rest. For a moment he thought night was coming on, so dark was it as he emerged from the tunnel, but as he glanced up at the opening above his head he saw that the shadows came from masses of blue-black clouds that swirled together ominously and dropped lower even as he watched. A dull pulsing shook the air, as of huge drums thudding afar off. Lightning ripped across the clouds, so close that Mather heard its white-hot crackle an instant before the smash of the thunder beat against his brain. He threw an arm across his face to shut out the flash and what it revealed—thousands of noisome, hairy beasts

The Bamboo Trap

that came scuttling on fat legs through the opening to take refuge from the storm.

Then it rained. The heavens opened and crashed down. A torrent of mud and water poured through the cave roof, ripping the opening to twice its former size. Like a huge bucket the cave caught and held the flood. Momentarily the water rose—to Mather's ankles, his knees, his waist. The spiders struggled in it, dropping from walls and roof by dozens. They swarmed over him horribly as they fought with each other for safety on his body and head. He tried to brush them off, to drown them by sousing himself under the cascade that spilled down from above, but they clung to him like leeches.

The water was up to his chest, now. Presently he was swimming, his head a mass of spiders that thickened by the minute and nearly suffocated him. For an age he struggled, growing weaker and weaker, knowing that in the end he must sink under that chaotic mass. The thought of it nerved him to a few more feeble strokes, a final effort to rid his head of the clammy bodies. Then, miraculously, a clatter and splash of falling rocks and earth, a sucking sound as from a giant sluice pipe suddenly cleared, and his feet touched bottom.

He staggered blindly, trying to gain his balance on the uneven rocks. With arms arched he crushed and rubbed his head free of its loathsome blanket and saw that the water was but waist deep and falling rapidly. Through the lightening darkness he could make out the whirlpool which told where, at the end of the tunnel he had been digging, the wall had given way before the pressure from within. Even as he looked the last of the water swashed out, and stooping down, he caught a glimpse of daylight. On hands and knees he crept through the opening and emerged to the free sweep of the hills, soft and dripping and peaceful against the background of the retreating storm.

For minutes he lay there, a sodden, shaken figure,

looking out across that far-flung view with hollow eyes from which the stare of horror slowly faded. Then he got to his knees, his feet, and drew a great, shuddering breath. His eyes dropped to the slope immediately before him, strewn with scores of drowned spiders.

"Well," he said shakily, "it looks as though there are enough here for all the museums in the world. I'll make a good haul while I'm about it."

With swollen, bruised hands, he began gathering up the draggled bodies and piling them beside a rock.

Leiningen versus the Ants

by Carl Stephenson

"Unless they alter their course and there's no reason why they should, they'll reach your plantation in two days at the latest."

Leiningen sucked placidly at a cigar about the size of a corncob and for a few seconds gazed without answering at the agitated District Commissioner. Then he took the cigar from his lips, and leaned slightly forward. With his bristling grey hair, bulky nose, and lucid eyes, he had the look of an aging and shabby eagle.

"Decent of you," he murmured, "paddling all this way just to give me the tip. But you're pulling my leg of course when you say I must do a bunk. Why, even a herd of saurians couldn't drive me from this plantation of mine."

The Brazilian official threw up lean and lanky arms and clawed the air with wildly distended fingers. "Leiningen!" he shouted. "You're insane! They're not creatures you can fight—they're an elemental—an 'act of God!' Ten miles long, two miles wide—ants, nothing but ants! And every single one of them a fiend from hell; before you can spit three times they'll eat a full-grown buffalo to the bones. I tell you if you don't clear out at once there'll be nothing left of you but a skeleton picked as clean as your own plantation."

Leiningen grinned. "Act of God, my eye! Anyway, I'm not an old woman; I'm not going to run for it just because an elemental's on the way. And don't think

I'm the kind of fathead who tries to fend off lightning with his fists, either. I use my intelligence, old man. With me, the brain isn't a second blindgut; I know what it's there for. When I began this model farm and plantation three years ago, I took into account all that could conceivably happen to it. And now I'm ready for anything and everything—including your ants."

The Brazilian rose heavily to his feet. "I've done my best," he gasped. "Your obstinacy endangers not only yourself, but the lives of your four hundred workers. You don't know these ants!"

Leiningen accompanied him down to the river, where the Government launch was moored. The vessel cast off. As it moved downstream, the exclamation mark neared the rail and began waving its arms frantically. Long after the launch had disappeared round the bend, Leiningen thought he could still hear that dimming, imploring voice, "You don't know them, I tell you! *You don't know them!*"

But the reported enemy was by no means unfamiliar to the planter. Before he started work on his settlement, he had lived long enough in the country to see for himself the fearful devastations sometimes wrought by these ravenous insects in their campaigns for food. But since then he had planned measures of defence accordingly, and these, he was convinced, were in every way adequate to withstand the approaching peril.

Moreover, during his three years as a planter, Leiningen had met and defeated drought, flood, plague and all other "acts of God" which had come against him—unlike his fellow-settlers in the district, who had made little or no resistance. This unbroken success he attributed solely to the observance of his lifelong motto: *The human brain needs only to become fully aware of its powers to conquer even the elements.* Dullards reeled senselessly and aimlessly into the abyss; cranks, however brilliant, lost their heads when circumstances suddenly altered or accelerated and ran into stone walls, sluggards drifted with the current until they were caught in whirlpools and dragged under. But such disasters, Leiningen contended, merely strengthened his argument that intelligence, directed aright, invariably makes man the master of his fate.

Yes, Leiningen had always known how to grapple with life. Even here, in this Brazilian wilderness, his brain had triumphed over every difficulty and danger it had so far encountered. First he had vanquished primal forces by cunning and organization, then he had enlisted the resources of modern science to increase miraculously the yield of his plantation. And now he was sure he would prove more than a match for the "irresistible" ants.

That same evening, however, Leiningen assembled his workers. He had no intention of waiting till the news reached their ears from other sources. Most of them had been born in the district; the cry "The ants are coming!" was to them an imperative signal for instant, panic-stricken flight, a spring for life itself. But so great was the Indians' trust in Leiningen, in Leiningen's word, and in Leiningen's wisdom, that they received his curt tidings, and his orders for the imminent struggle, with the calmness with which they were given. They waited, unafraid, alert, as if for the beginning of a new game or hunt which he had just described to them. The ants were indeed mighty, but not so mighty as the boss. Let them come!

They came at noon the second day. Their approach was announced by the wild unrest of the horses, scarcely controllable now either in stall or under rider, scenting from afar a vapor instinct with horror.

It was announced by a stampede of animals, timid and savage, hurtling past each other; jaguars and pumas flashing by nimble stags of the pampas, bulky tapirs, no longer hunters, themselves hunted, outpacing fleet kinkajous, maddened herds of cattle, heads lowered, nostrils snorting, rushing through tribes of loping monkeys, chattering in a dementia of terror; then followed the creeping and springing denizens of bush and steppe, big and little rodents, snakes, and lizards.

Pell-mell the rabble swarmed down the hill to the plantation, scattered right and left before the barrier of the water-filled ditch, then sped onwards to the river, where, again hindered, they fled along its bank out of sight.

This water-filled ditch was one of the defence measures which Leiningen had long since prepared against the advent of the ants. It encompassed three sides of the plantation like a huge horseshoe. Twelve feet across, but not very deep, when dry it could hardly be described as an obstacle to either man or beast. But the ends of the "horseshoe" ran into the river which formed the northern boundary, and fourth side, of the plantation. And at the end nearer the house and outbuildings in the middle of the plantation, Leiningen had constructed a dam by means of which water from the river could be diverted into the ditch.

So now, by opening the dam, he was able to fling an imposing girdle of water, a huge quadrilateral with the river as its base, completely around the plantation, like the moat encircling a medieval city. Unless the ants were clever enough to build rafts, they had no hope of reaching the plantation, Leiningen concluded.

The twelve-foot water ditch seemed to afford in itself all the security needed. But while awaiting the arrival of the ants, Leiningen made a further improvement. The western section of the ditch ran along the edge of a tamarind wood, and the branches of some great trees reached over the water. Leiningen now had them lopped so that ants could not descend from them within the "moat."

The women and children, then the herds of cattle, were escorted by peons on rafts over the river, to remain on the other side in absolute safety until the plunderers had departed. Leiningen gave this instruction, not because he believed the non-combatants were in any danger, but in order to avoid hampering the efficiency of the defenders. "Critical situations first become crises," he explained to his men, "when oxen or women get excited."

Finally, he made a careful inspection of the "inner moat"—a smaller ditch lined with concrete, which extended around the hill on which stood the ranch house, barns, stables and other buildings. Into this concrete ditch emptied the inflow pipes from three great petrol tanks. If by some miracle the ants managed to cross the water and reached the plantation, this "rampart of petrol" would be an absolutely impassable protection for the beseiged and their dwellings and stock. Such, at least, was Leiningen's opinion.

He stationed his men at irregular distances along the water ditch, the first line of defence. Then he lay down in his hammock and puffed drowsily away at his pipe until a peon came with the report that the ants had been observed far away in the South.

Leiningen mounted his horse, which at the feel of its master seemed to forget its uneasiness, and rode leisurely in the direction of the threatening offensive. The southern stretch of ditch—the upper side of the quadrilateral—was nearly three miles long; from its center one could survey the entire countryside. This was destined to be the scene of the outbreak of war between Leiningen's brain and twenty square miles of life-destroying ants.

It was a sight one could never forget. Over the range of hills, as far as eye could see, crept a darkening hem, ever longer and broader, until the shadow spread across the slope from east to west, then downwards, downwards, uncannily swift, and all the green herbage of that wide vista was being mown as by a giant sickle, leaving only the vast moving shadow, extending, deepening, and moving rapidly nearer.

When Leiningen's men, behind their barrier of water, perceived the approach of the long-expected foe, they gave vent to their suspense in screams and imprecations. But as the distance began to lessen between the "sons of hell" and the water ditch, they relapsed into silence. Before the advance of that awe-inspiring throng, their belief in the powers of the boss began to steadily dwindle.

Even Leiningen himself, who had ridden up just in time to restore their loss of heart by a display of unshakable calm, even he could not free himself from a qualm of malaise. Yonder were thousands of millions of voracious jaws bearing down upon him and only a suddenly insignificant, narrow ditch lay between him and his men and being gnawed to the bones "before you can spit three times."

Hadn't this brain for once taken on more than it could manage? If the blighters decided to rush the ditch, fill it to the brim with their corpses, there'd still be more than enough to destroy every trace of that cranium of his. The planter's chin jutted; they hadn't got him yet, and he'd see to it they never would. While he could think at all, he'd flout both death and the devil.

The hostile army was approaching in perfect formation; no human battalions, however well-drilled, could ever hope to rival the precision of that advance. Along a front that moved forward as uniformly as a straight line, the ants drew nearer and nearer to the water ditch. Then, when they learned through their scouts the nature of the obstacle, the two outlying wings of the army detached themselves from the main body and marched down the western and eastern sides of the ditch.

This surrounding maneuver took rather more than an hour to accomplish; no doubt the ants expected that at some point they would find a crossing.

During this outflanking movement by the wings, the army on the center and southern front remained still. The besieged were therefore able to contemplate at their leisure the thumb-long, reddish black, long-legged insects; some of the Indians believed they could see,

Leiningen versus the Ants

too, intent on them, the brilliant, cold eyes, and the razor-edged mandibles, of this host of infinity.

It is not easy for the average person to imagine that an animal, not to mention an insect, can *think*. But now both the European brain of Leiningen and the primitive brains of the Indians began to stir with the unpleasant foreboding that inside every single one of that deluge of insects dwelt a thought. And that thought was: Ditch or no ditch, we'll get to your flesh!

Not until four o'clock did the wings reach the "horseshoe" ends of the ditch, only to find these ran into the great river. Through some kind of secret telegraphy, the report must then have flashed very swiftly indeed along the entire enemy line. And Leiningen, riding— no longer casually—along his side of the ditch, noticed by energetic and widespread movements of troops that for some unknown reason the news of the check had its greatest effect on the southern front, where the main army was massed. Perhaps the failure to find a way over the ditch was persuading the ants to withdraw from the plantation in search of spoils more easily attainable.

An immense flood of ants, about a hundred yards in width, was pouring in a glimmering-black cataract down the far slope of the ditch. Many thousands were already drowning in the sluggish creeping flow, but they were followed by troop after troop, who clambered over their sinking comrades, and then themselves served as dying bridges to the reserves hurrying on in their rear.

Shoals of ants were being carried away by the current into the middle of the ditch, where gradually they broke asunder and then, exhausted by their struggles, vanished below the surface. Nevertheless, the wavering, floundering hundred-yard front was remorselessly if slowly advancing towards the beseiged on the other bank. Leiningen had been wrong when he supposed the enemy would first have to fill the ditch with their bodies before they could cross; instead, they merely needed to act as stepping-stones, as they swam and sank, to the hordes ever pressing onwards from behind.

Near Leiningen a few mounted herdsmen awaited his orders. He sent one to the weir—the river must be dammed more strongly to increase the speed and power of the water coursing through the ditch.

A second peon was dispatched to the outhouses to bring spades and petrol sprinklers. A third rode away to summon to the zone of the offensive all the men, except the observation posts, on the near-by sections of the ditch, which were not yet actively threatened.

The ants were getting across far more quickly than Leiningen would have deemed possible. Impelled by the mighty cascade behind them, they struggled nearer and nearer to the inner bank. The momentum of the attack was so great that neither the tardy flow of the stream nor its downward pull could exert its proper force; and into the gap left by every submerging insect, hastened forward a dozen more.

When reinforcements reached Leiningen, the invaders were halfway over. The planter had to admit to himself that it was only by a stroke of luck for him that the ants were attempting the crossing on a relatively short front: had they assaulted simultaneously along the entire length of the ditch, the outlook for the defenders would have been black indeed.

Even as it was, it could hardly be described as rosy, though the planter seemed quite unaware that death in a gruesome form was drawing closer and closer. As the war between his brain and the "act of God" reached its climax, the very shadow of annihilation began to pale to Leiningen, who now felt like a champion in a new Olympic game, a gigantic and thrilling contest, from which he was determined to emerge victor. Such, indeed, was his aura of confidence that the Indians forgot their stupefied fear of the peril only a yard or two away; under the planter's supervision, they began fervidly digging up to the edge of the bank and throwing clods of earth and spadefuls of sand into the midst of the hostile fleet.

The petrol sprinklers, hitherto used to destroy pests and blights on the plantation, were also brought into action. Streams of evil-reeking oil now soared and fell over an enemy already in disorder through the bombardment of earth and sand.

The ants responded to these vigorous and successful measures of defence by further developments of their offensive. Entire clumps of huddling insects began to roll down the opposite bank into the water. At the same time, Leiningen noticed that the ants were now attacking along an ever-widening front. As the numbers both of his men and his petrol sprinklers were severely limited, this rapid extension of the line of battle was becoming an overwhelming danger.

To add to his difficulties, the very clods of earth they flung into that black floating carpet often whirled fragments toward the defenders' side, and here and there dark ribbons were already mounting the inner bank. True, wherever a man saw these they could still be driven back into the water by spadefuls of earth or jets of petrol. But the file of defenders was too sparse and scattered to hold off at all points these landing parties, and though the peons toiled like madmen, their plight became momentarily more perilous.

One man struck with his spade at an enemy clump, did not draw it back quickly enough from the water; in a trice the wooden haft swarmed with upward scurrying insects. With a curse, he dropped the spade into the ditch; too late, they were already on his body. They lost no time; wherever they encountered bare flesh they bit deeply; a few, bigger than the rest, carried in their hind-quarters a sting which injected a burning and paralyzing venom. Screaming, frantic with pain, the peon danced and twirled like a dervish.

Realizing that another such casualty, yes, perhaps this alone, might plunge his men into confusion and destroy their morale, Leiningen roared in a bellow louder than the yells of the victim: "Into the petrol, idiot! Douse your paws in the petrol!" The dervish ceased his pirouette as if transfixed, then tore off his shirt and plunged his arm and the ants hanging to it up to the shoulder in one of the large open tins of petrol. But even then the fierce mandibles did not slacken; another peon had to help him squash and detach each separate insect.

Distracted by the episode, some defenders had turned away from the ditch. And now cries of fury, a thudding of spades, and a wild trampling to and fro, showed that the ants had made full use of the interval, though luckily only a few had managed to get across. The men set to work again desperately with the barrage of earth and sand. Meanwhile an old Indian, who acted as medicine-man to the plantation workers, gave the bitten peon a drink he had prepared some hours before, which, he claimed, possessed the virtue of dissolving and weakening ants' venom.

Leiningen surveyed his position. A dispassionate observer would have estimated the odds against him at a thousand to one. But then such an onlooker would have reckoned only by what he saw—the advance of myriad battalions of ants against the futile efforts of a few defenders—and not by the unseen activity that can go on in a man's brain.

For Leiningen had not erred when he decided he would fight elemental with elemental. The water in the ditch was beginning to rise; the stronger damming of the river was making itself apparent.

Visibly the swiftness and power of the masses of water increased, swirling into quicker and quicker movement its living black surface, dispersing its pattern, carrying away more and more of it on the hastening current.

Victory had been snatched from the very jaws of defeat. With a hysterical shout of joy, the peons feverishly intensified their bombardment of earth clods and sand.

Leiningen versus the Ants

And now the wide cataract down the opposite bank was thinning and ceasing, as if the ants were becoming aware that they could not attain their aim. They were scurrying back up the slope to safety.

All the troops so far hurled into the ditch had been sacrificed in vain. Drowned and floundering insects eddied in thousands along the flow, while Indians running on the bank destroyed every swimmer that reached the side.

Not until the ditch curved towards the east did the scattered ranks assemble again in a coherent mass. And now, exhausted and half-numbed, they were in no condition to ascend the bank. Fusillades of clods drove them round the bend towards the mouth of the ditch and then into the river, wherein they vanished without leaving a trace.

The news ran swiftly along the entire chain of outposts, and soon a long scattered line of laughing men could be seen hastening along the ditch towards the scene of victory.

For once they seemed to have lost all their native reserve, for it was in wild abandon now they celebrated the triumph—as if there were no longer thousands of millions of merciless, cold and hungry eyes watching them from the opposite bank, watching and waiting.

The sun sank behind the rim of the tamarind wood and twilight deepened into night. It was not only hoped but expected that the ants would remain quiet until dawn. But to defeat any forlorn attempt at a crossing, the flow of water through the ditch was powerfully increased by opening the dam still further.

In spite of this impregnable barrier, Leiningen was not yet altogether convinced that the ants would not venture another surprise attack. He ordered his men to camp along the bank overnight. He also detailed parties of them to patrol the ditch in two of his motor cars and ceaselessly to illuminate the surface of the water with headlights and electric torches.

After having taken all the precautions he deemed

necessary, the farmer ate his supper with considerable appetite and went to bed. His slumbers were in no wise disturbed by the memory of the waiting, live, twenty square miles.

Dawn found a thoroughly refreshed and active Leiningen riding along the edge of the ditch. The planter saw before him a motionless and unaltered throng of beseigers. He studied the wide belt of water between them and the plantation, and for a moment almost regretted that the fight had ended so soon and so simply. In the comforting, matter-of-fact light of morning, it seemed to him now that the ants hadn't the ghost of a chance to cross the ditch. Even if they plunged headlong into it on all three fronts at once, the force of the now powerful current would inevitably sweep them away. He had got quite a thrill out of the fight—a pity it was already over.

He rode along the eastern and southern sections of the ditch and found everything in order. He reached the western section, opposite the tamarind wood, and here, contrary to the other battle fronts, he found the enemy very busy indeed. The trunks and branches of the trees and the creepers of the lianas, on the far bank of the ditch, fairly swarmed with industrious insects. But instead of eating the leaves there and then, they were merely gnawing through the stalks, so that a thick green shower fell steadily to the ground.

No doubt they were victualing columns sent out to obtain provender for the rest of the army. The discovery did not surprise Leiningen. He did not need to be told that ants are intelligent, that certain species even use others as milch cows, watchdogs and slaves. He was well aware of their power of adaptation, their sense of discipline, their marvelous talent for organization.

His belief that a foray to supply the army was in progress was strengthened when he saw the leaves that fell to the ground being dragged to the troops waiting

Leiningen versus the Ants

outside the wood. Then all at once he realized the aim that rain of green was intended to serve.

Each single leaf, pulled or pushed by dozens of toiling insects, was borne straight to the edge of the ditch. Even as Macbeth watched the approach of Birnam Wood in the hands of his enemies, Leiningen saw the tamarind wood move nearer and nearer in the mandibles of the ants. Unlike the fey Scot, however, he did not lose his nerve; no witches had prophesied his doom, and if they had he would have slept just as soundly. All the same, he was forced to admit to himself that the situation was far more ominous than that of the day before.

He had thought it impossible for the ants to build rafts for themselves—well, here they were, coming in thousands, more than enough to bridge the ditch. Leaves after leaves rustled down the slope into the water, where the current drew them away from the bank and carried them into midstream. And every single leaf carried several ants. This time the farmer did not trust to the alacrity of his messengers. He galloped away, leaning from his saddle and yelling orders as he rushed past outpost after outpost: "Bring petrol pumps to the southwest front! Issue spades to every man along the line facing the wood!" And arrived at the eastern and southern sections, he dispatched every man except the observation posts to the menaced west.

Then, as he rode past the stretch where the ants had failed to cross the day before, he witnessed a brief but impressive scene. Down the slope of the distant hill there came towards him a singular being, writhing rather than running, an animal-like blackened statue with shapeless head and four quivering feet that knuckled under almost ceaselessly. When the creature reached the far bank of the ditch and collapsed opposite Leiningen, he recognized it as a pampas stag, covered over and over with ants.

It had strayed near the zone of the army. As usual, they had attacked its eyes first. Blinded, it had reeled in the madness of hideous torment straight into the ranks of its persecutors, and now the beast swayed to and fro in its death agony.

With a shot from his rifle Leiningen put it out of its misery. Then he pulled out his watch. He hadn't a second to lose, but for life itself he could not have denied his curiosity the satisfaction of knowing how long the ants would take—for personal reasons, so to speak. After six minutes the white polished bones alone remained. That's how he himself would look before you can—Leiningen spat once, and put spurs to his horse.

The sporting zest with which the excitement of the novel contest had inspired him the day before had now vanished; in its place was a cold and violent purpose. He would send these vermin back to the hell where they belonged, somehow, anyhow. Yes, but how was indeed the question; as things stood at present it looked as if the devils would raze him and his men from the earth instead. He had underestimated the might of the enemy; he really would have to bestir himself if he hoped to outwit them.

The biggest danger now, he decided, was the point where the western section of the ditch curved southwards. And arrived there, he found his worst expectations justified. The very power of the current had huddled the leaves and their crews of ants so close together at the bend that the bridge was almost ready.

True, streams of petrol and clumps of earth still prevented a landing. But the number of floating leaves was increasing ever more swiftly. It could not be long now before a stretch of water a mile in length was decked by a green pontoon over which the ants could rush in millions.

Leiningen galloped to the weir. The damming of the river was controlled by a wheel on its bank. The planter ordered the man at the wheel first to lower the water in the ditch almost to vanishing point, next to wait a moment, then suddenly to let the river in again. This maneuver of lowering and raising the surface, of decreasing then increasing the flow of water through the ditch was to be repeated over and over again until further notice.

This tactic was at first successful. The water in the ditch sank, and with it the film of leaves. The green fleet nearly reached the bed and the troops on the far bank swarmed down the slope to it. Then a violent flow of water at the original depth raced through the ditch, overwhelming leaves and ants, and sweeping them along.

This intermittent rapid flushing prevented just in time the almost completed fording of the ditch. But it also flung here and there squads of the enemy vanguard simultaneously up the inner bank. These seemed to know their duty only too well, and lost no time accomplishing it. The air rang with the curses of bitten Indians. They had removed their shirts and pants to detect the quicker the upwards-hastening insects; when they saw one, they crushed it; and fortunately the onslaught as yet was only by skirmishers.

Again and again, the water sank and rose, carrying leaves and drowned ants away with it. It lowered once more nearly to its bed; but this time the exhausted defenders waited in vain for the flush of destruction. Leiningen sensed disaster; something must have gone wrong with the machinery of the dam. Then a sweating peon tore up to him—

"They're over!"

While the besieged were concentrating upon the defence of the stretch opposite the wood, the seemingly unaffected line beyond the wood had become the theatre of decisive action. Here the defenders' front was sparse and scattered; everyone who could be spared had hurried away to the south.

Just as the man at the weir had lowered the water almost to the bed of the ditch, the ants on a wide front began another attempt at a direct crossing like that of the preceding day. Into the emptied bed poured an irresistible throng. Rushing across the ditch, they attained the inner bank before the slow-witted Indians fully grasped the situation. Their frantic screams dumfounded the man at the weir. Before he could direct the river anew into the safeguarding bed he saw himself surounded by raging ants. He ran like the others, ran for his life.

When Leiningen heard this, he knew the plantation was doomed. He wasted no time bemoaning the inevitable. For as long as there was the slightest chance of success, he had stood his ground, and now any further resistance was both useless and dangerous. He fired three revolver shots into the air—the prearranged signal for his men to retreat instantly within the "inner moat." Then he rode towards the ranch house.

This was two miles from the point of invasion. There was therefore time enough to prepare the second line of defence against the advent of the ants. Of the three great petrol cisterns near the house, one had already been half emptied by the constant withdrawals needed for the pumps during the fight at the water ditch. The remaining petrol in it was now drawn off through underground pipes into the concrete trench which encircled the ranch house and its outbuildings.

And there, drifting in twos and threes, Leiningen's men reached him. Most of them were obviously trying to preserve an air of calm and indifference, belied, however, by their restless glances and knitted brows. One could see their belief in a favorable outcome of the struggle was already considerably shaken.

The planter called his peons around him.

"Well, lads," he began, "we've lost the first round. But we'll smash the beggers yet, don't you worry. Anyone who thinks otherwise can draw his pay here and now and push off. There are rafts enough and to spare on the river and plenty of time still to reach 'em."

Not a man stirred.

Leiningen acknowledged his silent vote of confidence with a laugh that was half a grunt. "That's the stuff, lads. Too bad if you'd missed the rest of the show, eh? Well, the fun won't start till morning. Once these blighters turn tail, there'll be plenty of work for everyone and higher wages all round. And now run along and get something to eat; you've earned it all right."

In the excitement of the fight the greater part of the day had passed without the men once pausing to snatch a bite. Now that the ants were for the time being out of sight, and the "wall of petrol" gave a stronger feeling of security, hungry stomachs began to assert their claims.

The bridges over the concrete ditch were removed. Here and there solitary ants had reached the ditch; they gazed at the petrol meditatively, then scurried back again. Apparently they had little interest at the moment for what lay beyond the evil-reeking barrier; the abundant spoils of the plantation were the main attraction. Soon the trees, shrubs and beds for miles around were hulled with ants zealously gobbling the yield of long weary months of strenuous toil.

As twilight began to fall, a cordon of ants marched around the petrol trench, but as yet made no move towards its brink. Leiningen posted sentries with headlights and electric torches, then withdrew to his office, and began to reckon up his losses. He estimated these as large, but, in comparison with his bank balance, by no means unbearable. He worked out in some detail a scheme of intensive cultivation which would enable him, before very long, to more than compensate himself for the damage now being wrought to his crops. It was with a contented mind that he finally betook himself to bed where he slept deeply until dawn, undisturbed by any thought that next day little more might be left of him than a glistening skeleton.

He rose with the sun and went out on the flat roof of his house. And a scene like one from Dante lay around him; for miles in every direction there was nothing but a black, glittering multitude, a multitude of rested, sated, but none the less voracious ants: yes, look as far as one might, one could see nothing but that rustling black throng, except in the north, where the great river drew a boundary they could not hope to pass. But even the high stone breakwater, along the bank of the river, which Leiningen had built as a defence against inundations, was, like the paths, the shorn trees and shrubs, the ground itself, black with ants.

So their greed was not glutted in razing that vast plantation? Not by a long chalk; they were all the more eager now on a rich and certain booty—four hundred men, numerous horses, and bursting granaries.

At first it seemed that the petrol trench would serve its purpose. The besiegers sensed the peril of swimming it, and made no move to plunge blindly over its brink. Instead they devised a better maneuver; they began to collect shreds of bark, twigs and dried leaves and dropped these into the petrol. Everything green, which could have been similarly used, had long since been eaten. After a time, though, a long procession could be seen bringing from the west the tamarind leaves used as rafts the day before.

Since the petrol, unlike the water in the outer ditch, was perfectly still, the refuse stayed where it was thrown. It was several hours before the ants succeeded in covering an appreciable part of the surface. At length, however, they were ready to proceed to a direct attack.

Their storm troops swarmed down the concrete side, scrambled over the supporting surface of twigs and leaves, and impelled these over the few remaining streaks of open petrol until they reached the other side. Then they began to climb up this to make straight for the helpless garrison.

During the entire offensive, the planter sat peacefully, watching them with interest, but not stirring a muscle. Moreover, he had ordered his men not to disturb in any way whatever the advancing horde. So they

Leiningen versus the Ants

squatted listlessly along the bank of the ditch and waited for a sign from the boss.

The petrol was now covered with ants. A few had climbed the inner concrete wall and were scurrying towards the defenders.

"Everyone back from the ditch!" roared Leiningen. The men rushed away, without the slightest idea of his plan. He stooped forward and cautiously dropped into the ditch a stone which split the floating carpet and its living freight, to reveal a gleaming patch of petrol. A match spurted, sank down to the oily surface—Leiningen sprang back; in a flash a towering rampart of fire encompassed the garrison.

This spectacular and instant repulse threw the Indians into ecstasy. They applauded, yelled and stamped, like children at a pantomime. Had it not been for the awe in which they held the boss, they would infallibly have carried him shoulder high.

It was some time before the petrol burned down to the bed of the ditch, and the wall of smoke and flame began to lower. The ants had retreated in a wide circle from the devastation, and innumerable charred fragments along the outer bank showed that the flames had spread from the holocaust in the ditch well into the ranks beyond, where they had wrought havoc far and wide.

Yet the perseverance of the ants was by no means broken; indeed, each setback seemed only to whet it. The concrete cooled, the flicker of the dying flames wavered and vanished, petrol from the second tank poured into the trench—and the ants marched forward anew to the attack.

The foregoing scene repeated itself in every detail, except that on this occasion less time was needed to bridge the ditch, for the petrol was now already filmed by a layer of ash. Once again they withdrew; once again petrol flowed into the ditch. Would the creatures never learn that their self-sacrifice was utterly senseless? It really was senseless, wasn't it? Yes, of course it was senseless—provided the defenders had an *unlimited* supply of petrol.

When Leiningen reached this stage of reasoning, he felt for the first time since the arrival of the ants that his confidence was deserting him. His skin began to creep; he loosened his collar. Once the devils were over the trench there wasn't a chance in hell for him and his men. God, what a prospect, to be eaten alive like that!

For the third time the flames immolated the attacking troops, and burned down to extinction. Yet the ants were coming on again as if nothing had happened. And meanwhile Leiningen had made a discovery that chilled him to the bone—petrol was no longer flowing into the ditch. Something must be blocking the outflow pipe of the third and last cistern—a snake or a dead rat? Whatever it was, the ants could be held off no longer, unless petrol could by some method be led from the cistern into the ditch.

Then Leiningen remembered that in an outhouse nearby were two old disused fire engines. Spry as never before in their lives, the peons dragged them out of the shed, connected their pumps to the cistern, uncoiled and laid the hose. They were just in time to aim a stream of petrol at a column of ants that had already crossed and drive them back down the incline into the ditch. Once more an oily girdle surrounded the garrison, once more it was possible to hold the position—for the moment.

It was obvious, however, that this last resource meant only the postponement of defeat and death. A few of the peons fell on their knees and began to pray; others, shrieking insanely, fired their revolvers at the black, advancing masses, as if they felt their despair was pitiful enough to sway fate itself to mercy.

At length, two of the men's nerves broke: Leiningen saw a naked Indian leap over the north side of the petrol trench, quickly followed by a second. They sprinted with incredible speed towards the river. But their fleetness did not save them; long before they could attain the rafts, the enemy covered their bodies from head to foot.

In the agony of their torment, both sprang blindly into the wide river, where enemies no less sinister awaited them. Wild screams of mortal anguish informed the breathless onlookers that crocodiles and sword-toothed piranhas were no less ravenous than ants, and even nimbler in reaching their prey.

In spite of this bloody warning, more and more men showed they were making up their minds to run the blockade. Anything, even a fight midstream against alligators, seemed better than powerlessly waiting for death to come and slowly consume their living bodies.

Leiningen flogged his brain till it reeled. Was there nothing on earth could sweep this devil's spawn back into the hell from which it came?

Then out of the inferno of his bewilderment rose a terrifying inspiration. Yes, one hope remained, and one alone. It might be possible to dam the great river completely, so that its waters would fill not only the water ditch but overflow into the entire gigantic "saucer" of land in which lay the plantation.

The far bank of the river was too high for the waters to escape that way. The stone breakwater ran between the river and the plantation; its only gaps occurred where the "horseshoe" ends of the water-ditch passed into the river. So its waters would not only be forced to inundate into the plantation, they would also be held there by the breakwater until they rose to its own high level. In half an hour, perhaps even earlier, the plantation and its hostile army of occupation would be flooded.

The ranch house and outbuildings stood upon rising ground. Their foundations were higher than the breakwater, so the flood would not reach them. And any remaining ants trying to ascend the slope could be repulsed by petrol.

It was possible—yes, if one could only get to the dam!

A distance of nearly two miles lay between the ranch house and the weir—two miles of ants. Those two peons had managed only a fifth of that distance at the cost of their lives. Was there an Indian daring enough after that to run the gauntlet five times as far? Hardly likely; and if there were, his prospect of getting back was almost nil.

No, there was only one thing for it, he'd have to make the attempt himself; he might just as well be running as sitting still, anyway, when the ants finally got him. Besides, there was a bit of a chance. Perhaps the ants weren't so almighty, after all; perhaps he had allowed the mass suggestion of that evil black throng to hypnotize him, just as a snake fascinates and overpowers.

The ants were building their bridges. Leiningen got up on a chair. "Hey, lads, listen to me!" he cried. Slowly and listlessly, from all sides of the trench, the men began to shuffle towards him, the apathy of death already stamped on their faces.

"Listen, lads!" he shouted. "You're frightened of those beggars, but you're a damn sight more frightened of me, and I'm proud of you. There's still a chance to save our lives—by flooding the plantation from the river. Now one of you might manage to get as far as the weir—but he'd never come back. Well, I'm not going to let you try it; if I did I'd be worse than one of those ants. No, I called the tune, and now I'm going to pay the piper.

"The moment I'm over the ditch, set fire to the petrol. That'll allow time for the flood to do the trick. Then all you have to do is wait here all snug and quiet till I'm back. Yes, I'm coming back, trust me"—he grinned—"when I've finished my slimming-cure."

He pulled on high leather boots, drew heavy gauntlets over his hands, and stuffed the spaces between breeches and boots, gauntlets and arms, shirt and neck, with rags soaked in petrol. With close-fitting mosquito goggles he shielded his eyes, knowing too well the ants' dodge of first robbing their victim of sight. Finally, he plugged his nostrils and ears with cotton-wool, and let the peons drench his clothes with petrol.

He was about to set off, when the old Indian medicine man came up to him; he had a wondrous salve, he said, prepared from a species of chafer whose odor was intolerable to ants. Yes, this odor protected these chafers from the attacks of even the most murderous ants. The Indian smeared the boss' boots, his gauntlets, and his face over and over with the extract.

Leiningen then remembered the paralyzing effect of ants' venom, and the Indian gave him a gourd full of the medicine he had administered to the bitten peon at the water ditch. The planter drank it down without noticing its bitter taste; his mind was already at the weir.

He started off towards the northwest corner of the trench. With a bound he was over—and among the ants.

The beleaguered garrison had no opportunity to watch Leiningen's race against death. The ants were climbing the inner bank again—the lurid ring of petrol blazed aloft. For the fourth time that day the reflection from the fire shone on the sweating faces of the imprisoned men, and on the reddish-black cuirasses of their oppressors. The red and blue, dark-edged flames leaped vividly now, celebrating what? The funeral pyre of the four hundred, or of the hosts of destruction?

Leiningen ran. He ran in long, equal strides, with only one thought, one sensation, in his being—he *must* get through. He dodged all trees and shrubs; except for the split seconds his soles touched the ground the ants should have no opportunity to alight on him. That they would get to him soon, despite the salve on his boots, the petrol in his clothes, he realized only too well, but he knew even more surely that he must, and that he would, get to the weir.

Apparently the salve was some use after all; not until

he reached halfway did he feel ants under his clothes, and a few on his face. Mechanically, in his stride, he struck at them, scarcely conscious of their bites. He saw he was drawing appreciably nearer the weir—the distance grew less and less—sank to five hundred—three—two—one hundred yards.

Then he was at the weir and gripping the ant-hulled wheel. Hardly had he seized it when a horde of infuriated ants flowed over his hands, arms and shoulders. He started the wheel—before it turned once on its axis the swarm covered his face. Leiningen strained like a madman, his lips pressed tight; if he opened them to draw breath. . . .

He turned and turned; slowly the dam lowered until it reached the bed of the river. Already the water was overflowing the ditch. Another minute, and the river was pouring through the near-by gap in the breakwater. The flooding of the plantation had begun.

Leiningen let go the wheel. Now, for the first time, he realized he was coated from head to foot with a layer of ants. In spite of the petrol, his clothes were full of them, several had got to his body or were clinging to his face. Now that he had completed his task, he felt the smart raging over his flesh from the bites of sawing and piercing insects.

Frantic with pain, he almost plunged into the river. To be ripped and splashed to shreds by piranhas? Already he was running the return journey, knocking ants from his gloves and jacket, brushing them from his bloodied face, squashing them to death under his clothes.

One of the creatures bit him just below the rim of his goggles; he managed to tear it away, but the agony of the bite and its etching acid drilled into the eye nerves; he saw now through circles of fire into a milky mist, then he ran for a time almost blinded, knowing that if he once tripped and fell. . . . The old Indian's brew didn't seem much good; it weakened the poison a bit, but didn't get rid of it. His heart pounded as if it would burst; blood roared in his ears; a giant's fist battered his lungs.

Then he could see again, but the burning girdle of petrol appeared infinitely far away; he could not last half that distance. Swift-changing pictures flashed through his head, episodes in his life, while in another part of his brain a cool and impartial onlooker informed this ant-blurred, gasping, exhausted bundle named Leiningen that such a rushing panorama of scenes from one's past is seen only in the moment before death.

A stone in the path . . . too weak to avoid it . . . the planter stumbled and collapsed. He tried to rise . . . he must be pinned under a rock . . . it was impossible . . . the slightest movement was impossible. . . .

Then all at once he saw, starkly clear and huge, and, right before his eyes, furred with ants, towering and swaying in its death agony, the pampas stag. In six minutes—gnawed to the bones. God, he *couldn't* die like that! And something outside him seemed to drag him to his feet. He tottered. He began to stagger forward again.

Through the blazing ring hurtled an apparition which, as soon as it reached the ground on the inner side, fell full length and did not move. Leiningen, at the moment he made that leap through the flames, lost consciousness for the first time in his life. As he lay there, with glazing eyes and lacerated face, he appeared a man returned from the grave. The peons rushed to him, stripped off his clothes, tore away the ants from a body that seemed almost one open wound; in some places the bones were showing. They carried him into the ranch house.

As the curtain of flames lowered, one could see in place of the illimitable host of ants an extensive vista of water. The thwarted river had swept over the plantation, carrying with it the entire army. The water had collected and mounted in the great "saucer," while the ants had in vain attempted to reach the hill on which stood the ranch house. The girdle of flames held them back.

And so imprisoned between water and fire, they had been delivered into the annihilation that was their god. And near the farther mouth of the water-ditch, where the stone mole had its second gap, the ocean swept the lost battalions into the river, to vanish forever.

The ring of fire dwindled as the water mounted to the petrol trench, and quenched the dimming flames. The inundation rose higher and higher: because its outflow was impeded by the timber and underbrush it had carried along with it, its surface required some time to reach the top of the high stone breakwater and discharge over it the rest of the shattered army.

It swelled over ant-stippled shrubs and bushes, until it washed against the foot of the knoll whereon the besieged had taken refuge. For a while an alluvial of ants tried again and again to attain this dry land, only to be repulsed by streams of petrol back into the merciless flood.

Leiningen lay on his bed, his body swathed from head to foot in bandages. With fomentations and salves, they had managed to stop the bleeding, and had dressed his many wounds. Now they thronged around him, one question in every face. Would he recover? "He won't die," said the old man who had bandaged him, "if he doesn't want to."

The planter opened his eyes. "Everything in order?" he asked.

"They're gone," said his nurse. "To hell." He held out to his master a gourd full of a powerful sleeping draught. Leiningen gulped it down.

"I told you I'd come back," he murmured, "even if I am a bit streamlined." He grinned and shut his eyes. He slept.

The Blue Cross

by G. K. Chesterton

Between the silver ribbon of morning and the green glittering ribbon of sea, the boat touched Harwich and let loose a swarm of folk like flies, among whom the man we must follow was by no means conspicuous—nor wished to be. There was nothing notable about him, except a slight contrast between the holiday gayety of his clothes and the official gravity of his face. His clothes included a slight, pale gray jacket, a white waistcoat, and a silver straw hat with a gray-blue ribbon. His lean face was dark by contrast, and ended in a curt black beard that looked Spanish and suggested an Elizabethan ruff. He was smoking a cigarette with the seriousness of an idler. There was nothing about him to indicate the fact that the gray jacket covered a loaded revolver, that the white waistcoat covered a police card, or that the straw hat covered one of the most powerful intellects in Europe. For this was Valentin himself, the head of the Paris police and the most famous investigator of the world; and he was coming from Brussels to London to make the greatest arrest of the century.

Flambeau was in England. The police of three countries had tracked the great criminal at last from Ghent to Brussels, from Brussels to the Hook of Holland; and it was conjectured that he would take some advantage of the unfamiliarity and confusion of the Eucharistic Congress, then taking place in London. Probably he would travel as some minor clerk or secretary connected with it; but, of course, Valentin could not be certain; nobody could be certain about Flambeau.

It is many years now since this colossus of crime suddenly ceased keeping the world in a turmoil; and when he ceased, as they said after the death of Roland, there was a great quiet upon the earth. But in his best days (I mean, of course, his worst) Flambeau was a figure as statuesque and international as the Kaiser. Almost every morning the daily paper announced that he had escaped the consequences of one extraordinary crime by committing another. He was a Gascon of gigantic stature and bodily daring; and the wildest tales were told of his outburst of athletic humor; how he turned the *juge d'instruction* upside down and stood him on his head, "to clear his mind"; how he ran down the Rue de Rivoli with a policeman under each arm. It is due to him to say that his fantastic physical strength was generally employed in such bloodless though undignified scenes; his real crimes were chiefly those of ingenious and wholesale robbery. But each of his thefts was almost a new sin, and would make a story by itself. It was he who ran the great Tyrolean Dairy Company in London, with no dairies, no cows, no carts, no milk, but with some thousand subscribers. These he served by the simple operation of moving the little milk cans outside people's doors to the doors of his own customers. It was he who had kept up an unaccountable and close correspondence with a young lady whose whole letter-bag was intercepted, by the extraordinary trick of photographing his messages infinitesimally small upon the slides of a microscope. A sweeping simplicity, however, marked many of his experiments. It is said that he once repainted all the numbers in a street in the dead of night merely to divert one traveler into a trap. It is quite certain that he invented a portable pillar-box, which he put up at corners in quiet suburbs on the chance of strangers dropping postal orders into it. Lastly, he was known to be a

The Blue Cross

startling acrobat; despite his huge figure, he could leap like a grasshopper and melt into the tree-tops like a monkey. Hence the great Valentin, when he set out to find Flambeau, was perfectly aware that his adventures would not end when he had found him.

But how was he to find him? On this the great Valentin's ideas were still in process of settlement.

There was one thing which Flambeau, with all his dexterity of disguise, could not cover, and that was his singular height. If Valentin's quick eye had caught a tall apple-woman, a tall grenadier, or even a tolerably tall duchess, he might have arrested them on the spot. But all along his train there was nobody that could be a disguised Flambeau, any more than a cat could be a disguised giraffe. About the people on the boat he had already satisfied himself; and the people picked up at Harwich or on the journey limited themselves with certainty to six. There was a short railway official traveling up to the terminus, three fairly short market gardeners picked up two stations afterwards, one very short widow lady going up from a small Essex town, and a very short Roman Catholic priest going up from a small Essex village. When it came to the last case, Valentin gave it up and almost laughed. The little priest was so much the essence of those Eastern flats; he had a face as round and dull as a Norfolk dumpling; he had eyes as empty as the North Sea; he had several brown paper parcels, which he was quite incapable of collecting. The Eucharistic Congress had doubtless sucked out of their local stagnation many such creatures, blind and helpless, like moles disinterred. Valentin was a skeptic in the severe style of France, and could have no love for priests. But he could have pity for them, and this one might have provoked pity in anybody. He had a large, shabby umbrella, which constantly fell on the floor. He did not seem to know which was the right end of his return ticket. He explained with a moon-calf simplicity to everybody in the carriage that he had to be careful, because he had something made of real silver "with blue stones" in one of his brown-paper parcels. His quaint blending of Essex flatness with saintly simplicity continuously amused the Frenchman till the priest arrived (somehow) at Tottenham with all his parcels, and came back for his umbrella. When he did the last, Valentin even had the good nature to warn him not to take care of the silver by telling everybody about it. But to whomever he talked, Valentin kept his eye open for some one else; he looked out steadily for any one, rich or poor, male or female, who was well up to six feet; for Flambeau was four inches above it.

He alighted at Liverpool Street, however, quite conscientiously secure that he had not missed the criminal so far. He then went to Scotland Yard to regularize his position and arrange for help in case of need; he then lit another cigarette and went for a long stroll in the streets of London. As he was walking in the streets and squares beyond Victoria, he paused suddenly and stood. It was a quaint, quiet square, very typical of London, full of an accidental stillness. The tall, flat houses round looked at once prosperous and uninhabited; the square of shrubbery in the center looked as deserted as a green Pacific islet. One of the four sides was much higher than the rest, like a dais; and the line of this side was broken by one of London's admirable accidents—a restaurant that looked as if it had strayed from Soho. It was an unreasonably attractive object, with dwarf plants in pots and long, striped blinds of lemon yellow and white. It stood specially high above the street, and in the usual patchwork way of London, a flight of steps from the street ran up to meet the front door almost as a fire-escape might run up to a first-floor window. Valentin stood and smoked in front of the yellow-white blinds and considered them long.

The most incredible thing about miracles is that they happen. A few clouds in heaven do come together into the staring shape of one human eye. A tree does stand up in the landscape of a doubtful journey in the exact and elaborate shape of a note of interrogation. I have seen both these things myself within the last few days. Nelson does die in the instant of victory; and a man named Williams does quite accidentally murder a man named Williamson; it sounds like a sort of infanticide. In short, there is in life an element of elfin coincidence which people reckoning on the prosaic may perpetually miss. As it has been well expressed in the paradox of Poe, wisdom should reckon on the unforeseen.

Aristide Valentin was unfathomably French; and the French intelligence is intelligence specially and solely. He was not "a thinking machine"; for that is a brainless phrase of modern fatalism and materialism. A machine only *is* a machine because it cannot think. But he was a thinking man, and a plain man at the same time. All his wonderful successes, that looked like conjuring, had been gained by plodding logic, by clear and commonplace French thought. The French electrify the world not by starting any paradox, they electrify it by carrying out a truism. They carry a truism so far—as in the French Revolution. But exactly because Valentin understood reason, he understood the limits of reason. Only a man who knows nothing of motors talks of motoring without petrol; only a man who knows nothing of reason talks of reasoning without strong, undisputed first principles. Here he had no strong first principles. Flambeau had been missed at Harwich; and if he was in London at all, he might be anything from a tall tramp on Wimbledon Common to a tall toastmaster at the Hôtel Métropole. In such a naked state of nescience, Valentin had a view and a method of his own.

In such cases he reckoned on the unforeseen. In such cases, when he could not follow the train of the reasonable, he coldly and carefully followed the train of the unreasonable. Instead of going to the right places— banks, police stations, rendezvous—he systematically went to the wrong places; knocked at every empty house, turned down every *cul de sac,* went up every lane blocked with rubbish, went round every crescent that led him uselessly out of the way. He defended this crazy course quite logically. He said that if one had a clue this was the worst way; but if one had no clue at all it was the best, because there was just the chance that any oddity that caught the eye of the pursuer might be the same that had caught the eye of the pursued. Somewhere a man must begin, and it had better be just where another man might stop. Something about that flight of steps up to the shop, something about the quietude and quaintness of the restaurant, roused all the detective's rare romantic fancy and made him resolve to strike at random. He went up the steps, and sitting down at a table by the window, asked for a cup of black coffee.

It was half-way through the morning, and he had not breakfasted; the slight litter of other breakfasts stood about on the table to remind him of his hunger; and adding a poached egg to his order, he proceeded musingly to shake some white sugar into his coffee, thinking all the time about Flambeau. He remembered how Flambeau had escaped, once by a pair of nail scissors, and once by a house on fire; once by having to pay for an unstamped letter, and once by getting people to look through a telescope at a comet that might destroy the world. He thought his detective brain as good as the criminal's, which was true. But he fully realized the disadvantage. "The criminal is the creative artist; the detective only the critic," he said with a sour smile, and lifted his coffee cup to his lips slowly, and put it down very quickly. He had put salt in it.

He looked at the vessel from which the silvery powder had come; it was certainly a sugar-basin; as unmistakably meant for sugar as a champagne bottle for champagne. He wondered why they should keep salt in it. He looked to see if there were any more orthodox vessels. Yes; there were two salt-cellars quite full. Perhaps there was some specialty in the condiment in the

The Blue Cross 55

salt-cellars. He tasted it; it was sugar. Then he looked round at the restaurant with a refreshed air of interest, to see if there were any other traces of that singular artistic taste which puts the sugar in the salt-cellars and the salt in the sugar-basin. Except for an odd splash of some dark fluid on one of the white-papered walls, the whole place appeared neat, cheerful and ordinary. He rang the bell for the waiter.

When that official hurried up, fuzzy-haired and somewhat blear-eyed at that early hour, the detective (who was not without an appreciation of the simpler forms of humor) asked him to taste the sugar and see if it was up to the high reputation of the hotel. The result was that the waiter yawned suddenly and woke up.

"Do you play this delicate joke on your customers every morning?" inquired Valentin. "Does changing the salt and sugar never pall on you as a jest?"

The waiter, when this irony grew clearer, stammeringly assured him that the establishment had certainly no such intention; it must be a most curious mistake. He picked up the sugar-basin and looked at it; he picked up the salt-cellar and looked at that, his face growing more and more bewildered. At last he abruptly excused himself, and hurrying away, returned in a few seconds with the proprietor. The proprietor also examined the sugar-basin and then the salt-cellar; the proprietor also looked bewildered.

Suddenly the waiter seemed to grow inarticulate with a rush of words.

"I zink," he stuttered eagerly, "I zink it is those two clergymen."

"What two clergymen?"

"The two clergymen," said the waiter, "that threw soup at the wall."

"Threw soup at the wall?" repeated Valentin, feeling sure this must be some singular Italian metaphor.

"Yes, yes," said the attendant excitedly, and pointing at the dark splash on the white paper; "threw it over there on the wall."

Valentin looked his query at the proprietor, who came to his rescue with fuller reports.

"Yes, sir," he said, "it's quite true, though I don't suppose it has anything to do with the sugar and salt. Two clergymen came in and drank soup here very early, as soon as the shutters were taken down. They were both very quiet, respectable people; one of them paid the bill and went out; the other, who seemed a slower coach altogether, was some minutes longer getting his things together. But he went at last. Only, the instant before he stepped into the street he deliberately picked up his cup, which he had only half emptied, and threw the soup slap on the wall. I was in the back room myself, and so was the waiter; so I could only rush out in time to find the wall splashed and the shop empty. It don't do any particular damage, but it was confounded cheek; and I tried to catch the men in the street. They were too far off though; I only noticed they went round the next corner into Carstairs Street."

The detective was on his feet, hat settled and stick in his hand. He had already decided that in the universal darkness of his mind he could only follow the first odd finger that pointed; and this finger was odd enough. Paying his bill and clashing the glass doors behind him, he was soon swinging round into the other street.

It was fortunate that even in such fevered moments his eye was cool and quick. Something in a shop-front went by him like a mere flash; yet he went back to look at it. The shop was a popular greengrocer and fruiterer's, an array of goods set out in the open air and plainly ticketed with their names and prices. In the two most prominent compartments were two heaps, of oranges and of nuts respectively. On the heap of nuts lay a scrap of cardboard, on which was written in bold, blue chalk, "Best tangerine oranges, two a penny." On the oranges was the equally clear and exact description, "Finest Brazil nuts, 4d. a lb." M. Valentin looked at these two placards and fancied he had met this highly subtle form of humor before, and that somewhat recently. He drew the attention of the red-faced fruiterer, who was looking rather sullenly up and down the street, to this inaccuracy in his advertisements. The fruiterer said nothing, but sharply put each card into its proper place. The detective, leaning elegantly on his walking-cane, continued to scrutinize the shop. At last he said. "Pray excuse my apparent irrelevance, my good sir, but I should like to ask you a question in experimental psychology and the asociation of ideas."

The red-faced shopman regarded him with an eye of menace; but he continued gayly, swinging his cane. "Why," he pursued, "why are two tickets wrongly placed in a greengrocer's shop like a shovel hat that has come to London for a holiday? Or, in case I do not make myself clear, what is the mystical association which connects the idea of nuts marked as oranges with the idea of two clergymen, one tall and the other short?"

The eyes of the tradesman stood out of his head like a snail's; he really seemed for an instant likely to fling himself upon the stranger. At last he stammered angrily: "I don't know what you 'ave to do with it, but if you're one of their friends, you can tell 'em from me that I'll knock their silly 'eads off, parsons or no parsons, if they upset my apples again."

"Indeed," asked the detective, with great sympathy. "Did they upset your apples?"

"One of 'em did," said the heated shopman; "rolled 'em all over the street. I'd 'ave caught the fool but for havin' to pick 'em up."

"Which way did these parsons go?" asked Valentin.

"Up that second road on the left-hand side, and then across the square," said the other promptly.

"Thanks," replied Valentin, and vanished like a fairy. On the other side of the second square he found a policeman, and said: "This is urgent, constable; have you seen two clergymen in shovel hats?"

The policeman began to chuckle heavily. "I 'ave, sir; and if you arst me, one of 'em was drunk. He stood in the middle of the road that bewildered that—"

"Which way did they go?" snapped Valentin.

"They took one of them yellow busses over there," answered the man; "them that go to Hampstead."

Valentin produced his official card and said very rapidly: "Call up two of your men to come with me in pursuit," and crossed the road with such contagious energy that the ponderous policeman was moved to almost agile obedience. In a minute and a half the French detective was joined on the opposite pavement by an inspector and a man in plain clothes.

"Well, sir," began the former, with smiling importance, "and what may—?"

Valentin pointed suddenly with his cane. "I'll tell you on the top of that omnibus," he said, and was darting and dodging across the tangle of the traffic. When all three sank panting on the top seats of the yellow vehicle, the inspector said: "We could go four times as quick in a taxi."

"Quite true," replied their leader placidly, "if we only had an idea of where we were going."

"Well, where *are* you going?" asked the other, staring.

Valentin smoked frowningly for a few seconds; then, removing his cigarette, he said: "If you *know* what a man's doing, get in front of him; but if you want to guess what he's doing, keep behind him. Stray when he strays; stop when he stops; travel as slowly as he. Then you may see what he saw and may act as he acted. All we can do is to keep our eyes skinned for a queer thing."

"What sort of queer thing do you mean?" asked the inspector.

"Any sort of queer thing," answered Valentin, and relapsed into obstinate silence.

The yellow omnibus crawled up the northern roads for what seemed like hours on end; the great detective

The Blue Cross

would not explain further, and perhaps his assistants felt a silent and growing doubt of his errand. Perhaps, also, they felt a silent and growing desire for lunch, for the hours crept long past the normal luncheon hour, and the long roads of the North London suburbs seemed to shoot out into length after length like an infernal telescope. It was one of those journeys on which a man perpetually feels that now at last he must have come to the end of the universe, and then finds he has only come to the beginning of Tufnell Park. London died away in draggled taverns and dreary scrubs, and then was unaccountably born again in blazing high streets and blatant hotels. It was like passing through thirteen separate vulgar cities all just touching each other. But though the winter twilight was already threatening the road ahead of them, the Parisian detective still sat silent and watchful, eyeing the frontage of the streets that slid by on either side. By the time they had left Camden Town behind, the policemen were nearly asleep; at least, they gave something like a jump as Valentin leaped erect, struck a hand on each man's shoulder, and shouted to the driver to stop.

They tumbled down the steps into the road without realizing why they had been dislodged; when they looked round for enlightenment they found Valentin triumphantly pointing his finger towards a window on the left side of the road. It was a large window, forming part of the long façade of a gilt and palatial public-house; it was the part reserved for respectable dining, and labeled "Restaurant." This window, like all the rest along the frontage of the hotel, was of frosted and figured glass; but in the middle of it was a big, black smash, like a star in the ice.

"Our cue at last," cried Valentin, waving his stick: "the place with the broken window."

"What window? What cue?" asked his principal assistant. "Why, what proof is there that this has anything to do with them?"

Valentin almost broke his bamboo stick with rage.

"Proof!" he cried. "Good God! the man is looking for proof! Why, of course, the chances are twenty to one that it has *nothing* to do with them. But what else can we do? Don't you see we must either follow one wild possibility or else go home to bed?" He banged his way into the restaurant, followed by his companions, and they were soon seated at a late luncheon at a little table, and looking at the star of smashed glass from the inside. Not that it was very informative to them even then.

"Got your window broken, I see," said Valentin to the waiter as he paid the bill.

"Yes, sir," answered the attendant, bending busily over the change, to which Valentin silently added an enormous tip. The waiter straightened himself with mild but unmistakable animation.

"Ah, yes, sir," he said. "Very odd thing, that, sir."

"Indeed? Tell us about it," said the detective with careless curiosity.

"Well, two gents in black came in," said the waiter; "two of those foreign parsons that are running about. They had a cheap and quiet little lunch, and one of them paid for it and went out. The other was just going out to join him when I looked at my change again and found he'd paid me more than three times too much. 'Here,' I says to the chap who was nearly out of the door, 'you've paid too much.' 'Oh,' he says, very cool, 'have we?' 'Yes,' I says, and picks up the bill to show him. Well, that was a knockout."

"What do you mean?" asked his interlocutor.

"Well, I'd have sworn on seven Bibles that I'd put 4s. on that bill. But now I saw I'd put 14s., as plain as paint."

"Well?" cried Valentin, moving slowly, but with burning eyes, "and then?"

"The parson at the door he says all serene, 'Sorry to confuse your accounts, but it'll pay for the window.' 'What window?' I says. 'The one I'm going to break,'

The Blue Cross

he says, and smashed that blessed pane with his umbrella."

All three inquirers made an exclamation; and the inspector said under his breath, "Are we after escaped lunatics?" The waiter went on with some relish for the ridiculous story:

"I was so knocked silly for a second, I couldn't do anything. The man marched out of the place and joined his friend just round the corner. Then they went so quick up Bullock Street that I couldn't catch them, though I ran round the bars to do it."

"Bullock Street," said the detective, and shot up that thoroughfare as quickly as the strange couple he pursued.

Their journey now took them through bare brick ways like tunnels; streets with few lights and even with few windows; streets that seemed built out of the blank backs of everything and everywhere. Dusk was deepening, and it was not easy even for the London policemen to guess in what exact direction they were treading. The inspector, however, was pretty certain that they would eventually strike some part of Hampstead Heath. Abruptly one bulging gas-lit window broke the blue twilight like a bull's-eye lantern; and Valentin stopped an instant before a little garish sweetstuff shop. After an instant's hesitation he went in; he stood amid the gaudy colors of the confectionery with entire gravity and bought thirteen chocolate cigars with a certain care. He was clearly preparing an opening, but he did not need one.

An angular, elderly young woman in the shop had regarded his elegant appearance with a merely automatic inquiry; but when she saw the door behind him blocked with the blue uniform of the inspector, her eyes seemed to wake up.

"Oh," she said, "if you've come about that parcel, I've sent it off already."

"Parcel!" repeated Valentin; and it was his turn to look inquiring.

"I mean the parcel the gentleman left—the clergyman gentleman."

"For goodness' sake," said Valentin, leaning forward with his first real confession of eagerness, "for Heaven's sake tell us what happened exactly."

"Well," said the woman a little doubtfully, "the clergymen came in about half an hour ago and bought some peppermints and talked a bit, and then went off towards the Heath. But a second after, one of them runs back into the shop and says, 'Have I left a parcel?' Well, I looked everywhere and couldn't see one; so he says, 'Never mind; but if it should turn up, please post it to this address,' and he left me the address and a shilling for my trouble. And sure enough, though I thought I'd looked everywhere, I found he'd left a brown paper parcel, so I posted it to the place he said. I can't remember the address now; it was somewhere in Westminster. But as the thing seemed so important, I thought perhaps the police had come about it."

"So they have," said Valentin shortly. "Is Hampstead Heath near here?"

"Straight on for fifteen minutes," said the woman, "and you'll come right out on the open." Valentin sprang out of the shop and began to run. The other detectives followed him at a reluctant trot.

The street they threaded was so narrow and shut in by shadows that when they came out unexpectedly into the void common and vast sky they were startled to find the evening still so light and clear. A perfect dome of peacock-green sank into gold amid the blackening trees and the dark violet distances. The glowing green tint was just deep enough to pick out in points of crystal one or two stars. All that was left of the daylight lay in a golden glitter across the edge of Hampstead and that popular hollow which is called the Vale of Health. The holiday makers who roam this region had not wholly dispersed; a few couples sat shapelessly on benches; and here and there a distant girl still shrieked in one of the swings. The glory of heaven deepened and darkened around the sublime vulgarity of man; and standing on the slope and looking across the valley, Valentin beheld the thing which he sought.

Among the black and breaking groups in that distance was one especially black which did not break—a group of two figures clerically clad. Though they seemed as small as insects, Valentin could see that one of them was much smaller than the other. Though the other had a student's stoop and an inconspicuous manner, he could see that the man was well over six feet high. He shut his teeth and went forward, whirling his stick impatiently. By the time he had substantially diminished the distance and magnified the two black figures as in a vast microscope, he had perceived something else; something which startled him, and yet which he had somehow expected. Whoever was the tall priest, there could be no doubt about the identity of the short one. It was his friend of the Harwich train, the stumpy little *curé* of Essex whom he had warned about his brown paper parcels.

Now, so far as this went, everything fitted in finally and rationally enough. Valentin had learned by his inquiries that morning that a Father Brown from Essex was bringing up a silver cross with sapphires, a relic of considerable value, to show some of the foreign priests at the congress. This undoubtedly was the "silver with blue stones"; and Father Brown undoubtedly was the little greenhorn in the train. Now there was nothing wonderful about the fact that what Valentin had found out Flambeau had also found out; Flambeau found out everything. Also there was nothing wonderful in the fact that when Flambeau heard of a sapphire cross he should try to steal it; that was the most natural thing in all natural history. And most certainly there was nothing wonderful about the fact that Flambeau should have it all his own way with such a silly sheep as the man with the umbrella and the parcels. He was the sort of man whom anybody could lead on a string to the North Pole; it was not surprising that an actor like Flambeau, dressed as another priest, could lead him to Hampstead Heath. So far the crime seemed clear enough; and while the detective pitied the priest for his helplessness, he almost despised Flambeau for condescending to so gullible a victim. But when Valentin thought of all that had happened in between, of all that had led him to his triumph, he racked his brains for the smallest rhyme or reason in it. What had the stealing of a blue-and-silver cross from a priest from Essex to do with chucking soup at wall paper? What had it to do with calling nuts oranges, or with paying for windows first and breaking them afterwards? He had come to the end of his chase; yet somehow he had missed the middle of it. When he failed (which was seldom), he had usually grasped the clue, but nevertheless missed the criminal. Here he had grasped the criminal, but still he could not grasp the clue.

The two figures that they followed were crawling like black flies across the huge green contour of a hill. They were evidently sunk in conversation, and perhaps did not notice where they were going; but they were certainly going to the wilder and more silent heights of the Heath. As their pursuers gained on them, the latter had to use the undignified attitudes of the deer-stalker, to crouch behind clumps of trees and even to crawl prostrate in deep grass. By these ungainly ingenuities the hunters even came close enough to the quarry to hear the murmur of the discussion, but no word could be distinguished except the word "reason" recurring frequently in a high and almost childish voice. Once over an abrupt dip of land and a dense tangle of thickets, the detectives actually lost the two figures they were following. They did not find the trail again for an agonizing ten minutes, and then it led round the brow of a great dome of hill overlooking an amphitheater of rich and desolate sunset scenery. Under a tree in this commanding yet neglected spot was an old ramshackle wooden seat. On this seat sat the two priests still in serious speech together. The gorgeous green and gold

The Blue Cross

still clung to the darkening horizon; but the dome above was turning slowly from peacock-green to peacock-blue, and the stars detached themselves more and more like solid jewels. Mutely motioning to his followers, Valentin contrived to creep up behind the big branching tree, and, standing there in deathly silence, heard the words of the strange priests for the first time.

After he had listened for a minute and a half, he was gripped by a devilish doubt. Perhaps he had dragged the two English policemen to the wastes of a nocturnal heath on an errand no saner than seeking figs on its thistles. For the two priests were talking exactly like priests, piously, with learning and leisure, about the most aerial enigmas of theology. The little Essex priest spoke the more simply, with his round face turned to the strengthening stars; the other talked with his head bowed, as if he were not even worthy to look at them. But no more innocently clerical conversation could have been heard in any white Italian cloister or black Spanish cathedral.

The first he heard was the tail of one of Father Brown's sentences, which ended: ". . . what they really meant in the Middle Ages by the heavens being incorruptible."

The taller priest nodded his bowed head and said:

"Ah, yes, these modern infidels appeal to their reason; but who can look at those millions of worlds and not feel that there may well be wonderful universes above us where reason is utterly unreasonable?"

"No," said the other priest: "reason is always reasonable, even in the last limbo, in the lost borderland of things. I know that people charge the Church with lowering reason, but it is just the other way. Alone on earth, the Church makes reason really supreme. Alone on earth, the Church affirms that God himself is bound by reason."

The other priest raised his austere face to the spangled sky and said:

"Yet who knows if in that infinite universe—?"

"Only infinite physically," said the little priest, turning sharply in his seat, "not infinite in the sense of escaping from the laws of truth."

Valentin behind his tree was tearing his finger-nails with silent fury. He seemed almost to hear the sniggers of the English detectives whom he had brought so far on a fantastic guess only to listen to the metaphysical gossip of two mild old parsons. In his impatience he lost the equally elaborate answer of the tall cleric, and when he listened again it was Father Brown who was speaking:

"Reason and justice grip the remotest and loneliest star. Look at those stars. Don't they look as if they were single diamonds and sapphires? Well, you can imagine any mad botany or geology you please. Think of forests of adamant with leaves of brilliants. Think the moon is a blue moon, a single elephantine sapphire. But don't fancy that all that frantic astronomy would make the smallest difference to the reason and justice of conduct. On plains of opal, under cliffs cut out of pearl, you would still find a notice-board, 'Thou shalt not steal.'"

Valentin was just in the act of rising from his rigid and crouching attitude and creeping away as softly as might be, felled by the one great folly of his life. But something in the very silence of the tall priest made him stop until the latter spoke. When at last he did speak, he said simply, his head bowed and his hands on his knees:

"Well, I still think that other worlds may perhaps rise higher than our reason. The mystery of heaven is unfathomable, and I for one can only bow my head."

Then, with brow yet bent and without changing by the faintest shade his attitude or voice, he added:

"Just hand over that sapphire cross of yours, will you? We're all alone here, and I could pull you to pieces like a straw doll."

The utterly unaltered voice and attitude added a

The Blue Cross

strange violence to that shocking change of speech. But the guarder of the relic only seemed to turn his head by the smallest section of the compass. He seemed still to have a somewhat foolish face turned to the stars. Perhaps he had not understood. Or, perhaps, he had understood and sat rigid with terror.

"Yes," said the tall priest, in the same low voice and in the same still posture, "yes, I am Flambeau."

Then, after a pause, he said:

"Come, will you give me that cross?"

"No," said the other, and the monosyllable had an odd sound.

Flambeau suddenly flung off all his pontifical pretensions. The great robber leaned back in his seat and laughed low but long.

"No," he cried, "you won't give it me, you proud prelate. You won't give it me, you little celibate simpleton. Shall I tell you why you won't give it me? Because I've got it already in my own breast-pocket."

The small man from Essex turned what seemed to be a dazed face in the dusk, and said, with the timid eagerness of "The Private Secretary":

"Are—are you sure?"

Flambeau yelled with delight.

"Really, you're as good as a three-act farce," he cried. "Yes, you turnip, I am quite sure. I had the sense to make a duplicate of the right parcel, and now, my friend, you've got the duplicate and I've got the jewels. An old dodge, Father Brown—a very old dodge."

"Yes," said Father Brown, and passed his hand through his hair with the same strange vagueness of manner. "Yes, I've heard of it before."

The colossus of crime leaned over to the little rustic priest with a sort of sudden interest.

"*You* have heard of it?" he asked. "Where have *you* heard of it?"

"Well, I mustn't tell you his name, of course," said the little man simply. "He was a penitent, you know. He had lived prosperously for about twenty years entirely on duplicate brown paper parcels. And so, you see, when I began to suspect you, I thought of this poor chap's way of doing it at once."

"Began to suspect me?" repeated the outlaw with increased intensity. "Did you really have the gumption to suspect me just because I brought you up to this bare part of the heath?"

"No, no," said Father Brown with an air of apology. "You see, I suspected you when we first met. It's that little bulge up the sleeve where you people have the spiked bracelet."

"How in Tartarus," cried Flambeau, "did you ever hear of the spiked bracelet?"

"Oh, one's little flock, you know!" said Father Brown, arching his eyebrows rather blankly. "When I was a curate in Hartlepool, there were three of them with spiked bracelets. So, as I suspected you from the first, don't you see, I made sure that the cross should go safe, anyhow. I'm afraid I watched you, you know. So at last I saw you change the parcels. Then, don't you see, I changed them back again. And then I left the right one, behind."

"Left it behind?" repeated Flambeau, and for the first time there was another note in his voice beside his triumph.

"Well, it was like this," said the little priest, speaking in the same unaffected way. "I went back to that sweetshop and asked if I'd left a parcel, and gave them a particular address if it turned up. Well, I knew I hadn't; but when I went away again I did. So, instead of running after me with that valuable parcel, they have sent it flying to a friend of mine in Westminster." Then he added rather sadly: "I learnt that, too, from a poor fellow in Hartlepool. He used to do it with handbags he stole at railway stations, but he's in a monastery now. Oh, one gets to know, you know," he added, rubbing his head again with the same sort of desperate apology. "We can't help it being priests. People come and tell us these things."

Flambeau tore a brown paper parcel out of his inner pocket and rent it in pieces. There was nothing but paper and sticks of lead inside it. He sprang to his feet with a gigantic gesture, and cried:

"I don't believe you. I don't believe a bumpkin like you could manage all that. I believe you've still got the stuff on you, and if you don't give it up—why, we're all alone, and I'll take it by force!"

"No," said Father Brown simply, and stood up also, "you won't take it by force. First, because I really haven't still got it. And, second, because we are not alone."

Flambeau stopped in his stride forward.

"Behind that tree," said Father Brown, pointing, "are two strong policemen and the greatest detective alive. How did they come here, do you ask? Why, I brought them, of course! How did I do it? Why, I'll tell you if you like! Lord bless you, we have to know twenty such things when we work among the criminal classes! Well, I wasn't sure you were a thief, and it would never do to make a scandal against one of our own clergy. So I just tested you to see if anything would make you show yourself. A man generally makes a small scene if he finds salt in his coffee; if he doesn't, he has some reason for keeping quiet. I changed the salt and sugar, and *you* kept quiet. A man generally objects if his bill is three times too big. If he pays it, he has some motive for passing unnoticed. I altered your bill, and *you* paid it."

The world seemed waiting for Flambeau to leap like a tiger. But he was held back as by a spell; he was stunned with the utmost curiosity.

"Well," went on Father Brown, with lumbering lucidity, "as you wouldn't leave any tracks for the police, of course somebody had to. At every place we went to, I took care to do something that would get us talked about for the rest of the day. I didn't do much harm— a splashed wall, spilt apples, a broken window; but I saved the cross, as the cross will always be saved. It is at Westminster by now. I rather wonder you didn't stop it with the Donkey's Whistle."

"With the what?" asked Flambeau.

"I'm glad you've never heard of it," said the priest, making a face. "It's a foul thing. I'm sure you're too good a man for a Whistler. I couldn't have countered it even with the Spots myself; I'm not strong enough in the legs."

"What on earth are you talking about?" asked the other.

"Well, I did think you'd know the Spots," said Father Brown, agreeably surprised. "Oh, you can't have gone so very wrong yet!"

"How in blazes do you know all these horrors?" cried Flambeau.

The shadow of a smile crossed the round, simple face of his clerical opponent.

"Oh, by being a celibate simpleton, I suppose," he said. "Has it never struck you that a man who does next to nothing but hear men's real sins is not likely to be wholly unaware of human evil? But, as a matter of fact, another part of my trade, too, made me sure you weren't a priest."

"What?" asked the thief, almost gaping.

"You attacked reason," said Father Brown. "It's bad theology."

And even as he turned away to collect his property, the three policemen came out from under the twilight trees. Flambeau was an artist and a sportsman. He stepped back and swept Valentin a great bow.

"Do not bow to me, *mon ami*," said Valentin with silver clearness. "Let us both bow to our master."

And they both stood an instant uncovered while the little Essex priest blinked about for his umbrella.

The Most Dangerous Game

by *Richard Connell*

"Off there to the right—somewhere—is a large island," said Whitney. "It's rather a mystery—"

"What island is it?" Rainsford asked.

"The old charts call it 'Ship-Trap Island,'" Whitney replied. "A suggestive name, isn't it? Sailors have a curious dread of the place. I don't know why some superstition—"

"Can't see it," remarked Rainsford, trying to peer through the dank tropical night that was palpable as it pressed its thick, warm blackness in upon the yacht.

"You've good eyes," said Whitney, with a laugh, "and I've seen you pick off a moose moving in the brown fall bush at four hundred yards, but even you can't see four miles or so through a moonless Caribbean night."

"Not four yards," admitted Rainsford. "Ugh! It's like moist black velvet."

"It will be light enough where we're going," promised Whitney. "We should make it in a few days. I hope the jaguar guns have come. We'll have good hunting up the Amazon. Great sport, hunting."

"The best sport in the world," agreed Rainsford.

"For the hunter," amended Whitney. "Not for the jaguar."

"Don't talk rot, Whitney," said Rainsford. "You're a big-game hunter, not a philosopher. Who cares how a jaguar feels?"

"Perhaps the jaguar does," observed Whitney.

"Bah! They've no understanding."

"Even so, I rather think they understand one thing—fear. The fear of pain and the fear of death."

"Nonsense," laughed Rainsford. "This hot weather is making you soft, Whitney. Be a realist. The world is made up of two classes—the hunters and the hunted. Luckily, you and I are hunters. Do you think we've passed that island yet?"

"I can't tell in the dark. I hope so."

"Why?" asked Rainsford.

"The place has a reputation—a bad one."

"Cannibals?" suggested Rainsford.

"Hardly. Even cannibals wouldn't live in such a God-forsaken place. But it's got into sailor lore, somehow. Didn't you notice that the crew's nerves seemed a bit jumpy today?"

"They were a bit strange, now you mention it. Even Captain Nielson—"

"Yes, even that tough-minded old Swede, who'd go to the devil himself and ask him for a light. Those fishy blue eyes held a look I never saw there before. All I could get out of him was: 'This place has an evil name among seafaring men, sir.' Then he said to me, very gravely: 'Don't you feel anything?'—as if the air about us was actually poisonous. Now you mustn't laugh when I tell you this—I did feel something like a sudden chill.

"There was no breeze. The sea was as flat as a plate-glass window. We were drawing near the island then. What I felt was a—a mental chill; a sort of sudden dread."

"Pure imagination," said Rainsford. "One superstitious sailor can taint the whole ship's company with his fear."

"Maybe. But sometimes I think sailors have an extra sense that tells them when they are in danger. Sometimes I think evil is a tangible thing—with wave lengths, just as sound and light have. An evil place can, so to speak, broadcast vibrations of evil. Anyhow, I'm glad we're getting out of the zone. Well, I think I'll turn in now, Rainsford."

"I'm not sleepy," said Rainsford. "I'm going to smoke another pipe up on the afterdeck."

"Good night, then, Rainsford. See you at breakfast."

"Good night, Whitney."

There was no sound in the night as Rainsford sat there but the muffled throb of the engine that drove the yacht swiftly through the darkness, and the swish and ripple of the wash of the propeller.

Rainsford, reclining in a steamer chair, indolently puffed on his favorite briar. The sensuous drowsiness of the night was on him. "It's so dark," he thought, "that I could sleep without closing my eyes; the night would be my eyelids—"

An abrupt sound startled him. Off to the right he heard it, and his ears, expert in such matters, could not be mistaken. Again he heard the sound, and again. Somewhere, off in the blackness, someone had fired a gun three times.

Rainsford sprang up and moved quickly to the rail, mystified. He strained his eyes in the direction from which the reports had come, but it was like trying to see through a blanket. He leaped upon the rail and balanced himself there, to get greater elevation; his pipe, striking a rope, was knocked from his mouth. He lunged for it; a short, hoarse cry came from his lips as he realized he had reached too far and had lost his balance. The cry was pinched off short as the blood-warm waters of the Caribbean Sea closed over his head.

He struggled up to the surface and tried to cry out, but the wash from the speeding yacht slapped him in the face and the salt water in his open mouth made him gag and strangle. Desperately he struck out with strong strokes after the receding lights of the yacht, but he stopped before he had swum fifty feet. A certain cool-headedness had come to him; it was not the first time he had been in a tight place. There was a chance that his cries could be heard by someone aboard the yacht, but that chance was slender, and grew more slender as the yacht raced on. He wrestled himself out of his clothes, and shouted with all his power. The lights of the yacht became faint and ever-vanishing fireflies; then they were blotted out entirely by the night.

Rainsford remembered the shots. They had come from the right, and doggedly he swam in that direction, swimming with slow, deliberate strokes, conserving his strength. For a seemingly endless time he fought the sea. He began to count his strokes; he could do possibly a hundred more and then—

Rainsford heard a sound. It came out of the darkness, a high, screaming sound, the sound of an animal in an extremity of anguish and terror.

He did not recognize the animal that made the sound—he did not try to; with fresh vitality he swam toward the sound. He heard it again; then it was cut short by another noise, crisp, staccato.

"Pistol shot," muttered Rainsford, swimming on.

Ten minutes of determined effort brought another sound to his ears—the most welcome he had ever heard —the muttering and growling of the sea breaking on a rocky shore. He was almost on the rocks before he saw them; on a night less calm he would have been shattered against them. With his remaining strength he dragged himself from the swirling waters. Jagged crags appeared to jut into the opaqueness; he forced himself upward, hand over hand. Gasping, his hands raw, he reached a flat place at the top. Dense jungle came down to the very edge of the cliffs. What perils that tangle of trees and underbrush might hold for him did not concern Rainsford just then. All he knew was that he was safe from his enemy, the sea, and that utter weariness was on him. He flung himself down at the jungle edge and tumbled headlong into the deepest sleep of his life.

When he opened his eyes he knew from the position of the sun that it was late in the afternoon. Sleep had given him new vigor; a sharp hunger was picking at him. He looked about him, almost cheerfully.

The Most Dangerous Game

"Where there are pistol shots, there are men. Where there are men, there is food," he thought. But what kind of men, he wondered, in so forbidding a place? An unbroken front of snarled and jagged jungle fringed the shore.

He saw no sign of a trail through the closely knit web of weeds and trees; it was easier to go along the shore, and Rainsford floundered along by the water. Not far from where he had landed, he stopped.

Some wounded thing, by the evidence a large animal, had thrashed about in the underbrush; the jungle weeds were crushed down and the moss was lacerated; one patch of weeds was stained crimson. A small, glittering object not far away caught Rainsford's eye and he picked it up. It was an empty cartridge.

"A twenty-two," he remarked. "That's odd. It must have been a fairly large animal too. The hunter had his nerve with him to tackle it with such a light gun. It's clear that the brute put up a good fight. I suppose the first three shots I heard were when the hunter flushed his quarry and wounded it. The last shot was when he trailed it here and finished it."

He examined the ground closely and found what he had hoped to find—the print of hunting boots. They pointed along the cliff in the direction he had been going. Eagerly he hurried along, now slipping on a rotten log or a loose stone, but making headway. Night was beginning to settle down on the island.

Bleak darkness was blacking out the sea and jungle when Rainsford sighted the lights. He came upon them as he turned a crook in the coast line, and his first thought was that he had come upon a village, for there were many lights. But as he forged along he saw to his great astonishment that all the lights were in one enormous building—a lofty structure with pointed towers plunging upward into the gloom. His eyes made out the shadowy outlines of a palatial château; it was set on a high bluff, and on three sides of it cliffs dived down to where the sea licked greedy lips in the shadows.

"Mirage," thought Rainsford. But it was no mirage, he found, when he opened the tall spiked iron gate. The steps were real enough; the massive door with a leering gargoyle for a knocker was real enough; yet about it all hung an air of unreality.

He lifted the knocker, and it creaked up stiffly, as if it had never before been used. He let it fall, and it startled him with its booming loudness. He thought he heard steps within; the door remained closed. Again Rainsford lifted the heavy knocker, and let it fall. The door opened then, opened as suddenly as if it were on a spring, and Rainsford stood blinking in the river of glaring gold light that poured out. The first thing his eyes discerned was the largest man he had ever seen— a gigantic creature, solidly made and black-bearded to the waist. In his hand the man held a long-barreled revolver, and he was pointing it straight at Rainsford's heart.

Out of the snarl of beard two small eyes regarded Rainsford.

"Don't be alarmed," said Rainsford, with a smile which he hoped was disarming. "I'm no robber. I fell off a yacht. My name is Sanger Rainsford of New York City."

The menacing look in the eyes did not change. The revolver pointed as rigidly as if the giant were a statue. He gave no sign that he understood Rainsford's words, or that he had even heard them. He was dressed in uniform, a black uniform trimmed with gray astrakhan.

"I'm Sanger Rainsford of New York," Rainsford began again. "I fell off a yacht. I am hungry."

The man's only answer was to raise with his thumb the hammer of his revolver. Then Rainsford saw the man's free hand go to his forehead in a military salute, and he saw him click his heels together and stand at attention. Another man was coming down the broad marble steps, an erect, slender man in evening clothes. He advanced and held out his hand.

In a cultivated voice marked by a slight accent that

gave it added precision and deliberateness, he said: "It is a very great pleasure and honor to welcome Mr. Sanger Rainsford, the celebrated hunter, to my home." Automatically Rainsford shook the man's hand.

"I've read your book about hunting snow leopards in Tibet, you see," explained the man. "I am General Zaroff."

Rainsford's first impression was that the man was singularly handsome; his second was that there was an original, almost bizarre quality about the general's face. He was a tall man, past middle age, for his hair was a vivid white; but his thick eyebrows and pointed military mustache were as black as the night from which Rainsford had come. His eyes, too, were black and very bright. He had high cheekbones, a sharp-cut nose, a spare, dark face, the face of a man used to giving orders, the face of an aristocrat. Turning to the giant in uniform, the general made a sign. The giant put away his pistol, saluted, withdrew.

"Ivan is an incredibly strong fellow," remarked the general, "but he has the misfortune to be deaf and dumb. A simple fellow, but, I'm afraid, like all his race, a bit of a savage."

"Is he Russian?"

"He is a Cossack," said the general, and his smile showed red lips and pointed teeth. "So am I.

"Come," he said, "we shouldn't be chatting here. We can talk later. Now you want clothes, food, rest. You shall have them. This is a most restful spot."

Ivan had re-appeared, and the general spoke to him with lips that moved but gave forth no sound.

"Follow Ivan, if you please, Mr. Rainsford," said the general. "I was about to have my dinner when you came. I'll wait for you. You'll find that my clothes will fit you, I think."

It was to a huge, beam-ceilinged room with a canopied bed big enough for six men that Rainsford followed the silent giant. Ivan laid out an evening suit, and Rainsford, as he put it on, noticed that it came from a London tailor who ordinarily cut and sewed for none below the rank of a duke.

The dining room to which Ivan conducted him was in many ways remarkable. There was a medieval magnificence about it; it suggested a baronial hall of feudal times with its oaken panels, its high ceiling, its vast refectory table where two score men could sit down to eat. About the hall were the mounted heads of many animals—lions, tigers, elephants, moose, bears; larger or more perfect specimens Rainsford had never seen before. At the great table the general was sitting, alone.

"You'll have a cocktail, Mr. Rainsford," he suggested. The cocktail was surpassingly good; and, Rainsford noted, the table appointments were of the finest—the linen, the crystal, the silver, the china.

They were eating *borsch*, the rich, red soup with whipped cream so dear to Russian palates. Half apologetically General Zaroff said: "We try to preserve the amenities of civilization here. Please forgive any lapses. We are well off the beaten track, you know. Do you think the champagne has suffered from its long ocean trip?"

"Not in the least," declared Rainsford. He was finding the general a most thoughtful and affable host, a true cosmopolite. But there was one trait of the general's that made Rainsford uncomfortable. Whenever he looked up he found the general studying him, appraising him narrowly.

"Perhaps," said General Zaroff, "you were surprised that I recognized your name. You see, I read all books on hunting published in English, French, and Russian. I have but one passion in my life, Mr. Rainsford, and it is the hunt."

"You have some wonderful heads here," said Rainsford as he ate a particularly well-cooked filet mignon. "That Cape buffalo is the largest I ever saw."

"Oh, that fellow. Yes, he was a monster."

"Did he charge you?"

"Hurled me against a tree," said the general. "Fractured my skull. But I got the brute."

"I've always thought," said Rainsford, "that the Cape buffalo is the most dangerous of all big game."

For a moment the general did not reply; he was smiling his curious red-lipped smile. Then he said slowly: "No. You are wrong, sir. The Cape buffalo is not the most dangerous big game." He sipped his wine. "Here in my preserve on this island," he said in the same slow tone, "I hunt more dangerous game."

Rainsford expressed his surprise. "Is there big game on this island?"

The general nodded. "The biggest."

"Really?"

"Oh, it isn't here naturally, of course. I have to stock the island."

"What have you imported, General?" Rainsford asked. "Tigers?"

The general smiled. "No," he said. "Hunting tigers ceased to interest me some years ago. I exhausted their possibilities, you see. No thrill left in tigers, no real danger. I live for danger, Mr. Rainsford."

The general took from his pocket a gold cigarette case and offered his guest a long black cigarette with a silver tip; it was perfumed and gave off a smell like incense.

"We will have some capital hunting, you and I," said the general. "I shall be most glad to have your society."

"But what game—" began Rainsford.

"I'll tell you," said the general. "You will be amused, I know. I think I may say, in all modesty, that I have done a rare thing. I have invented a new sensation. May I pour you another glass of port, Mr. Rainsford?"

"Thank you, General."

The general filled both glasses, and said: "God makes some men poets. Some He makes kings, some beggars. Me He made a hunter. My hand was made for the trigger, my father said. He was a very rich man with a quarter of a million acres in the Crimea, and he was an ardent sportsman. When I was only five years old he gave me a little gun, specially made in Moscow for me, to shoot sparrows with. When I shot some of his prize turkeys with it, he did not punish me; he complimented me on my marksmanship. I killed my first bear in the Caucasus when I was ten. My whole life had been one prolonged hunt. I went into the army—it was expected of noblemen's sons—and for a time commanded a division of Cossack cavalry, but my real interest was always the hunt. I have hunted every kind of game in every land. It would be impossible for me to tell you how many animals I have killed."

The general puffed at his cigarette.

"After the debacle in Russia I left the country, for it was imprudent for an officer of the Czar to stay there. Many noble Russians lost everything. I, luckily, had invested heavily in American securities, so I shall never have to open a tearoom in Monte Carlo or drive a taxi in Paris. Naturally, I continued to hunt—grizzlies in your Rockies, crocodiles in the Ganges, rhinoceroses in East Africa. It was in Africa that the Cape buffalo hit me and laid me up for six months. As soon as I recovered, I started for the Amazon to hunt jaguars, for I had heard they were unusually cunning. They weren't." The Cossack sighed. "They were no match at all for a hunter with his wits about him, and a high-powered rifle. I was bitterly disappointed. I was lying in my tent with a splitting headache one night when a terrible thought rushed into my mind. Hunting was beginning to bore me! And hunting, remember, had been my life. I have heard that in America businessmen often go to pieces when they give up the business that has been their life."

"Yes, that's so," said Rainsford.

The general smiled. "I had no wish to go to pieces," he said. "I must do something. Now, mine is an analytical mind, Mr. Rainsford. Doubtless that is why I enjoy the problems of the chase."

"No doubt, General Zaroff."

"So," continued the general, "I asked myself why the hunt no longer fascinated me. You are much younger than I am, Mr. Rainsford, and have not hunted as much, but you perhaps can guess the answer."

"What was it?"

"Simply this: hunting had ceased to be what you call a 'sporting proposition.' It had become too easy. I always got my quarry. Always. There is no greater bore than perfection."

The general lit a fresh cigarette.

"No animal had a chance with me any more. That is no boast; it is a mathematical certainty. The animal had nothing but his legs and his instinct. Instinct is no match for reason. When I thought of this, it was a tragic moment for me, I can tell you."

Rainsford leaned across the table, absorbed in what his host was saying.

"It came to me as an inspiration what I must do," the general said.

"And that was?"

The general smiled the quiet smile of one who has faced an obstacle and surmounted it with success. "I had to invent a new animal to hunt," he said.

"A new animal? You're joking."

"Not at all," said the general. "I never joke about hunting. I needed a new animal. I found one. So I bought this island, built this house, and here I do my hunting. The island is perfect for my purposes—there are jungles with a maze of trails in them, hills, swamps—"

"But the animal, General Zaroff?"

"Oh," said the general, "it supplies me with the most exciting hunting in the world. No other hunting compares with it for an instant. Every day I hunt, and I never grow bored now, for I have a quarry with which I can match my wits."

Rainsford's bewilderment showed in his face.

"I wanted the ideal animal to hunt," explained the general. "So I said: 'What are the attributes of an ideal quarry?' And the answer was, of course: 'It must have courage, cunning, and, above all, it must be able to reason.'"

"But no animal can reason," objected Rainsford.

"My dear fellow," said the general, "there is one that can."

"But you can't mean—" gasped Rainsford.

"And why not?"

"I can't believe you are serious, General Zaroff. This is a grisly joke."

"Why should I not be serious? I am speaking of hunting."

"Hunting? Good God, General Zaroff, what you speak of is murder."

The general laughed with entire good nature. He regarded Rainsford quizzically. "I refuse to believe that so modern and civilized a young man as you harbors romantic ideas about the value of human life. Surely your experiences in the war—"

"Did not make me condone cold-blooded murder," finished Rainsford stiffly.

Laughter shook the general. "How extraordinarily droll you are!" he said. "One does not expect nowadays to find a young man of the educated class, even in America, with such a naïve and, if I may say so, mid-Victorian point of view. It's like finding a snuffbox in a limousine. Ah, well, doubtless you had Puritan ancestors. So many Americans appear to have had. I'll wager you'll forget your notions when you go hunting with me. You've a genuine new thrill in store for you, Mr. Rainsford."

"Thank you, I'm a hunter, not a murderer."

"Dear me," said the general, quite unruffled, "again that unpleasant word. But I think I can show you that your scruples are quite unfounded."

"Yes?"

The Most Dangerous Game

"Life is for the strong, to be lived by the strong, and, if needs be, taken by the strong. The weak of the world were put here to give the strong pleasure. I am strong. Why should I not use my gift? If I wish to hunt, why should I not? I hunt the scum of the earth—sailors from tramp ships—lascars, blacks, Chinese, whites, mongrels—a thoroughbred horse or hound is worth more than a score of them."

"But they are men," said Rainsford hotly.

"Precisely," said the general. "That is why I use them. It gives me pleasure. They can reason, after a fashion. So they are dangerous."

"But where do you get them?"

The general's left eyelid fluttered down in a wink. "This island is called Ship Trap," he answered. "Sometimes an angry god of the high seas sends them to me. Sometimes, when Providence is not so kind, I help Providence a bit. Come to the window with me."

Rainsford went to the window and looked out toward the sea.

"Watch! Out there!" exclaimed the general, pointing into the night. Rainsford's eyes saw only blackness, and then, as the general pressed a button, far out to sea Rainsford saw the flash of lights.

The general chuckled. "They indicate a channel," he said, "where there's none: giant rocks with razor edges crouch like a sea monster with wide-open jaws. They can crush a ship as easily as I crush this nut." He dropped a walnut on the hardwood floor and brought his heel grinding down on it. "Oh, yes," he said, casually, as if in answer to a question, "I have electricity. We try to be civilized here."

"Civilized? And you shoot down men?"

A trace of anger was in the general's black eyes, but it was there for but a second, and he said, in his most pleasant manner: "Dear me, what a righteous young man you are! I assure you I do not do the thing you suggest. That would be barbarous. I treat these visitors with every consideration. They get plenty of good food and exercise. They get into splendid physical condition. You shall see for yourself tomorrow."

"What do you mean?"

"We'll visit my training school," smiled the general. "It's in the cellar. I have about a dozen pupils down there now. They're from the Spanish bark, 'San Lucar,' that had the bad luck to go on the rocks out there. A very inferior lot, I regret to say. Poor specimens and more accustomed to the deck than to the jungle."

He raised his hand, and Ivan, who served as waiter, brought thick Turkish coffee. Rainsford, with an effort, held his tongue in check.

"It's a game, you see," pursued the general blandly. "I suggest to one of them that we go hunting. I give him a supply of food and an excellent hunting knife. I give him three hours' start. I am to follow, armed only with a pistol of the smallest caliber and range. If my quarry eludes me for three whole days, he wins the game. If I find him," the general smiled, "he loses."

"Suppose he refuses to be hunted?"

"Oh," said the general, "I give him his option, of course. He need not play that game if he doesn't wish to. If he does not wish to hunt I turn him over to Ivan. Ivan once had the honor of serving as official knouter to the Great White Czar, and he has his own ideas of sport. Invariably, Mr. Rainsford, invariably they choose the hunt."

"And if they win?"

The smile on the general's face widened. "To date I have not lost," he said.

Then he added, hastily: "I don't wish you to think me a braggart, Mr. Rainsford. Many of them afford only the most elementary sort of problem. Occasionally I strike a tartar. One almost did win. I eventually had to use the dogs."

"The dogs?"

"This way, please. I'll show you."

The general steered Rainsford to a window. The

lights from the window sent a flickering illumination that made grotesque patterns on the courtyard below, and Rainsford could see moving about there a dozen or so huge black shapes; as they turned toward him, their eyes glittered greenly.

"A rather good lot, I think," observed the general. "They are let out at seven every night. If anyone should try to get into my house—or out of it—something extremely regrettable would occur to him." He hummed a snatch of song from the *Folies Bergère*.

"And now," said the general, "I want to show you my new collection of heads. Will you come with me to the library?"

"I hope," said Rainsford, "that you will excuse me tonight, General Zaroff. I'm really not feeling at all well."

"Ah, indeed?" the general inquired solicitously. "Well, I suppose that's only natural, after your long swim. You need a good, restful night's sleep. Tomorrow you'll feel like a new man, I'll wager. Then we'll hunt, eh? I've one rather promising prospect—"

Rainsford was hurrying from the room.

"Sorry you can't go with me tonight," called the general. "I expect rather fair sport—a big, strong black. He looks resourceful—well, good night, Mr. Rainsford; I hope you have a good night's rest."

The bed was good, and the pajamas of the softest silk, and he was tired in every fiber of his being, but nevertheless Rainsford could not quiet his brain with the opiate of sleep. He lay, eyes wide open. Once he thought he heard stealthy steps in the corridor outside his room. He sought to throw open the door; it would not open. He went to the window and looked out. His room was high up in one of the towers. The lights of the château were out now, and it was dark and silent; but there was a fragment of sallow moon, and by its wan light he could see, dimly, the courtyard; there, weaving in and out in the pattern of shadow, were black, noiseless forms; the hounds heard him at the window and looked up, expectantly, with their green eyes. Rainsford went back to the bed and lay down. By many methods he tried to put himself to sleep. He had achieved a doze when, just as morning began to come, he heard, far off in the jungle, the faint report of a pistol.

General Zaroff did not appear until luncheon. He was dressed faultlessly in the tweeds of a country squire. He was solicitous about the state of Rainsford's health.

"As for me," sighed the general, "I do not feel so well. I am worried, Mr. Rainsford. Last night I detected traces of my old complaint."

To Rainsford's questioning glance the general said: "Ennui. Boredom."

Then, taking a second helping of Crêpes Suzette, the general explained: "The hunting was not good last night. The fellow lost his head. He made a straight trail that offered no problems at all. That's the trouble with these sailors; they have dull brains to begin with, and they do not know how to get about in the woods. They do excessively stupid and obvious things. It's most annoying. Will you have another glass of Chablis, Mr. Rainsford?"

"General," said Rainsford firmly, "I wish to leave this island at once."

The general raised his thickets of eyebrows; he seemed hurt. "But, my dear fellow," the general protested, "you've only just come. You've had no hunting—"

"I wish to go today," said Rainsford. He saw the dead black eyes of the general on him, studying him. General Zaroff's face suddenly brightened.

He filled Rainsford's glass with venerable Chablis from a dusty bottle.

"Tonight," said the general, "we will hunt—you and I."

Rainsford shook his head. "No, General," he said. "I will not hunt."

The general shrugged his shoulders and nibbled delicately at a hothouse grape. "As you wish, my friend," he said. "The choice rests entirely with you. But may I not venture to suggest that you will find my idea of sport more diverting than Ivan's?"

He nodded toward the corner where the giant stood, scowling, his thick arms crossed on his hogshead of chest.

"You don't mean—" cried Rainsford.

"My dear fellow," said the general, "have I not told you I always mean what I say about hunting? This is really an inspiration. I drink to a foeman worthy of my steel—at last."

The general raised his glass, but Rainsford sat staring at him.

"You'll find this game worth playing," the general said enthusiastically. "Your brain against mine. Your woodcraft against mine. Your strength and stamina against mine. Outdoor chess. And the stake is not without value, eh?"

"And if I win—" began Rainsford huskily.

"I'll cheerfully admit myself defeated if I do not find you by midnight of the third day," said General Zaroff. "My sloop will place you on the mainland near a town."

The general read what Rainsford was thinking.

"Oh, you can trust me," said the Cossack. "I will give you my word as a gentleman and a sportsman. Of course you, in turn, must agree to say nothing of your visit here."

"I'll agree to nothing of the kind," said Rainsford.

"Oh," said the general, "in that case— But why discuss that now? Three days hence we can discuss it over a bottle of Veuve Cliquot, unless—"

The general sipped his wine.

Then a businesslike air animated him. "Ivan," he said to Rainsford, "will supply you with hunting clothes, food, a knife. I suggest you wear moccasins; they leave a poorer trail. I should suggest too that you avoid the big swamp in the southeast corner of the island. We call it Death Swamp. There's quicksand there. One foolish fellow tried it. The deplorable part of it was that Lazarus followed him. You can imagine my feelings, Mr. Rainsford. I loved Lazarus; he was the finest hound in my pack. Well, I must beg you to excuse me now. I always take a siesta after lunch. You'll hardly have time for a nap, I fear. You'll want to start, no doubt. I shall not follow till dusk. Hunting at night is so much more exciting than by day, don't you think? Au revoir, Mr. Rainsford, au revoir."

General Zaroff, with a deep, courtly bow, strolled from the room.

From another door came Ivan. Under one arm he carried khaki hunting clothes, a haversack of food, a leather sheath containing a long-bladed hunting knife; his right hand rested on a cocked revolver thrust in the crimson sash around his waist. . . .

Rainsford had fought his way through the bush for two hours. "I must keep my nerve. I must keep my nerve," he said through his tight teeth.

He had not been entirely clear-headed when the château gates snapped shut behind him. His whole idea at first was to put distance between himself and General Zaroff, and, to this end, he had plunged along, spurred on by the sharp rowels of something very like panic. Now he had got a grip on himself, had stopped, and was taking stock of himself and the situation.

He saw that straight flight was futile; inevitably it would bring him face to face with the sea. He was in a picture with the frame of water, and his operations, clearly, must take place within that frame.

"I'll give him a trail to follow," muttered Rainsford, and struck off from the rude path he had been following into the trackless wilderness. He executed a series of intricate loops; he doubled on his trail again and again, recalling all the lore of the fox hunt, and all the dodges of the fox. Night found him leg-weary, with hands and face lashed by the branches, on a thickly wooded ridge. He knew it would be insane to blunder on through the dark, even if he had the strength. His need for rest was imperative and he thought: "I have played the fox, now I must be the cat of the fable." A big tree with a thick trunk and outspread branches was near by, and taking care to leave not the slightest mark, he climbed up into the crotch and, stretching out on one of the broad limbs, after a fashion, rested. Rest brought him new confidence and almost a feeling of security. Even so zealous a hunter as General Zaroff could not trace him there, he told himself; only the devil himself could follow that complicated trail through the jungle after dark. But perhaps the general was a devil—

An apprehensive night crawled slowly by like a wounded snake, and sleep did not visit Rainsford, although the silence of a dead world was on the jungle. Toward morning when a dingy gray was varnishing the sky, the cry of some startled bird focused Rainsford's attention in that direction. Something was coming through the bush, coming slowly, carefully, coming by the same winding way Rainsford had come. He flattened himself down on the limb, and through a screen of leaves almost as thick as tapestry, he watched. The thing that was approaching was a man.

It was General Zaroff. He made his way along with his eyes fixed in utmost concentration on the ground before him. He paused almost beneath the tree, dropped to his knees, and studied the ground before him. Rainsford's impulse was to hurl himself down like a panther, but he saw that the general's right hand held something small and metallic—an automatic pistol.

The hunter shook his head several times as if he were puzzled. Then he straightened up and took from his case one of his black cigarettes; its pungent incense-like smoke floated up to Rainsford's nostrils.

Rainsford held his breath. The general's eyes had left the ground and were traveling inch by inch up the tree. Rainsford froze there, every muscle tensed for a spring. But the sharp eyes of the hunter stopped before they reached the limb where Rainsford lay; a smile spread over his brown face. Very deliberately he blew a smoke ring into the air; then he turned his back on the tree and walked carelessly away, back along the trail he had come. The swish of the underbrush against his hunting boots grew fainter and fainter.

The pent-up air burst hotly from Rainsford's lungs. His first thought made him feel sick and numb. The general could follow a trail through the woods at night; he could follow an extremely difficult trail; he must have uncanny powers; only by the merest chance had the Cossack failed to see his quarry.

Rainsford's second thought was even more terrible. It sent a shudder of cold horror through his whole being. Why had the general smiled? Why had he turned back?

Rainsford did not want to believe what his reason told him was true, but the truth was as evident as the sun that had by now pushed through the morning mists. The general was playing with him. The general was saving him for another day's sport! The Cossack was the cat; he was the mouse. Then it was that Rainsford knew the full meaning of terror.

"I will not lose my nerve. I will not."

He slid down from the tree, and struck off again into the woods. His face was set and he forced the machinery of his mind to function. Three hundred yards from his hiding place he stopped where a huge dead tree leaned precariously on a smaller living one. Throwing off his sack of food, Rainsford took his knife from its sheath and began to work with all his energy.

The job was finished at last, and he threw himself down behind a fallen log a hundred feet away. He did not have to wait long. The cat was coming again to play with the mouse.

Following the trail with the sureness of a bloodhound came General Zaroff. Nothing escaped those searching black eyes, no crushed blade of grass, no bent twig, no mark, no matter how faint, in the moss. So intent was the Cossack on his stalking that he was upon the thing Rainsford had made before he saw it. His foot touched the protruding bough that was the trigger. Even as he touched it, the general sensed his danger and leaped back with the agility of an ape. But he was not quite quick enough; the dead tree, delicately adjusted to rest on the cut living one, crashed down and struck the general a glancing blow on the shoulder as it fell; but for his alertness, he must have been smashed beneath it. He staggered, but he did not fall; nor did he drop his revolver. He stood there rubbing his injured shoulder, and Rainsford, with fear again gripping his heart, heard the general's mocking laugh ring through the jungle.

"Rainsford," called the general, "if you are within sound of my voice, as I suppose you are, let me congratulate you. Not many men know how to make a Malay mancatcher. Luckily, for me, I too have hunted in Malacca. You are proving interesting, Mr. Rainsford. I am going now to have my wound dressed; it's only a slight one. But I shall be back. I shall be back."

When the general, nursing his bruised shoulder, had gone, Rainsford took up his flight again. It was flight now, a desperate, hopeless flight, that carried him on for some hours. Dusk came, then darkness, and still he pressed on. The ground grew softer under his moccasins; the vegetation grew ranker, denser; insects bit him savagely. Then, as he stepped forward his foot sank into the ooze. He tried to wrench it back, but the muck sucked viciously at his foot as if it were a giant leech. With a violent effort, he tore his foot loose. He knew where he was now. Death Swamp and its quicksand.

His hands were tight closed as if his nerve were something tangible that someone in the darkness was trying to tear from his grip. The softness of the earth had given him an idea. He stepped back from the quicksand a dozen feet or so and, like some huge prehistoric beaver, he began to dig.

Rainsford had dug himself in in France when a second's delay meant death. That had been a placid pastime compared to his digging now. The pit grew deeper; when it was above his shoulders, he climbed out and from some hard saplings cut stakes and sharpened them to a fine point. These stakes he planted in the bottom of the pit with the points sticking up. With flying fingers he wove a rough carpet of weeds and branches and with it covered the mouth of the pit. Then, wet with sweat and aching with tiredness, he crouched behind the stump of a lightning-charred tree.

He knew his pursuer was coming; he heard the padding sound of feet on the soft earth, and the night breeze brought him the perfume of the general's cigarette. It seemed to Rainsford that the general was coming with unusual swiftness; he was not feeling his way along, foot by foot. Rainsford, crouching there, could not see the general, nor could he see the pit. He lived a year in a minute. Then he felt an impulse to cry aloud with joy, for he heard the sharp crackle of the breaking branches as the cover of the pit gave way; he heard the sharp scream of pain as the pointed stakes found their mark. He leaped up from his place of concealment. Then he cowered back. Three feet from the pit a man was standing, with an electric torch in his hand.

"You've done well, Rainsford," the voice of the general called. "Your Burmese tiger pit has claimed one of my best dogs. Again you score. I think, Mr. Rainsford, I'll see what you can do against my whole pack. I'm going home for a rest now. Thank you for a most amusing evening."

At daybreak Rainsford, lying near the swamp, was awakened by a sound that made him know that he had new things to learn about fear. It was a distant sound, faint and wavering, but he knew it. It was the baying of a pack of hounds.

Rainsford knew he could do one of two things. He

The Most Dangerous Game

could stay where he was and wait. That was suicide. He could flee. That was postponing the inevitable. For a moment he stood there, thinking. An idea that held a wild chance came to him, and tightening his belt, he headed away from the swamp. The baying of the hounds grew nearer, then still nearer, nearer, ever nearer. On a ridge, Rainsford climbed a tree. Down a watercourse, not a quarter of a mile away, he could see the bush moving. Straining his eyes, he saw the lean figure of General Zaroff; just ahead of him Rainsford made out another figure whose wide shoulders surged through the jungle weeds; it was the giant Ivan, and he seemed pulled forward by some unseen force; Rainsford knew that Ivan must be holding the pack in leash.

They would be on him any minute now. His mind worked frantically. He thought of a native trick he had learned in Uganda. He slid down the tree. He caught hold of a springy young sapling and to it he fastened his hunting knife, with the blade pointing down the trail; with a bit of wild grapevine he tied back the sapling. Then he ran for his life. The hounds raised their voices as they hit the fresh scent. Rainsford knew now how an animal at bay feels.

He had to stop to get his breath. The baying of the hounds stopped abruptly, and Rainsford's heart stopped too. They must have reached the knife.

He shinned excitedly up a tree and looked back. His pursuers had stopped. But the hope that was in Rainsford's brain when he climbed died, for he saw in the shallow valley that General Zaroff was still on his feet. But Ivan was not. The knife, driven by the recoil of the springing tree, had not wholly failed.

Rainsford had hardly tumbled to the ground when the pack resumed the chase.

"Nerve, nerve, nerve!" he panted, as he dashed along. A blue gap showed between the trees dead ahead. Ever nearer drew the hounds. Rainsford forced himself on toward that gap. He reached it. It was the shore of the sea. Across a cove he could see the gloomy gray stone of the château. Twenty feet below him the sea rumbled and hissed. Rainsford hesitated. He heard the hounds. Then he leaped far out into the sea. . . .

When the general and his pack reached the place by the sea, the Cossack stopped. For some minutes he stood regarding the blue-green expanse of water. He shrugged his shoulders. Then he sat down, took a drink of brandy from a silver flask, lit a perfumed cigarette, and hummed a bit from *Madame Butterfly*.

General Zaroff had an exceedingly good dinner in his great paneled dining hall that evening. With it he had a bottle of Pol Roger and a half bottle of Chambertin. Two slight annoyances kept him from perfect enjoyment. One was the thought that it would be difficult to replace Ivan; the other was that his quarry had escaped him; of course, the American hadn't played the game—so thought the general as he tasted his after-dinner liqueur. In his library he read, to soothe himself, from the works of Marcus Aurelius. At ten we went up to his bedroom. He was deliciously tired, he said to himself, as he locked himself in. There was a little moonlight, so, before turning on his light, he went to the window and looked down at the courtyard. To the great hounds he called: "Better luck another time!" Then he switched on the light.

"Rainsford!" screamed the general. "How in God's name did you get here?"

"Swam," said Rainsford. "I found it quicker than walking through the jungle."

The general sucked in his breath and smiled. "I congratulate you," he said. "You have won the game."

Rainsford did not smile. "I am still a beast at bay," he said, in a low voice. "Get ready, General Zaroff."

The general made one of his deepest bows. "I see," he said. "Splendid! One of us is to furnish a repast for the hounds. The other will sleep in this very excellent bed. On guard, Rainsford!" . . .

He had never slept in a better bed, Rainsford decided.

The Fourth Man

by John Russell

The raft might have been taken for a swath of cut sedge or a drifting tangle of roots as it slid out of the shadowy river mouth at dawn and dipped into the first ground swell. But while the sky brightened and the breeze came fresh offshore it picked a way among shoals and swampy islets with purpose and direction, and when at last the sun leaped up and cleared his bright eye of the morning mists it had passed the wide entrance to the bay and stood to open sea.

It was a curious craft for such a venture, of a type that survives here and there in the obscure corners of the world. The coracle maker would have scorned it. The first navigating pithecanthrope built nearly as well with his log and bush. A mat of pandanus leaves served for its sail and a paddle of niaouli wood for its helm. But it had a single point of real seaworthiness. Its twin floats, paired as a catamaran, were woven of reed bundles and bamboo sticks upon triple rows of bladders. It was light as a bladder itself, elastic, fit to ride any weather. One other quality this raft possessed which recommended it beyond all comfort and safety to its present crew. It was very nearly invisible. They had only to unstep its mast and lie flat in the cup of its soggy platform and they could not be spied half a mile away.

Four men occupied the raft. Three of them were white. Their bodies had been scored with brambles and blackened with dried blood, and on wrist and ankle they bore the black and wrinkled stain of the gyves. The hair upon them was long and matted. They wore only the rags of blue canvas uniforms. But they were whites, members of the superior race—members of a highly superior race according to those philosophers who rate criminal aberration as a form of genius.

The fourth was a man who had built the raft and was now sailing it. There was nothing superior about him. His skin was a layer of soot. His prognathous jaw carried out the angle of a low forehead. No line of beauty redeemed his lean limbs and knobby joints. Nature had set upon him her plainest stamp of inferiority, and his only attempts to relieve it were the twist of bark about his middle and the prong of pig ivory through the cartilage of his nose. Altogether a very ordinary specimen of one of the lowest branches of the human family—the Canaques of New Caledonia.

The three whites sat together well forward, and so they had sat in silence for hours. But at sunrise, as if some spell had been raised by the clang of that great copper gong in the east, they stirred and breathed deep of the salt air and looked at one another with hope in their haggard faces, and then back toward the land which was now no more than a gray-green smudge behind them.

"Friends," said the eldest, whose temples were bound with a scrap of crimson scarf, "Friends—the thing is done."

With a gesture like conjuring he produced from the breast of his tattered blouse three cigarettes, fresh and round, and offered them.

"Nippers!" cried the one at his right. "True nippers —name of a little good man! And here? Doctor, I always said you were a marvel. See if they be not new from the box!"

Dr. Dubosc smiled. Those who had known him in very different circumstances about the boulevards, the lobbies, the clubs, would have known him again and in spite of all disfigurement by that smile. And here, at

The Fourth Man

the bottom of the earth, it had set him still apart in the prisons, the cobalt mines, the chain gangs of a community not much given to mirth. Many a crowded lecture hall in Montpellier had seen him touch some intellectual firework with just a twinkle behind his bristly gray brows, with just such a thin curl of the lip.

"By way of celebration," he explained. "Consider. There are seventy-five evasions from Noumea every six months, of which not more than one succeeds. I had the figures myself from Dr. Pierre at the infirmary. He is not much of a physician, but a very honest fellow. Could anybody win on that percentage without dissipating? I ask you."

"Therefore you prepared for this?"

"It is now three weeks since I bribed the night guard to get these same nippers."

The other regarded him with admiration. Sentiment came readily upon this beardless face, tender and languid, but overdrawn, with eyes too large and soft and mouth too long. It was one of those faces familiar enough to the police which might serve as model for an angel were it not associated with some revolting piece of deviltry. Fenayrou himself had been condemned "to perpetuity" as an incorrigible.

"Is not our doctor a wonder?" he inquired as he handed a cigarette along to the third white man. "He thinks of everything. You should be ashamed to grumble. See—we are free, after all. Free!"

The third was a gross, pock-marked man with hairless lids, known sometimes as Niniche, Trois Huit, Le Tordeur, but chiefly among copains as Perroquet—a name derived perhaps from his beaked nose, or from some perception of his jailbird character. He was a garroter by profession, accustomed to rely upon his fists only for the exchange of amenities. Dubosc might indulge a fancy and Fenayrou seek to carry it as a pose, but The Parrot remained a gentleman of strictly serious turn. There is perhaps a tribute to the practical spirit of penal administration in the fact that while

Dubosc was the most dangerous of these three and Fenayrou the most depraved, Perroquet was the one with the official reputation, whose escape would be signaled first among the "Wanted." He accepted the cigarette because he was glad to get it, but he said nothing until Dubosc passed a tin box of matches and the first gulp of picadura filled his lungs. . . .

"Wait till you've got your two feet on a pavé, my boy. That will be the time to talk of freedom. What? Suppose there came a storm."

"It is not the season of storms," observed Dubosc.

But The Parrot's word had given them a check. Such spirits as these, to whom the land had been a horror, would be slow to feel the terror of the sea. Back there they had left the festering limbo of a convict colony, oblivion. Out here they had reached the rosy threshold of the big round world again. They were men raised from the dead, charged with all the furious appetites of lost years, with the savor of life strong and sweet on their lips. And yet they paused and looked about in quickened perception, with the clutch at the throat that takes landsmen on big waters. The spaces were so wide and empty. The voices in their ears were so wide and murmurous. There was a threat in each wave that came from the depths, a sinister vibration. None of them knew the sea. None knew its ways, what tricks it might play, what traps it might spread—more deadly than those of the jungle.

The raft was running now before a brisk chop with alternate spring and wallow, while the froth bubbled in over the prow and ran down among them as they sat.

"Where is that cursed ship that was to meet us here?" demanded Fenayrou.

"It will meet us right enough." Dubosc spoke carelessly, though behind the blown wisp of his cigarette he had been searching the outer horizon with keen glance. "This is the day, as agreed. We will be picked up off the mouth of the river."

"You say," growled Perroquet. "But where is any

The Fourth Man

river now? Or any mouth? Sacred name! this wind will blow us to China if we keep on."

"We dare not lie in any closer. There is a government launch at Torrien. Also the traders go armed hereabouts, ready for chaps like us. And don't imagine that the native trackers have given us up. They are likely to be following still in their proas."

"So far!"

Fenayrou laughed, for The Parrot's dread of their savage enemies had a morbid tinge.

"Take care, Perroquet. They will eat you yet."

"Is it true?" demanded the other, appealing to Dubosc. "I have heard it is even permitted these devils to keep all runaways they can capture—Name of God!— to fatten on."

"An idle tale," smiled Dubosc. "They prefer the reward. But one hears of convicts being badly mauled. There was a forester who made a break from Baie du Sud and came back lacking an arm. Certainly these people have not lost the habit of cannibalism."

"Piecemeal," chuckled Fenayrou. "They will only sample you, Perroquet. Let them make a stew of your brains. You would miss nothing."

But The Parrot swore.

"Name of a name—what brutes!" he said, and by a gesture recalled the presence of that fourth man who was of their party and yet so completely separated from them that they had almost forgotten him.

The Canaque was steering the raft. He sat crouched at the stern, his body glistening like varnished ebony with spray. He held the steering paddle, immobile as an image, his eyes fixed upon the course ahead.

There was no trace whatever of expression on his face, no hint of what he thought or felt or whether he thought or felt anything. He seemed not even aware of their regard, and each one of them experienced somehow that twinge of uneasiness with which the white always confronts his brother of color—this enigma brown or yellow or black he is fated never wholly to understand or to fathom. . . .

"It occurs to me," said Fenayrou in a pause, "that our friend here who looks like a shiny boot is able to steer us God knows where. Perhaps to claim the reward."

"Reassure yourself," answered Dubosc. "He steers by my order. Besides, it is a simple creature—an infant, truly, incapable of any but the most primitive reasoning."

"Is he incapable of treachery?"

"Of any that would deceive us. Also, he is bound by his duty. I made my bargain with his chief, up the river, and this one is sent to deliver us on board our ship. It is the only interest he has in us.

"And he will do it. Such is the nature of the native."

"I am glad you feel so," returned Fenayrou, adjusting himself indolently among the drier reeds and nursing the last of his cigarette. "For my part I wouldn't trust a figurehead like that for two sous. Mazette! What a monkey face!"

"Brute!" repeated Perroquet, and this man, sprung from some vile river-front slum of Argenteuil, whose home had been the dock pilings, the grog shop, and the jail, even this man viewed the black Canaque from an immeasurable distance with the look of hatred and contempt. . . .

Under the heat of the day the two younger convicts lapsed presently into dozing. But Dubosc did not doze. His tormented soul peered out behind its mask as he stood to sweep the sky line again under shaded hand. His theory had been so precise, the fact was so different. He had counted absolutely on meeting the ship—some small schooner, one of those flitting, half-piratical traders of the copra islands that can be hired like cabs in a dark street for any questionable enterprise. Now there was no ship, and here was no crossroads where one might sit and wait. Such a craft as the catamaran could not be made to lie to.

The Fourth Man

The doctor foresaw ugly complications for which he had prepared and whereof he must bear the whole burden. The escape had been his own conception, directed by him from the start. He had picked his companions deliberately from the whole forced labor squad, Perroquet for his great strength, Fenayrou as a ready echo. He had made it plain since their first dash from the mine, during their skirmish with the military guards, their subsequent wanderings in the brush with bloodhounds and trackers on the trail—through every crisis—that he alone should be the leader.

For the others, they had understood well enough which of their number was the chief beneficiary. Those mysterious friends on the outside that were reaching half round the world to further their release had never heard of such individuals as Fenayrou and The Parrot. Dubosc was the man who had pulled the wires: that brilliant physician whose conviction for murder had followed so sensationally, so scandalously, upon his sweep of academic and social honors. There would be clacking tongues in many a Parisian salon, and white faces in some, when news should come of his escape. Ah, yes, for example, they knew the highflyer of the band, and they submitted—so long as he led them to victory. They submitted, while reserving a depth of jealousy, the inevitable remnant of caste still persisting in this democracy of stripes and shame.

By the middle of the afternoon the doctor had taken certain necessary measures.

"Ho," said Fenayrou sleepily. "Behold our colors at the masthead. What is that for, comrade?"

"To help them sight us when the ship comes."

"What wisdom!" cried Fenayrou. "Always he thinks of everything, our doctor; everything—"

He stopped with the phrase on his lips and his hand outstretched toward the center of the platform. Here, in a damp depression among the reeds, had lain the wicker-covered bottle of green glass in which they carried their water. It was gone.

"Where is that flask?" he demanded. "The sun has grilled me like a bone."

"You will have to grill some more," said Dubosc grimly. "This crew is put on rations."

Fenayrou stared at him wide-eyed, and from the shadow of a folded mat The Parrot thrust his purpled face. "What do you sing me there? Where is that water?"

"I have it," said Dubosc.

They saw, in fact, that he held the flask between his knees, along with their single packet of food in its wrapping of cocoanut husk.

"I want a drink," challenged Perroquet.

"Reflect a little. We must guard our supplies like reasonable men. One does not know how long we may be floating here. . . ."

Fell a silence among them, heavy and strained, in which they heard only the squeaking of the frail basketwork as their raft labored in the wash. Slow as was their progress, they were being pushed steadily outward and onward, and the last cliffs of New Caledonia were no longer even a smudge in the west, but only a hazy line. And still they had seen no moving thing upon the great round breast of the sea that gleamed in its corselet of brass plates under a brazen sun.

"So that is the way you talk now?" began The Parrot, half choking. "You do not know how long? But you were sure enough when we started."

"I am still sure," returned Dubosc. "The ship will come. Only she cannot stay for us in one spot. She will be cruising to and fro until she intercepts us. We must wait."

"Ah, good! We must wait. And in the meantime, what? Fry here in the sacred heat with our tongues hanging out while you deal us drop by drop—*hein?*"

"Perhaps."

"But no!" The garroter clenched his hands. "Blood of God, there is no man big enough to feed me with a spoon!"

The Fourth Man

Fenayrou's chuckle came pat, as it had more than once, and Dubosc shrugged.

"You laugh!" cried Perroquet, turning in fury. "But how about this Lascar of a captain that lets us put to sea unprovided? What? He thinks of everything, does he? He thinks of everything! . . . Sacred farceur—let me hear you laugh again!"

Somehow Fenayrou was not so minded.

"And now he bids us be reasonable," concluded The Parrot. "Tell that to the devils in hell. You and your cigarettes, too. Bah—comedian!"

"It is true," muttered Fenayrou, frowning. "A bad piece of work for a captain of runaways."

But the doctor faced mutiny with his thin smile.

"All this alters nothing. Unless we would die very speedily, we must guard our water."

"By whose fault?"

"Mine," acknowledged the doctor. "I admit it. What then? We can't turn back. Here we are. Here we must stay. We can only do our best with what we have."

"I want a drink," repeated The Parrot, whose throat was afire since he had been denied.

"You can claim your share, of course. But take warning of one thing. After it is gone, do not think to sponge on us—on Fenayrou and me."

"He would be capable of it, the pig!" exclaimed Fenayrou, to whom this thrust had been directed. "I know him. See here, my old, the doctor is right. Fair for one, fair for all."

"I want a drink."

Dubosc removed the wooden plug from the flask.

"Very well," he said quietly.

With the delicacy that lent something of legerdemain to all his gestures, he took out a small canvas wallet, the crude equivalent of the professional black bag, from which he drew a thimble. Meticulously he poured a brimming measure, and Fenayrou gave a shout at the grumbler's fallen jaw as he accepted that tiny cup between his big fingers. Dubosc served Fenayrou and himself with the same amount before he recorked the bottle.

"In this way we should have enough to last us three days—maybe more—with equal shares among the three of us."

Such was his summing of the demonstration, and it passed without comment, as a matter of course in the premises, that he should count as he did—ignoring that other who sat alone at the stern of the raft, the black Canaque, the fourth man.

Perroquet had been outmaneuvered, but he listened sullenly while for the hundredth time Dubosc recited his easy and definite plan for their rescue, as arranged with his secret correspondents.

"That sounds very well," observed The Parrot at last. "But what if these jokers only mock themselves of you. What if they have counted it good riddance to let you rot here? And us? Sacred name, that would be a famous jest! To let us wait for a ship and they have no ship!"

"Perhaps the doctor knows better than we how sure a source he counts upon," suggested Fenayrou slyly.

"That is so," said Dubosc with great good humor. "My faith, it would not be well for them to fail me. Figure to yourselves that there is a safety vault in Paris full of papers to be opened at my death. Certain friends of mine could hardly afford to have some little confessions published that would be found there. . . . Such a tale as this, for instance—"

And to amuse them he told an indecent anecdote of high life, true or fictitious, it mattered nothing, so he could make Fenayrou's eyes glitter and The Parrot growl in wonder. Therein lay his means of ascendancy over such men, the knack of eloquence and vision. Harried, worn, oppressed by fears that he could sense so much more sharply than they, he must expend himself now in vulgar marvels to distract these ruder minds. He succeeded so far that when the wind fell at sunset they were almost cheerful, ready to believe that the morning would bring relief. They dined on dry biscuit and another thimbleful of water apiece and took watch by amiable agreement. And through that long clear night of stars, whenever the one of the three who lay awake between his comrades chanced to look aft, he could see the vague blot of another figure—the naked Canaque, who slumbered there apart.

It was an evil dawning. Fenayrou, on the morning trick, was aroused by a foot as hard as a hoof, and started up at Perroquet's wrathful face, with the doctor's graver glance behind.

"Idler! Good-for-nothing! Will you wake at least before I smash your ribs? Name of God, here is a way to stand watch!"

"Keep off!" cried Fenayrou wildly. "Keep off! Don't touch me!"

"Eh, and why not, fool? Do you know that the ship could have missed us? A ship could have passed us a dozen times while you slept!"

"Bourrique!"

"Vache!"

They spat the insults of the prison while Perroquet knotted his great fists over the other, who crouched away catlike, his mobile mouth twisted to a snarl. Dubosc stood aside in watchful calculation until against the angry red sunrise in which they floated there flashed the naked red gleam of steel. Then he stepped between.

"Enough. Fenayrou, put up that knife."

"The dog kicked me."

"You were at fault," said Dubosc sternly. "Perroquet!"

"Are we all to die that he may sleep?" stormed The Parrot.

"The harm is done. Listen now, both of you. Things are bad enough already. We may need all our energies. Look about."

They looked and saw the far, round horizon and the empty desert of the sea and their own long shadows that slipped slowly before them over its smooth, slow heaving, and nothing else. The land had sunk away from them in the night—some one of the chance currents that sweep among the islands had drawn them none could say where or how far. The trap had been sprung.

"Good God, how lonely it is!" breathed Fenayrou in a hush.

No more was said. They dropped their quarrel. Silently they shared their rations as before, made shift to eat something with their few drops of water, and sat down to pit themselves one against another in the vital struggle that each could feel was coming—a sort of tacit test of endurance.

A calm had fallen as it does between trades in this flawed belt, an absolute calm. The air hung weighted. The sea showed no faintest crinkle, only the maddening, unresting heave and fall in polished undulations on which the lances of the sun broke and drove in under their eyelids as white, hot splinters; a savage sun that kindled upon them with the power of a burning glass, that sucked the moisture from poor human bits of jelly and sent them crawling to the shelter of their mats and brought them out again, gasping, to shrivel anew. The water, the world of water, seemed sleek and thick as oil. They came to loathe it and the rotting smell of it, and when the doctor made them dip themselves overside they found little comfort. It was warm and sluggish, slimed. But a curious thing resulted. . . .

While they clung along the edge of the raft they all faced inboard, and there sat the black Canaque. He did not join them. He did not glance at them. He sat hunkered on his heels in the way of the native, with arms hugging his knees. He stayed in his place at the stern, motionless under that shattering sun, gazing out into vacancy. Whenever they raised their eyes, they saw him. He was the only thing to see.

"Here is one who appears to enjoy himself quite well," remarked Dubosc.

"I was thinking so myself," said Fenayrou.

"The animal!" rumbled Perroquet.

They observed him, and for the first time with direct interest, with thought of him as a fellow being—with the beginning of envy.

"He does not seem to suffer."

"What is going on in his brain? What does he dream of there? One would say he despises us."

"The beast!"

"Perhaps he is waiting for us to die," suggested Fenayrou with a harsh chuckle. "Perhaps he is waiting for the reward. He would not starve on the way home at least. And he could deliver us—piecemeal."

They studied him.

"How does he do it, doctor? Has he no feeling?"

"I have been wondering," said Dubosc. "It may be that his fibres are tougher—his nerves."

"Yet we have had water and he none."

"But look at his skin, fresh and moist."

"And his belly, fat as a football!"

The Parrot hauled himself aboard.

"Don't tell me this black beast knows thirst!" he cried with a strange excitement. "Is there any way he could steal our supplies?"

"Certainly not."

"Then, name of a dog, what if he has supplies of his own hidden about?"

The same monstrous notion struck them all, and the others swarmed to help. They knocked the black aside. They searched the platform where he sat, burrowing among the rushes, seeking some hidden cache, another bottle or a gourd. They found nothing.

"We were mistaken," said Dubosc.

But Perroquet had a different expression for disappointment. He turned on the Canaque and caught him by the kinky mop of hair and proceeded to give him what is known as gruel in the cobalt mines. This was a little specialty of The Parrot's. He paused only when he himself was breathless and exhausted and threw the limp, unresisting body from him.

"There, lump of dirt! That will teach you. Maybe you're not so chipper now, my boy—*hein?* Not quite so satisfied with your luck. Pig! That will make you feel...."

It was a ludicrous, a wanton, a witless thing. But the others said nothing. The learned Dubosc made no protest. Fenayrou had none of his usual jests at the garroter's stupidity. They looked on as at the satisfaction of a common grudge. The white trampled the black with or without cause, and that was natural. And the black crept away into his place with his hurts and his wrongs and made no sign and struck no blow. And that was natural too.

The sun declined into a blazing furnace whereof the gates stood wide, and they prayed to hasten it and cursed because it hung so long enchanted. But when it was gone their blistered bodies still held the heat like things incandescent. The night closed down over them like a purple bowl, glazed and impermeable. They would have divided the watches again, though none of them thought of sleep, but Fenayrou made a discovery.

"Idiots!" he rasped. "Why should we look and look? A whole navy of ships cannot help us now. If we are becalmed, why so are they!"

The Parrot was singularly put out.

"Is this true?" he asked Dubosc.

"Yes, we must hope for a breeze first."

"Then, name of God, why didn't you tell us so? Why did you keep on playing out the farce?"

He pondered it for a time. "See here," he said. "You are wise, eh? You are very wise. You know things we do not and you keep them to yourself." He leaned forward to peer into the doctor's face. "Very good. But if you think you are going to use that cursed smartness to get the best of us in any way—see here, my zig, I pull your gullet out like the string of an orange.... Like that. What?"

The Fourth Man

Fenayrou gave a nervous giggle and Dubosc shrugged, but it was perhaps about this time that he began to regret his intervention in the knife play.

For there was no breeze and there was no ship.

By the third morning each had sunk within himself, away from the rest. The doctor was lost in a profound depression, Perroquet in dark suspicion, and Fenayrou in bodily suffering, which he supported ill. Only two effective ties still bound their confederacy. One was the flask which Dubosc had slung at his side by a strip of wickerwork. Every move he made with it, every drop he poured, was followed with burning eyes. And he knew and he had no advantage of them in knowing that the will to live was working its relentless formula aboard that raft. Under his careful saving there still remained nearly half of their original store.

The other bond, as it had come to be by strange mutation, was the presence of the black Canaque.

There was no forgetting the fourth man now, no overlooking him. He loomed upon their consciousness, more formidable, more mysterious, more exasperating with every hour. Their own powers were ebbing. The naked savage had yet to give the slightest sign of complaint or weakness.

During the night he had stretched himself out on the platform as before, and after a time he had slept. Through the hours of darkness and silence while each of the whites wrestled with despair, this black man had slept as placidly as a child, with easy, regular breathing. Since then he had resumed his place aft. And so he remained, unchanged, a fixed fact and a growing wonder.

The brutal rage of Perroquet, in which he had vented his distorted hate of the native, had been followed by superstitious doubts.

"Doctor," he said at last, in awed huskiness, "is this a man or a fiend?"

"It is a man."

"A miracle," put in Fenayrou.

But the doctor lifted a finger in a way his pupils would have remembered.

"It is a man," he repeated, "and a very poor and wretched example of a man. You will find no lower type anywhere. Observe his cranial angle, the high ears, the heavy bones of his skull. He is scarcely above the ape. There are educated apes more intelligent."

"Ah? Then what?"

"He has a secret," said the doctor.

That was a word to transfix them.

"A secret! But we see him—every move he makes, every instant. What chance for a secret?"

The doctor rather forgot his audience, betrayed by chagrin and bitterness.

"How pitiful!" he mused. "Here are we three—children of the century, products of civilization—I fancy none would deny that, at least. And here is this man who belongs before the Stone Age. In a set trial of fitness, of wits, of resource, is he to win? Pitiful!"

"What kind of a secret?" demanded Perroquet, fuming.

"I cannot say," admitted Dubosc with a baffled gesture. "Possibly some method of breathing, some peculiar posture that operates to cheat the sensations of the body. Such things are known among primitive peoples—known and carefully guarded—like the properties of certain drugs, the uses of hypnotism and complex natural laws. Then, again, it may be psychologic—a mental attitude persistently held. Who knows? . . .

"To ask him? Useless. He will not tell. Why should he? We scorn him. We give him no share with us. We abuse him. He simply remains inscrutable—as he has always been and will always be. He never tells those innermost secrets. They are the means by which he has survived from the depth of time, by which he may yet survive when all our wisdom is dust."

"I know several very excellent ways of learning secrets," said Fenayrou as he passed his dry tongue over his lips. "Shall I begin?"

Dubosc came back with a start and looked at him.

"It would be useless. He could stand any torture you could invent. No, that is not the way."

"Listen to me," said Perroquet with sudden violence. "Me, I am wearied of the gab. You say he is a man. Very well. If he is a man, he must have blood in his veins. That would be, anyway, good to drink."

"No," returned Dubosc. "It would be hot. Also it would be salt. For food—perhaps. But we do not need food."

"Kill the animal then, and throw him over."

"We gain nothing."

"Well, sacred name, what do you want?"

"To beat him!" cried the doctor, curiously agitated. "To beat him at the game—that's what I want! For our own sakes, for our racial pride, we must, we must. To outlast him, to prove ourselves his masters. By better brain, by better organization and control. Watch him, watch him, friends—that we may ensnare him, that we may detect and defeat him in the end!"

But the doctor was miles beyond them.

"Watch?" growled The Parrot. "I believe you, old windbag. It is all one watch. I sleep no more and leave any man alone with that bottle."

To this the issue finally sharpened. Such craving among such men could not be stayed much longer by driblets. They watched. They watched the Canaque. They watched each other. And they watched the falling level in their flask—until the tension gave.

Another dawn upon the same dead calm, rising like a conflagration through the puddled air, cloudless, hopeless! Another day of blinding, slow-drawn agony to meet. And Dubosc announced that their allowance must be cut to half the thimbleful.

There remained perhaps a quarter of a liter—a miserable reprieve of bare life among the three of them, but one good swallow for a yearning throat.

At the sight of the bottle, at the tinkle of its limpid

content, so cool and silvery green inside the glass, Fenayrou's nerves snapped.

"More!" he begged, with pleading hands. "I die. More!"

When the doctor refused him, he groveled among the reeds, then rose suddenly to his knees and tossed his arms abroad with a hoarse cry.

"A ship! A ship!"

The others spun about. They saw the thin, unbroken ring of this greater and more terrible prison to which they had exchanged; and that was all they saw, though they stared and stared. They turned back to Fenayrou and found him in the act of tilting the bottle. A cunning slash of his knife had loosed it from its sling at the doctor's side. . . . Even now he was sucking at the mouth, spilling the precious liquid—

With one sweep Perroquet caught up their paddle and flattened him, crushed him.

Springing across the prostrate man, Dubosc snatched the flask upright and put the width of the raft between himself and the big garroter who stood wide-legged, his bloodshot eyes alight, rumbling in his chest.

"There is no ship," said The Parrot. "There will be no ship. We are done. Because of you and your rotten promises that have brought us here—doctor, liar, ass!"

Dubosc stood firm.

"Come a step nearer and I break bottle and all over your head."

They stood regarding each other, and Perroquet's brows gathered in a slow effort of thought.

"Consider," urged Dubosc with his quaint touch of pedantry. "Why should you and I fight? We are rational men. We can see this trouble through and win yet. Such weather cannot last forever. Besides, here are only two of us to divide the water now."

"That is true," nodded The Parrot. "That is true, isn't it? Fenayrou kindly leaves us his share. An inheritance—what? A famous idea. I'll take mine now."

Dubosc probed him keenly.

The Fourth Man

"My share at once, if you please," insisted Perroquet, with heavy docility. "Afterwards we shall see. Afterwards."

The doctor smiled his grim and wan little smile.

"So be it."

Without relinquishing the flask, he brought out his canvas wallet once more—that wallet which replaced the professional black bag—and rolled out the thimble by some swift sleight of his flexible fingers while he held Perroquet's glance with his own.

"I will measure it for you."

He poured the thimbleful and handed it over quickly, and when Perroquet had tossed it off he filled again and again.

"Four—five," he counted. "That is enough."

But The Parrot's big grip closed quietly around his wrist at the last offering and pinioned him and held him helpless.

"No, it is not enough. Now I will take the rest. Ha, wise man! Have I fooled you at last?"

There was no chance to struggle and Dubosc did not try, only stayed smiling up at him, waiting.

Perroquet took the bottle.

"The best man wins," he remarked. "Eh, my zig? A bright notion of yours. The—best—"

His lips moved, but no sound issued. A look of the most intense surprise spread upon his round face. He stood swaying a moment, and collapsed like a huge hinged toy when the string is cut.

Dubosc stooped and caught the bottle again, looking down at his big adversary, who sprawled in a brief convulsion and lay still, a bluish scum oozing between his teeth. . . .

"Yes, the best man wins," repeated the doctor, and laughed as he in turn raised the flask for a draft.

"The best man wins!" echoed a voice in his ear.

Fenayrou, writhing up and striking like a wounded snake, drove the knife home between his shoulders.

The bottle fell and rolled to the middle of the platform, and there, while each strove vainly to reach it, it poured out its treasure in a tiny stream that trickled away and was lost.

It may have been minutes or hours later—for time has no count in emptiness—when next a sound proceeded from that frail slip of a raft, hung like a mote between sea and sky. It was a phrase of song, a wandering strain in half tones and fluted accidentals, not unmelodious. The black Canaque was singing. He sang without emotion or effort, quite casually and softly to himself. So he might sing by his forest hut to ease some hour of idleness. Clasping his knees and gazing out into space, untroubled, unmoved, enigmatic to the end, he sang—he sang.

And, after all, the ship came.

She came in a manner befitting the sauciest little tops'l schooner between Nukahiva and the Pelews—as her owner often averred and none but the envious denied—in a manner worthy too of that able Captain Jean Guilbert, the merriest little scamp that ever cleaned a pearl bank or snapped a cargo of labor from a scowling coast. Before the first whiff out of the west came the *Petite Suzanne,* curtsying and skipping along with a flash of white frill by her forefoot, and brought up startled and stood shaking her skirts and keeping herself quite daintily to windward.

"And 'ere they are sure enough, by dam!" said the polyglot Captain Jean in the language of commerce and profanity. "Zose passengers for us, hey? They been here all the time, not ten mile off—I bet you, Marteau. Ain't it 'ell? What you zink, by gar?"

His second, a tall and excessively bony individual of gloomy outlook, handed back the glasses.

"More bad luck. I never approved this job. And now—see—we have had our voyage for nothing. What misfortune!"

"Marteau, if that good Saint Pierre gives you some day a gold 'arp, still you would holler bad luck—bad job!" retorted Captain Jean. "Do I 'ire you to stand zere and cry about ze luck? Get a boat over, and quicker zan zat!"

M. Marteau aroused himself sufficiently to take command of the boat's crew that presently dropped away to investigate. . . .

"It is even as I thought," he called up from the quarter when he returned with his report. "I told you how it would be, Captain Jean."

"Hey?" Captain Jean cried, bouncing at the rail. "Have you got those passengers yet, *enfant de salaud?*"

"I have not," said Marteau in the tone of lugubrious triumph. There was nothing in the world that could have pleased him quite so much as this chance to prove Captain Jean the loser on a venture. "We are too late. Bad luck, bad luck—that calm. What misfortune! They are all dead!"

"Will you mind your business?" shouted the skipper.

"But still the gentlemen are dead—"

"What is zat to me? All ze better, they will cost nozing to feed."

"But how—"

"Hogsheads, my gar," said Captain Jean paternally. "Zose hogsheads in the afterhold. Fill them nicely with brine, and zere we are!" And after having drawn all possible satisfaction from the other's amazement, he sprang the nub of his joke with a grin. "Ze gentlemen's passage is all paid, Marteau. Before we left Sydney, Marteau. I contrac' to bring back three escape' convicts and so by 'ell I do—in pickle! And now if you'll kindly get zose passengers aboard like I said and bozzer less about ze goddam luck, I be much oblige'. Also, zere is no green on my eye, Marteau, and you can dam well smoke it!"

Marteau recovered himself with difficulty in time to recall another trifling detail. "There is a fourth man on board that raft, Captain Jean. He is a Canaque—still alive. What shall we do with him?"

"A Canaque?" snapped Captain Jean. "A Canaque!

I had no word in my contrac' about any Canaque....
Leave him zere.... He is only a dam nigger. He'll do
well enough where he is."

And Captain Jean was right, perfectly right, for
while the *Petite Suzanne* was taking aboard her grisly
cargo the wind freshened from the west, and just about
the time she was shaping away for Australia the "dam
nigger" spread his own sail of pandanus leaves and
twirled his own helm of niaouli wood and headed the
catamaran eastward, back toward New Caledonia.

Feeling somewhat dry after his exertions, he plucked
at random from the platform a hollow reed with a
sharp end and, stretching himself at full length in his
accustomed place at the stern, he thrust the reed down
into one of the bladders underneath and drank his fill
of the sweet water....

He had a dozen such storage bladders remaining,
built into floats at intervals above the water line—quite
enough to last him safely home again.

The Interlopers

by "Saki" (H. H. Munro)

In a forest of mixed growth somewhere on the eastern spurs of the Carpathians, a man stood one winter night watching and listening, as though he waited for some beast of the woods to come within the range of his vision, and, later, of his rifle. But the game for whose presence he kept so keen an outlook was none that figured in the sportsman's calendar as lawful and proper for the chase; Ulrich von Gradwitz patrolled the dark forest in quest of a human enemy.

The forest lands of Gradwitz were of wide extent and well stocked with game; the narrow strip of precipitous woodland that lay on its outskirt was not remarkable for the game it harboured or the shooting it afforded, but it was the most jealously guarded of all its owner's territorial possessions. A famous lawsuit, in the days of his grandfather, had wrested it from the illegal possession of a neighbouring family of petty landowners; the dispossessed party had never acquiesced in the judgment of the Courts, and a long series of poaching affrays and similar scandals had embittered the relationships between the families for three generations. The neighbour feud had grown into a personal one since Ulrich had come to be head of his family; if there was a man in the world whom he detested and wished ill to it was Georg Znaeym, the inheritor of the quarrel and the tireless game-snatcher and raider of the disputed border-forest. The feud might, perhaps, have died down or been compromised if the personal ill-will of the two men had not stood in the way; as boys they had thirsted for one another's blood, as men each prayed that misfortune might fall on the other, and this wind-scourged winter night Ulrich had banded together his foresters to watch the dark forest, not in quest of four-footed quarry, but to keep a look-out for the prowling thieves whom he suspected of being afoot from across the land boundary. The roebuck, which usually kept in the sheltered hollows during a storm-wind, were running like driven things tonight, and there was movement and unrest among the creatures that were wont to sleep through the dark hours. Assuredly there was a disturbing element in the forest, and Ulrich could guess the quarter from whence it came.

He strayed away by himself from the watchers whom he had placed in ambush on the crest of the hill, and wandered far down the steep slopes amid the wild tangle of undergrowth, peering through the tree-trunks and listening through the whistling and skirling of the wind and the restless beating of the branches for sight or sound of the marauders. If only on this wild night, in this dark, lone spot, he might come across Georg Znaeym, man to man, with none to witness— that was the wish that was uppermost in his thoughts. And as he stepped round the trunk of a huge beech he came face to face with the man he sought.

The two enemies stood glaring at one another for a long silent moment. Each had a rifle in his hand, each had hate in his heart and murder uppermost in his mind. The chance had come to give full play to the passions of a lifetime. But a man who has been brought up under the code of a restraining civilization cannot easily nerve himself to shoot down his neighbour in cold blood and without word spoken, except for an offence against his hearth and honour. And before the moment of hesitation had given way to action a deed of Nature's own violence overwhelmed them both. A fierce shriek of the storm had been answered by a splitting crash over their heads, and ere they could leap

The Interlopers

aside a mass of falling beech tree had thundered down on them. Ulrich von Gradwitz found himself stretched on the ground, one arm numb beneath him and the other held almost as helplessly in a tight tangle of forked branches, while both legs were pinned beneath the fallen mass. His heavy shooting-boots had saved his feet from being crushed to pieces, but if his fractures were not as serious as they might have been, at least it was evident that he could not move from his present position till someone came to release him. The descending twigs had slashed the skin of his face, and he had to wink away some drops of blood from his eyelashes before he could take in a general view of the disaster. At his side, so near that under ordinary circumstances he could almost have touched him, lay Georg Znaeym, alive and struggling, but obviously as helplessly pinioned down as himself. All round them lay a thick-strewn wreckage of splintered branches and broken twigs.

Relief at being alive and exasperation at his captive plight brought a strange medley of pious thank-offerings and sharp curses to Ulrich's lips. Georg, who was nearly blinded with the blood which trickled across his eyes, stopped his struggling for a moment to listen, and then gave a short, snarling laugh.

"So you're not killed, as you ought to be, but you're caught, anyway," he cried; "caught fast. Ho, what a jest, Ulrich von Gradwitz snarled in his stolen forest. There's real justice for you!"

And he laughed again, mockingly and savagely.

"I'm caught in my own forest-land," retorted Ulrich. "When my men come to release us you will wish, perhaps, that you were in a better plight than caught poaching on a neighbour's land, shame on you."

Georg was silent for a moment; then he answered quietly:

"Are you sure that your men will find much to release? I have men, too, in the forest tonight, close behind me, and *they* will be here first and do the releasing. When they drag me out from under these damned branches it won't need much clumsiness on their part to roll this mass of trunk right over on the top of you. Your men will find you dead under a fallen beech tree. For form's sake I shall send my condolences to your family."

"It is a useful hint," said Ulrich fiercely. "My men had orders to follow in ten minutes' time, seven of which must have gone by already, and when they get me out—I will remember the hint. Only as you will have met your death poaching on my lands I don't think I can decently send any message of condolence to your family."

"Good," snarled Georg, "good. We fight this quarrel out to death, you and I and our foresters, with no cursed interlopers to come between us. Death and damnation to you, Ulrich von Gradwitz."

"The same to you, Georg Znaeym, forest-thief, game-snatcher."

Both men spoke with the bitterness of possible defeat before them, for each knew that it might be long before his men would seek him out or find him; it was a bare matter of chance which party would arrive on the scene.

Both had now given up the useless struggle to free themselves from the mass of wood that held them down; Ulrich limited his endeavours to an effort to bring his one partially free arm near enough to his outer coatpocket to draw out his wine-flask. Even when he had accomplished that operation it was long before he could manage the unscrewing of the stopper or get any of the liquid down his throat. But what a Heaven-sent draught it seemed! It was an open winter, and little snow had fallen as yet, hence the captives suffered less from the cold than might have been the case at the season of the year; nevertheless, the wine was warming and reviving to the wounded man, and he looked across with something like a throb of pity to where his enemy lay, just keeping the groans of pain and weariness from crossing his lips.

"Could you reach this flask if I threw it over to you?" asked Ulrich suddenly; "there is good wine in it, and one may as well be as comfortable as one can. Let us drink, even if tonight one of us dies."

"No, I can scarcely see anything: there is so much blood caked round my eyes," said Georg, "and in any case I don't drink wine with an enemy."

Ulrich was silent for a few minutes, and lay listening to the weary screeching of the wind. An idea was slowly forming and growing in his brain, an idea that gained strength every time that he looked across at the man who was fighting so grimly against pain and exhaustion. In the pain and langour that Ulrich himself was feeling the old fierce hatred seemed to be dying down.

"Neighbour," he said presently, "do as you please if your men come first. It was a fair compact. But as for me, I've changed my mind. If my men are the first to come you shall be the first to be helped, as though you were my guest. We have quarrelled like devils all our lives over this stupid strip of forest, where the trees can't even stand upright in a breath of wind. Lying here tonight, thinking, I've come to think we've been rather fools; there are better things in life than getting the better of a boundary dispute. Neighbour, if you will help me to bury the old quarrel I—I will ask you to be my friend."

Georg Znaeym was silent for so long that Ulrich thought, perhaps, he had fainted with the pain of his injuries. Then he spoke slowly and in jerks.

"How the whole region would stare and gabble if we rode into the market-square together. No one living can remember seeing a Znaeym and a von Gradwitz talking to one another in friendship. And what peace there would be among the forester folk if we ended our feud tonight. And if we choose to make peace among our people there is none other to interfere, no interlopers from outside. . . . You would come and keep the Sylvester night beneath my roof, and I would come and feast on some high day at your castle. . . . I would never fire a shot on your land, save when you invited me as guest; and you should come and shoot with me down in the marshes where the wildfowl are. In all the countryside there are none that could hinder it if we willed to make peace. I never thought to have wanted to do other than hate you all my life, but I think I have changed my mind about things too, this last half-hour. And you offered me your wine-flask. . . . Ulrich von Gradwitz, I will be your friend."

For a space both men were silent, turning over in their minds the wonderful changes that this dramatic reconciliation would bring about. In the cold, gloomy forest, with the wind tearing in fitful gusts through the naked branches and whistling round the tree-trunks, they lay and waited for the help that would bring release and succour to both parties. And each prayed a private prayer that his men might be the first to arrive, so that he might be the first to show honourable attention to the enemy that had become a friend.

Presently, as the wind dropped for a moment, Ulrich broke silence.

"Let's shout for help," he said; "in this lull our voices may carry a little way."

"They won't carry far through the trees and undergrowth," said Georg, "but we can try. Together, then."

The two raised their voices in a prolonged hunting call.

"Together again," said Ulrich a few minutes later, after listening in vain for an answering halloo.

"I heard something that time, I think," said Ulrich.

"I heard nothing but the pestilential wind," said Georg hoarsely.

There was silence again for some minutes, and then Ulrich gave a joyful cry.

"I can see figures coming through the wood. They are following in the way I came down the hillside."

Both men raised their voices in as loud a shout as they could muster.

"They hear us! They've stopped. Now they see us. They're running down the hill towards us," cried Ulrich.

"How many of them are there?" asked Georg.

"I can't see distinctly," said Ulrich; "nine or ten."

"Then they are yours," said Georg; "I had only seven out with me."

"They are making all the speed they can, brave lads," said Ulrich gladly.

"Are they your men?" asked Georg. "Are they your men?" he repeated impatiently as Ulrich did not answer.

"No," said Ulrich with a laugh, the idiotic chattering laugh of a man unstrung with a hideous fear.

"Who are they?" asked Georg quickly, straining his eyes to see what the other would gladly not have seen.

"Wolves."

The Adventure of the Dancing Men

by Sir Arthur Conan Doyle

Holmes had been seated for some hours in silence with his long, thin back curved over a chemical vessel in which he was brewing a particularly malodorous product. His head was sunk upon his breast, and he looked from my point of view like a strange, lank bird, with dull gray plumage and a black topknot.

"So, Watson," said he, suddenly, "you do not propose to invest right now in South African securities?"

I gave a start of astonishment. Accustomed as I was to Holmes's curious faculties, this sudden intrusion into my most intimate thoughts was utterly inexplicable.

"How on earth do you know that?" I asked.

He wheeled round upon his stool, with a steaming test tube in his hand, and a gleam of amusement in his deep-set eyes.

"Now, Watson, confess yourself utterly taken aback," said he.

"I am."

"I ought to make you sign a paper to that effect."

"Why?"

"Because in five minutes you will say that it is all so absurdly simple."

"I am sure that I shall say nothing of the kind."

"You see, my dear Watson"—he propped his test tube in the rack, and began to lecture with the air of a professor addressing his class—"it is not really difficult to construct a series of inferences, each dependent upon

The Adventure of the Dancing Men

its predecessor and each simple in itself. If, after doing so, one simply knocks out all the central inferences and presents one's audience with the starting point and the conclusion, one may produce a startling, though possibly a meretricious, effect. Now, it was not really difficult, by an inspection of the groove between your left forefinger and thumb, to feel sure that you did *not* propose to invest your small capital in the gold fields."

"I see no connection."

"Very likely not, but I can quickly show you a close connection. Here are the missing links of the very simple chain: 1. You had chalk between your left finger and thumb when you returned from the club last night. 2. You put chalk there when you play billiards, to steady the cue. 3. You never play billiards except with Thurston. 4. You told me, four weeks ago, that Thurston had an option on some South African property, which would expire in a month, and which he desired you to share with him. 5. Your checkbook is locked in my drawer, and you have not asked for the key. 6. You do not propose to invest your money in this manner."

"How absurdly simple!" I cried.

"Quite so!" said he, a little nettled. "Every problem becomes very childish when once it is explained to you. Here is an unexplained one. See what you can make of that, friend Watson." He tossed a sheet of paper upon the table and turned once more to his chemical analysis.

I looked with amazement at the absurd hieroglyphics upon the paper.

"Why, Holmes, it is a child's drawing," I cried.

"Oh, that's your idea!"

"What else should it be?"

"That is what Mr. Hilton Cubitt, of Riding Thorpe Manor, Norfolk, is very anxious to know. This little conundrum came by the first post, and he was to follow by the next train. There's a ring at the bell, Watson. I should not be surprised if this were he."

A heavy step was heard upon the stairs, and an instant later there entered a tall, ruddy, clean-shaven gentleman, whose clear eyes and florid cheeks told of a life led far from the fogs of Baker Street. He seemed to bring a whiff of his strong, fresh, bracing, east-coast air with him as he entered. Having shaken hands with each of us, he was about to sit down, when his eye rested upon the paper with the curious markings, which I had just examined and left upon the table.

"Well, Mr. Holmes, what do you make of these?" he cried. "They told me that you were fond of queer mysteries, and I don't think you can find a queerer one than that. I sent the paper on ahead, so that you might have time to study it before I came."

"It is certainly rather a curious production," said Holmes. "At first sight it would appear to be some childish prank. It consists of a number of absurd little figures dancing across the paper upon which they are drawn. Why should you attribute any importance to so grotesque an object?"

"I never should, Mr. Holmes. But my wife does. It is frightening her to death. She says nothing, but I can see terror in her eyes. That's why I want to sift the matter to the bottom."

Holmes held up the paper so that the sunlight shone full upon it. It was a page torn from a notebook. The markings were done in pencil, and ran in this way:

Holmes examined it for some time, and then, folding it carefully up, he placed it in his pocketbook.

"This promises to be a most interesting and unusual case," said he. "You gave me a few particulars in your

The Adventure of the Dancing Men

letter, Mr. Hilton Cubitt, but I should be very much obliged if you would kindly go over it all again for the benefit of my friend, Dr. Watson."

"I'm not much of a storyteller," said our visitor, nervously clasping and unclasping his great, strong hands. "You'll just ask me anything that I don't make clear. I'll begin at the time of my marriage last year, but I want to say first of all that, though I'm not a rich man, my people have been at Riding Thorpe for a matter of five centuries, and there is no better known family in the County of Norfolk. Last year I came up to London for the Jubilee, and I stopped at a boarding-house in Russell Square, because Parker, the vicar of our parish, was staying in it. There was an American young lady there—Patrick was the name—Elsie Patrick. In some way we became friends, and before my month was up I was as much in love as man could be. We were quietly married at a registry office, and we returned to Norfolk a wedded couple. You'll think it very mad, Mr. Holmes, that a man of a good old family should marry a wife in this fashion, knowing nothing of her past or of her people, but if you saw her and knew her, it would indeed help you to understand.

"She was very straight about it, was Elsie. I can't say that she did not give me every chance of getting out of it if I wished to do so. 'I wish to forget all about them. I would rather never allude to the past, for it is very painful to me. If you take me, Hilton, you will take a woman who has nothing that she need be personally ashamed of; but you will have to be content with my word for it, and to allow me to be silent as to all that passed up to the time when I became yours. If these conditions are too hard, then go back to Norfolk, and leave me to the lonely life in which you found me.' It was only the day before our wedding that she said those very words to me. I told her that I was content to take her on her own terms, and I have been as good as my word.

"Well, we have been married now for a year, and

very happy we have been. But about a month ago, at the end of June, I saw for the first time signs of trouble. One day my wife received a letter from America. I saw the American stamp. She turned deadly white, read the letter, and threw it into the fire. She made no allusion to it afterwards, and I made none, for a promise is a promise; but she has never known an easy hour from that moment. There is always a look of fear upon her face—a look as if she were waiting and expecting. She would do better to trust me. She would find that I was her best friend. But until she speaks, I can say nothing. Mind you, she is a truthful woman, Mr. Holmes, and whatever trouble there may have been in her past life it has been no fault of hers. I am only a simple Norfolk squire, but there is not a man in England who ranks his family honor more highly than I do. She knows it well, and she knew it well before she married me. She would never bring any stain upon it—of that I am sure.

"Well, now I come to the queer part of my story. About a week ago—it was the Tuesday of last week—I found on one of the window sills a number of absurd little dancing figures like these upon the paper. They were scrawled with chalk. I thought that it was the stableboy who had drawn them, but the lad swore he knew nothing about it. Anyhow, they had come there during the night. I had them washed out, and I only mentioned the matter to my wife afterwards. To my surprise, she took it very seriously, and begged me if any more came to let her see them. None did come for a week, and then yesterday morning I found this paper lying on the sundial in the garden. I showed it to Elsie, and down she dropped in a dead faint. Since then she has looked like a woman in a dream, half dazed, and with terror always lurking in her eyes. It was then that I wrote and sent the paper to you, Mr. Holmes. It was not a thing that I could take to the police, for they would have laughed at me, but you will tell me what to do. I am not a rich man, but if there is any danger threatening my little woman, I would spend my last copper to shield her."

He was a fine creature, this man of the old English soil—simple, straight, and gentle, with his great, earnest blue eyes and broad, comely face. His love for his wife and his trust in her shone in his features. Holmes had listened to his story with the utmost attention, and now he sat for some time in silent thought.

"Don't you think, Mr. Cubitt," said he, at last, "that your best plan would be to make a direct appeal to your wife, and to ask her to share her secret with you?"

Hilton Cubitt shook his massive head.

"A promise is a promise, Mr. Holmes. If Elsie wished to tell me, she would. If not, it is not for me to force her confidence. But I am justified in taking my own line—and I will."

"Then I will help you with all my heart. In the first place, have you heard of any strangers being seen in your neighborhood?"

"No."

"I presume that it is a very quiet place. Any fresh face would cause comment?"

"In the immediate neighborhood, yes. But we have several small watering places not very far away. And the farmers take in lodgers."

"These hieroglyphics have evidently a meaning. If it is a purely arbitrary one, it may be impossible for us to solve it. If, on the other hand, it is systematic, I have no doubt that we shall get to the bottom of it. But this particular sample is so short that I can do nothing, and the facts which you have brought me are so indefinite that we have no basis for an investigation. I would suggest that you return to Norfolk, that you keep a keen lookout, and that you take an exact copy of any fresh dancing men which may appear. It is a thousand pities that we have not a reproduction of those which were done in chalk upon the window sill. Make a discreet inquiry also as to any strangers in the neighborhood. When you have collected some fresh evidence, come to me again. That is the best advice which I can give you, Mr. Hilton Cubitt. If there are any pressing fresh developments, I shall be always ready to run down and see you in your Norfolk home."

The interview left Sherlock Holmes very thoughtful, and several times in the next few days I saw him take his slip of paper from his notebook and look long and earnestly at the curious figures inscribed upon it. He made no allusion to the affair, however, until one afternoon a fortnight or so later. I was going out when he called me back.

"You had better stay here, Watson."

"Why?"

"Because I had a wire from Hilton Cubitt this morning. You remember Hilton Cubitt, of the dancing men? He was to reach Liverpool Street at one-twenty. He may be here at any moment. I gather from his wire that there have been some new incidents of importance."

We had not long to wait, for our Norfolk squire came straight from the station as fast as a hansom could bring him. He was looking worried and depressed, with tired eyes and a lined forehead.

"It's getting on my nerves, this business, Mr. Holmes," said he, as he sank, like a wearied man, into an armchair. "It's bad enough to feel that you are surrounded by unseen, unknown folk, who have some kind of design upon you; but when, in addition to that, you know that it is just killing your wife by inches, then it becomes as much as flesh and blood can endure. She's wearing away under it—just wearing away before my eyes."

"Has she said anything yet?"

"No, Mr. Holmes, she has not. And yet there have been times when the poor girl has wanted to speak, and yet could not quite bring herself to take the plunge. I have tried to help her, but I dare say I did it clumsily, and scared her from it. She has spoken about my old

The Adventure of the Dancing Men

family, and our reputation in the county, and our pride in our unsullied honor, and I always felt it was leading to the point, but somehow it turned off before we got there."

"But you have found out something for yourself?"

"A good deal, Mr. Holmes. I have several fresh dancing-men pictures for you to examine, and, what is more important, I have seen the fellow."

"What, the man who draws them?"

"Yes, I saw him at his work. But I will tell you everything in order. When I got back after my visit to you, the very first thing I saw next morning was a fresh crop of dancing men. They had been drawn in chalk upon the black wooden door of the tool house, which stands beside the lawn in full view of the front windows. I took an exact copy, and here it is." He unfolded a paper and laid it upon the table. Here are the hieroglyphics:

"Excellent!" said Holmes. "Excellent! Pray continue."

"When I had taken the copy, I rubbed out the marks, but, two mornings later, a fresh inscription had appeared. I have a copy of it here:"

Holmes rubbed his hands and chuckled with delight.

"Our material is rapidly accumulating," said he.

"Three days later a message was left scrawled upon paper, and placed under a pebble upon the sundial. Here it is. The characters are, as you see, exactly the same as the last one. After that I determined to lie in wait; so I got out my revolver and I sat up in my study, which overlooks the lawn and garden. About two in the morning I was seated by the window, all being dark save for the moonlight outside, when I heard steps behind me, and there was my wife in her dressing gown. She implored me to come to bed. I told her frankly that I wished to see who it was who played such absurd tricks upon us. She answered that it was some senseless practical joke, and that I should not take any notice of it.

" 'If it really annoys you, Hilton, we might go and travel, you and I, and so avoid this nuisance.'

" 'What, be driven out of our own house by a practical joker?' said I. 'Why, we should have the whole county laughing at us.'

" 'Well, come to bed,' said she, 'and we can discuss it in the morning.'

"Suddenly, as she spoke, I saw her white face grow whiter yet in the moonlight, and her hand tighten upon my shoulder. Something was moving in the shadow of the tool house. I saw a dark, creeping figure which crawled round the corner and squatted in front of the door. Seizing my pistol, I was rushing out, when my wife threw her arms round me and held me with convulsive strength. I tried to throw her off, but she clung to me most desperately. At last I got clear, but by the time I had opened the door and reached the house the creature was gone. He had left a trace of his presence, however, for there on the door was the very same arrangement of dancing men which had already twice appeared, and which I have copied on that paper. There was no other sign of the fellow anywhere, though I ran all over the grounds. And yet the amazing thing is that he must have been there all the time, for when I examined the door again in the morning, he had scrawled some more of his pictures under the line which I had already seen."

"Have you that fresh drawing?"

The Adventure of the Dancing Men

"Yes, it is very short, but I made a copy of it, and here it is."

Again he produced a paper. The new dance was in this form:

"Tell me," said Holmes—and I could see by his eyes that he was much excited—"was this a mere addition to the first or did it appear to be entirely separate?"

"It was on a different panel of the door."

"Excellent! This is far the most important of all for our purpose. It fills me with hopes. Now, Mr. Hilton Cubitt, please continue your most interesting statement."

"I have nothing more to say, Mr. Holmes, except that I was angry with my wife that night for having held me back when I might have caught the skulking rascal. She said that she feared that I might come to harm. For an instant it had crossed my mind that perhaps what she really feared was that *he* might come to harm; for I could not doubt that she knew who this man was, and what he meant by these strange signals. But there is a tone in my wife's voice, Mr. Holmes, and a look in her eyes which forbid doubt, and I am sure that it was indeed my own safety that was in her mind. There's the whole case and now I want your advice as to what I ought to do. My own inclination is to put half a dozen of my farm lads in the shrubbery, and when this fellow comes again, to give him such a hiding that he will leave us in peace for the future."

"I fear it is too deep a case for such simple remedies," said Holmes. "How long can you stay in London?"

"I must go back today. I would not leave my wife alone all night for anything. She is very nervous, and begged me to come back."

"I dare say you are right. But if you could have stopped, I might possibly have been able to return with you in a day or two. Meanwhile you will leave me these papers, and I think that it is very likely that I shall be able to pay you a visit shortly and to throw some light upon your case."

Sherlock Holmes preserved his calm professional manner until our visitor had left us, although it was easy for me, who knew him so well, to see that he was profoundly excited. The moment that Hilton Cubitt's broad back had disappeared through the door my comrade rushed to the table, laid out all the slips of paper containing dancing men in front of him, and threw himself into an intricate and elaborate calculation. For two hours I watched him as he covered sheet after sheet of paper with figures and letters, so completely absorbed in his task that he had evidently forgotten my presence. Sometimes he was making progress and whistled and sang at his work; sometimes he was puzzled, and would sit for long spells with a furrowed brow and a vacant eye. Finally he sprang from his chair with a cry of satisfaction, and walked up and down the room rubbing his hands together. Then he wrote a long telegram upon a cable form. "If my answer to this is as I hope, you will have a very pretty case to add to your collection, Watson," said he. "I expect that we shall be able to go down to Norfolk tomorrow, and to take our friend some very definite news as to the secret of his annoyance."

I confess that I was filled with curiosity, but I was aware that Holmes liked to make his disclosures at his own time and in his own way, so I waited until it should suit him to take me into his confidence.

But there was a delay in that answering telegram, and two days of impatience followed, during which Holmes pricked up his ears at every ring of the bell. On the evening of the second there came a letter from Hilton Cubitt. All was quiet with him, save that a long inscription had appeared that morning upon the pedestal of the sundial. He inclosed a copy of it, which is here reproduced:

Holmes bent over this grotesque frieze for some minutes, and then suddenly sprang to his feet with an exclamation of surprise and dismay. His face was haggard with anxiety.

"We have let this affair go far enough," said he. "Is there a train to North Walsham tonight?"

I turned up the timetable. The last had just gone.

"Then we shall breakfast early and take the very first in the morning," said Holmes. "Our presence is most urgently needed. Ah! here is our expected cablegram. One moment, Mrs. Hudson, there may be an answer. No, that is quite as I expected. This message makes it even more essential that we should not lose an hour in letting Hilton Cubitt know how matters stand, for it is a singular and a dangerous web in which our simple Norfolk squire is entangled."

So, indeed, it proved, and as I come to the dark conclusion of a story which had seemed to me to be only childish and bizarre, I experience once again the dismay and horror with which I was filled. Would that I had some brighter ending to communicate to my readers, but these are the chronicles of fact, and I must follow to their dark crisis the strange chain of events which for some days made Riding Thorpe Manor a household word through all the length and breadth of England.

We had hardly alighted at North Walsham, and mentioned the name of our destination, when the stationmaster hurried towards us. "I suppose that you are the detectives from London?" said he.

A look of annoyance passed over Holmes's face.

"What makes you think such a thing?"

"Because Inspector Martin from Norwich has just passed through. But maybe you are the surgeons. She's not dead—or wasn't by last accounts. You may be in time to save her yet—though it be for the gallows."

Holmes's brow was dark with anxiety.

"We are going to Riding Thorpe Manor," said he, "but we have heard nothing of what has passed there."

"It's a terrible business," said the stationmaster. "They are shot, both Mr. Hilton Cubitt and his wife. She shot him and then herself—so the servants say. He's dead, and her life is despaired of. Dear, dear, one of the oldest families in the county of Norfolk, and one of the most honored."

Without a word Holmes hurried to a carriage, and during the long seven miles' drive he never opened his mouth. Seldom have I seen him so utterly despondent. He had been uneasy during all our journey from town, and I had observed that he had turned over the morning papers with anxious attention, but now this sudden realization of his worst fears left him in a blank melancholy. He leaned back in his seat, lost in gloomy speculation. Yet there was much around to interest us, for we were passing through as singular a countryside as any in England, where a few scattered cottages represented the population of today; while on every hand enormous square-towered churches bristled up from the flat green landscape and told of the glory and prosperity of old East Anglia. At last the violet rim of the German Ocean appeared over the green edge of the Norfolk coast, and the driver pointed with his whip to two old brick and timber gables which projected from a grove of trees. "That's Riding Thorpe Manor," said he.

As we drove up to the porticoed front door, I observed in front of it, beside the tennis lawn, the black tool house and the pedestaled sundial with which we had such strange associations. A dapper little man, with a quick, alert manner and a waxed mustache, had just descended from a high dogcart. He introduced himself

The Adventure of the Dancing Men

as Inspector Martin, of the Norfolk Constabulary, and he was considerably astonished when he heard the name of my companion.

"Why, Mr. Holmes, the crime was only committed at three this morning. How could you hear of it in London and get to the spot as soon as I?"

"I anticipated it. I came in the hope of preventing it."

"Then you must have important evidence, of which we are ignorant, for they were said to be a most united couple."

"I have only the evidence of the dancing men," said Holmes. "I will explain the matter to you later. Meanwhile, since it is too late to prevent this tragedy, I am very anxious that I should use the knowledge which I possess in order to insure that justice be done. Will you associate me in your investigation, or will you prefer that I should act independently?"

"I should be proud to feel that we were acting together, Mr. Holmes," said the inspector, earnestly.

"In that case I should be glad to hear the evidence and to examine the premises without an instant of unnecessary delay."

Inspector Martin had the good sense to allow my friend to do things in his own fashion, and contented himself with carefully noting the results. The local surgeon, an old, white-haired man, had just come down from Mrs. Hilton Cubitt's room, and he reported that her injuries were serious, but not necessarily fatal. The bullet had passed through the front of her brain, and it would probably be some time before she could regain full consciousness.

On the question of whether she had been shot or had shot herself, he would not venture to express any decided opinion. Certainly the bullet had been discharged at very close quarters. There was only the one pistol found in the room, two barrels of which had been emptied. Mr. Hilton Cubitt had been shot through the heart. It was equally conceivable that he had shot her and then himself, or that she had been the criminal, for the revolver lay upon the floor midway between them.

"Has he been moved?" asked Holmes.

"We have moved nothing except the lady. We could not leave her lying wounded upon the floor."

"How long have you been here, Doctor?"

"Since four o'clock."

"Any one else?"

"Yes, the constable here."

"And you have touched nothing?"

"Nothing."

"You have acted with great discretion. Who sent for you?"

"The housemaid, Saunders."

"Was it she who gave the alarm?"

"She and Mrs. King, the cook."

"Where are they now?"

"In the kitchen, I believe."

"Then I think we had better hear their story at once."

The old hall, oak-paneled and high-windowed, had been turned into a court of investigation. Holmes sat in a great, old-fashioned chair, his inexorable eyes gleaming out of his haggard face. I could read in them a set purpose to devote his life to this quest until the client whom he had failed to save should at last be avenged. The trim Inspector Martin, the old, gray-headed country doctor, myself, and a stolid village policeman made up the rest of that strange company.

The two women told their story clearly enough. They had been aroused from their sleep by the sound of an explosion, which had been followed a minute later by a second one. They slept in adjoining rooms, and Mrs. King had rushed in to Saunders. Together they had descended the stairs. The door of the study was open, and a candle was burning upon the table. Their master lay upon his face in the center of the room. He was quite dead. Near the window his wife

The Adventure of the Dancing Men

was crouching, her head leaning against the wall. She was horribly wounded, and the side of her face was red with blood. She breathed heavily, but was incapable of saying anything. The passage, as well as the room, was full of smoke and the smell of powder. The window was certainly shut and fastened upon the inside. Both women were positive upon the point. They had at once sent for the doctor and for the constable. Then, with the aid of the groom and the stableboy, they had conveyed their injured mistress to her room. Both she and her husband had occupied the bed. She was clad in her dress—he in his dressing gown, over his night clothes. Nothing had been moved in the study. So far as they knew, there had never been any quarrel between husband and wife. They had always looked upon them as a very united couple.

These were the main points of the servants' evidence. In answer to Inspector Martin, they were clear that every door was fastened upon the inside, and that no one could have escaped from the house. In answer to Holmes, they both remembered that they were conscious of the smell of powder from the moment that they ran out of their rooms upon the top floor. "I commend that fact very carefully to your attention," said Holmes to his professional colleague. "And now I think that we are in a good position to undertake a thorough examination of the room."

The study proved to be a small chamber, lined on three sides with books, and with a writing table facing an ordinary window, which looked out upon the garden. Our first attention was given to the body of the unfortunate squire, whose huge frame lay stretched across the room. His disordered dress showed that he had been hastily aroused from sleep. The bullet had been fired at him from the front, and had remained in his body, after penetrating the heart. His death had certainly been instantaneous and painless. There was no powder marking either upon his dressing gown or on his hands. According to the country surgeon, the lady had stains upon her face, but none upon her hand.

"The absence of the latter means nothing, though its presence may mean everything," said Holmes. "Unless the powder from a badly fitting cartridge happens to spurt backward, one may fire many shots without leaving a sign. I would suggest that Mr. Cubitt's body may now be removed. I suppose, Doctor, you have not recovered the bullet which wounded the lady?"

"A serious operation will be necessary before that can be done. But there are still four cartridges in the revolver. Two have been fired and two wounds inflicted, so that each bullet can be accounted for."

"So it would seem," said Holmes. "Perhaps you can account also for the bullet which has so obviously struck the edge of the window?"

He had turned suddenly, and his long, thin finger was pointing to a hole which had been drilled right through the lower window sash, about an inch above the bottom.

"By George!" cried the inspector. "How ever did you see that?"

"Because I looked for it."

"Wonderful!" said the country doctor. "You are certainly right, sir. Then a third shot has been fired, and therefore a third person must have been present. But who could that have been, and how could he have got away?"

"That is the problem which we are now about to solve," said Sherlock Holmes. "You remember, Inspector Martin, when the servants said that on leaving their room they were at once conscious of a smell of powder, I remarked that the point was an extremely important one?"

"Yes, sir; but I confess I did not quite follow you."

"It suggested that at the time of the firing, the window as well as the door of the room had been open. Otherwise the fumes of powder could not have been blown so rapidly through the house. A draught in the

The Adventure of the Dancing Men

room was necessary for that. Both door and window were only open for a very short time, however."

"How do you prove that?"

"Because the candle was not guttered."

"Capital!" cried the inspector. "Capital!"

"Feeling sure that the window had been open at the time of the tragedy, I conceived that there might have been a third person in the affair, who stood outside this opening and fired through it. Any shot directed at this person might hit the sash. I looked, and there, sure enough, was the bullet mark!"

"But how came the window to be shut and fastened?"

"The woman's first instinct would be to shut and fasten the window. But, halloa! what is this?"

It was a lady's handbag which stood upon the study table—a trim little handbag of crocodile skin and silver. Holmes opened it and turned the contents out. There were twenty fifty-pound notes of the Bank of England, held together by an India-rubber band—nothing else.

"This must be preserved, for it will figure in the trial," said Holmes, as he handed the bag with its contents to the inspector. "It is now necessary that we should try to throw some light upon this third bullet, which has clearly, from the splintering of the wood, been fired from inside the room. I should like to see Mrs. King, the cook, again. You said, Mrs. King, that you were awakened by a *loud* explosion. When you said that, did you mean that it seemed to you to be louder than the second one?"

"Well, sir, it wakened me from my sleep, and so it is hard to judge. But it did seem very loud."

"You don't think that it might have been two shots fired almost at the same instant?"

"I am sure I couldn't say, sir."

"I believe that it was undoubtedly so. I rather think, Inspector Martin, that we have now exhausted all that this room can teach us. If you will kindly step round with me, we shall see what fresh evidence the garden has to offer."

A flower bed extended up to the study window, and we all broke into an exclamation as we approached it. The flowers were trampled down, and the soft soil was imprinted all over with footmarks. Large, masculine feet they were, with peculiarly long, sharp toes. Holmes hunted about among the grass and leaves like a retriever after a wounded bird. Then, with a cry of satisfaction, he bent forward and picked up a little brazen cylinder.

"I thought so," said he; "the revolver had an ejector, and here is the third cartridge. I really think, Inspector Martin, that our case is almost complete."

The county inspector's face had shown his intense amazement at the rapid and masterful progress of Holmes's investigation. At first he had shown some disposition to assert his own position, but now he was overcome with admiration, and ready to follow without question wherever Holmes led.

"Whom do you suspect?" he asked.

"I'll go into that later. There are several points in this problem which I have not been able to explain to you yet. Now that I have got so far, I had best proceed on my own lines, and then clear the whole matter up once and for all."

"Just as you wish, Mr. Holmes, so long as we get our man."

"I have no desire to make mysteries, but it is impossible at the moment of action to enter into long and complex explanations. I have the threads of this affair all in my hand. Even if this lady should never recover consciousness, we can still reconstruct the events of last night, and insure that justice be done. First of all, I wish to know whether there is any inn in this neighborhood known as 'Elrige's'?"

The servants were cross-questioned, but none of them had heard of such a place. The stableboy threw a light upon the matter by remembering that a farmer of that name lived some miles off, in the direction of East Ruston.

"Is it a lonely farm?"

"Very lonely, sir."

"Perhaps they have not heard yet of all that has happened here during the night?"

"Maybe not, sir."

Holmes thought for a little, and then a curious smile played over his face.

"Saddle a horse, my lad," said he. "I shall wish you to take a note to Elrige's farm."

He took from his pocket the various slips of the dancing men. With these in front of him, he worked for some time at the study table. Finally he handed a note to the boy, with directions to put it into the hands of the person to whom it was addressed, and especially to answer no questions of any sort which might be put to him. I saw the outside of the note, addressed in straggling, irregular characters, very unlike Holmes's usual precise hand. It was consigned to Mr. Abe Slaney, Elrige's Farm, East Ruston, Norfolk.

"I think, Inspector," Holmes remarked, "that you would do well to telegraph for an escort as, if my calculations prove to be correct, you may have a particularly dangerous prisoner to convey to the county jail. The boy who takes this note could no doubt forward your telegram. If there is an afternoon train to town, Watson, I think we should do well to take it, as I have a chemical analysis of some interest to finish, and this investigation draws rapidly to a close."

When the youth had been dispatched with the note, Sherlock Holmes gave his instructions to the servants. If any visitor were to call asking for Mrs. Hilton Cubitt, no information should be given as to her condition, but he was to be shown at once into the drawing room. He impressed these points upon them with the utmost earnestness. Finally he led the way into the drawing room, with the remark that the business was now out of our hands, and that we must while away the time as best we might until we could see what was in store for us. The doctor had departed to his patients, and only the inspector and myself remained.

"I think that I can help you to pass an hour in an interesting and profitable manner," said Holmes, drawing his chair up to the table, and spreading out in front of him the various papers upon which were recorded the antics of the dancing men. "As to you, friend Watson, I owe you every atonement for having allowed your natural curiosity to remain so long unsatisfied. To you, Inspector, the whole incident may appeal as a remarkable professional study. I must tell you, first of all, the interesting circumstances connected with the previous consultations which Mr. Hilton Cubitt has had with me in Baker Street." He then shortly recapitulated the facts which have already been recorded. "I have here in front of me these singular productions, at which one might smile, had they not proved themselves to be the forerunners of so terrible a tragedy. I am fairly familiar with all forms of secret writings, and am myself the author of a trifling monograph upon the subject, in which I analyze one hundred and sixty separate ciphers, but I confess that this is entirely new to me. The object of those who invented the system has apparently been to conceal that these characters convey a message, and to give the idea that they are the mere random sketches of children.

"Having once recognized, however, that the symbols stood for letters, and having applied the rules which guide us in all forms of secret writings, the solution was easy enough. The first message submitted to me was so short that it was impossible for me to do more than to say, with some confidence, that the symbol stood

for *E*. As you are aware, *E* is the most common letter in the English alphabet, and it predominates to so marked an extent that even in a short sentence one would expect to find it most often. Out of fifteen symbols in the first message, four were the same, so it was reasonable to set this down as *E*. It is true that in some cases the figure was bearing a flag, and in some cases not, but it was probable, from the way in which the flags were distributed, that they were used to break the sentence up into words. I accepted this as a hypothesis, and noted that *E* was represented by .

"But now came the real difficulty of the inquiry. The order of the English letters after *E* is by no means well marked, and any preponderance which may be shown in an average of a printed sheet may be reversed in a single short sentence. Speaking roughly, *T, A, O, I, N, S, H, R, D*, and *L* are the numerical order in which letters occur; but *T, A, O*, and *I* are very nearly abreast of each other, and it would be an endless task to try each combination until a meaning was arrived at. I therefore waited for fresh material. In my second interview with Mr. Hilton Cubitt he was able to give me two other short sentences and one message, which appeared—since there was no flag—to be a single word. Here are the symbols. Now, in the single word I have already got the two *E*'s coming second and fourth in a word of five letters. It might be 'sever,' or 'lever,' or 'never.' There can be no question that the latter as a reply to an appeal is far the most probable, and the circumstances pointed to its being a reply written by the lady. Accepting it as correct, we are now able to say that the symbols stand respectively for *N, V*, and *R*.

"Even now I was in considerable difficulty, but a happy thought put me in possession of several other letters. It occurred to me that if these appeals came, as I expected, from some one who had been intimate with the lady in her early life, a combination which contained two *E*'s with three letters between might very well stand for the name Elsie. On examination I found that such a combination formed the termination of the message which was three times repeated. It was certainly some appeal to Elsie. In this way I had got my *L, S,* and *I*. But what appeal could it be? There were only four letters in the word which preceded Elsie, and it ended in *E*. Surely the word must be *come*. I tried all other four letters ending in *E*, but could find none to fit the case. So now I was in possession of *C, O,* and *M,* and I was in a position to attack the first message once more, dividing it into words and putting dots for each symbol which was still unknown. So treated, it worked out in this fashion:

.M .ERE . .E SL.NE.

"Now the first letter *can* only be *A,* which is a most useful discovery, since it occurs no fewer than three times in this short sentence, and the *H* is also apparent in the second word. Now it becomes:

AM HERE A.E SLANE.

Or, filling in the obvious vacancies in the name:

AM HERE ABE SLANEY

I had so many letters now that I could proceed with considerable confidence to the second message, which worked out in this fashion:

A . ELRI . ES

Here I could only make sense by putting *T* and *G* for the missing letters, and supposing that the name was that of some house or inn at which the writer was staying."

Inspector Martin and I had listened with the utmost interest to the full and clear account of how my friend had produced results which had led to so complete a command over our difficulties.

"What did you do then, sir?" asked the inspector.

"I had every reason to suppose that this Abe Slaney was an American, since Abe is an American contraction, and since a letter from America had been the starting point of all the trouble. I had also every cause to think that there was some criminal secret in the matter. The lady's allusions to her past, and her refusal to take her husband into her confidence, both pointed in that direction. I therefore cabled to my friend, Wilson Hargreave, of the New York Police Bureau, who has more than once made use of my knowledge of London crime. I asked him whether the name Abe Slaney was known to him. Here is his reply: 'The most dangerous crook in Chicago.' On the very evening upon which I had his answer, Hilton Cubitt sent me the last message from Slaney. Working with known letters, it took this form:

ELSIE . RE . ARE TO MEET THY GO.

The addition of a *P* and a *D* completed a message which showed me that the rascal was proceeding from persuasion to threats, and my knowledge of the crooks of Chicago prepared me to find that he might very rapidly put his words into action. I at once came to Norfolk with my friend and colleague, Dr. Watson, but, unhappily, only in time to find that the worst had already occurred."

"It is a privilege to be associated with you in the handling of a case," said the inspector, warmly. "You will excuse me, however, if I speak frankly to you. You are only answerable to yourself, but I have to answer to my superiors. If this Abe Slaney, living at Elrige's, is indeed the murderer, and if he has made his escape while I am seated here, I should certainly get into serious trouble."

"You need not be uneasy. He will not try to escape."

"How do you know?"

"To fly would be a confession of guilt."

"Then let us go to arrest him."

"I expect him here every instant."

"But why should he come?"

"Because I have written and asked him."

"But this is incredible, Mr. Holmes! Why should he

come because you have asked him? Would not such a request rather rouse his suspicions and cause him to fly?"

"I think I have known how to frame the letter," said Sherlock Holmes. "In fact, if I am not very much mistaken, here is the gentleman himself coming up the drive."

A man was striding up the path which led to the door. He was a tall, handsome, swarthy fellow, clad in a suit of gray flannel, with a Panama hat, a bristling black beard, and a great, aggressive hooked nose, and flourishing a cane as he walked. He swaggered up the path as if the place belonged to him, and we heard his loud, confident peal at the bell.

"I think, gentlemen," said Holmes, quietly, "that we had best take up our position behind the door. Every precaution is necessary when dealing with such a fellow. You will need your handcuffs, Inspector. You can leave the talking to me."

We waited in silence for a minute—one of those minutes which one can never forget. Then the door opened and the man stepped in. In an instant Holmes clapped a pistol to his head, and Martin slipped the handcuffs over his wrists. It was all done so swiftly and deftly that the fellow was helpless before he knew that he was attacked. He glared from one to the other of us with a pair of blazing black eyes. Then he burst into a bitter laugh.

"Well, gentlemen, you have the drop on me this time. I seem to have knocked up against something hard. But I came here in answer to a letter from Mrs. Hilton Cubitt. Don't tell me that she is in this? Don't tell me that she helped to set a trap for me?"

"Mrs. Hilton Cubitt was seriously injured, and is at death's door."

The man gave a hoarse cry of grief, which rang through the house.

"You're crazy!" he cried, fiercely. "It was he that was hurt, not she. Who would have hurt little Elsie? I may

The Adventure of the Dancing Men

have threatened her—God forgive me!—but I would not have touched a hair of her pretty head. Take it back—you! Say that she is not hurt!"

"She was found, badly wounded, by the side of her dead husband."

He sank with a deep groan on to the settee, and buried his face in his manacled hands. For five minutes he was silent. Then he raised his face once more, and spoke with the cold composure of despair.

"I have nothing to hide from you, gentlemen," said he. "If I shot the man he had his shot at me, and there's no murder in that. But if you think I could have hurt that woman, then you don't know either me or her. I tell you, there was never a man in this world loved a woman more than I loved her. I had a right to her. She was pledged to me years ago. Who was this Englishman that he should come between us? I tell you that I had the first right to her, and that I was only claiming my own."

"She broke away from your influence when she found the man that you are," said Holmes, sternly. "She fled from America to avoid you, and she married an honorable gentleman in England. You dogged her and followed her and made her life a misery to her, in order to induce her to abandon the husband whom she loved and respected in order to fly with you, whom she feared and hated. You have ended by bringing about the death of a noble man and driving his wife to suicide. That is your record in this business, Mr. Abe Slaney, and you will answer for it to the law."

"If Elsie dies, I care nothing what becomes of me," said the American. He opened one of his hands, and looked at a note crumpled up in his palm. "See here, mister," he cried, with a gleam of suspicion in his eyes, "you're not trying to scare me over this, are you? If the lady is hurt as bad as you say, who was it that wrote this note?" He tossed it forward on the table.

"I wrote it, to bring you here."

"You wrote it? There was no one on earth outside the

Joint who knew the secret of the dancing men. How came you to write it?"

"What one man can invent another can discover," said Holmes. "There is a cab coming to convey you to Norwich, Mr. Slaney. But, meanwhile, you have time to make some small reparation for the injury you have wrought. Are you aware that Mrs. Hilton Cubitt has herself lain under grave suspicion of the murder of her husband, and that it was only my presence here, and the knowledge which I happened to possess, which has saved her from the accusation? The least that you owe her is to make it clear to the whole world that she was in no way, directly or indirectly, responsible for his tragic end."

"I ask nothing better," said the American. "I guess the very best case I can make for myself is the absolute naked truth."

"It is my duty to warn you that it will be used against you," cried the inspector, with the magnificent fair play of the British criminal law.

Slaney shrugged his shoulders.

"I'll chance that," said he. "First of all, I want you gentlemen to understand that I have known this lady since she was a child. There were seven of us in a gang in Chicago, and Elsie's father was the boss of the Joint. He was a clever man, was old Patrick. It was he who invented that writing, which would pass as a child's scrawl unless you just happened to have the key to it. Well, Elsie learned some of our ways, but she couldn't stand the business, and she had a bit of honest money of her own, so she gave us all the slip and got away to London. She had been engaged to me, and she would have married me, I believe, if I had taken over another profession, but she would have nothing to do with anything on the cross. It was only after her marriage to this Englishman that I was able to find out where she was. I wrote to her, but got no answer. After that I came over, and, as letters were no use, I put my messages where she could read them.

"Well, I have been here a month now. I lived in that farm, where I had a room down below, and could get in and out every night, and no one the wiser. I tried all I could to coax Elsie away. I knew that she read the messages, for once she wrote an answer under one of them. Then my temper got the better of me, and I began to threaten her. She sent me a letter then, imploring me to go away, and saying that it would break her heart if any scandal should come upon her husband. She said that she would come down when her husband was asleep at three in the morning, and speak with me through the end window, if I would go away afterwards and leave her in peace. She came down and brought money with her, trying to bribe me to go. This made me mad, and I caught her arm and tried to pull her through the window. At that moment in rushed the husband with his revolver in his hand. Elsie had sunk down upon the floor, and we were face to face. I was heeled also, and I held up my gun to scare him off and let me get away. He fired and missed me. I pulled off almost at the same instant, and down he dropped. I made away across the garden, and as I went I heard the window shut behind me. That's God's truth, gentlemen, every word of it; and I heard no more about it until that lad came riding up with a note which made me walk in here, like a jay, and give myself into your hands."

A cab had driven up whilst the American had been talking. Two uniformed policemen sat inside. Inspector Martin rose and touched his prisoner on the shoulder.

"It is time for us to go."

"Can I see her first?"

"No, she is not conscious. Mr. Sherlock Holmes, I only hope that, if ever again I have such an important case, I shall have the good fortune to have you by my side."

We stood at the window and watched the cab drive away. As I turned back, my eye caught the pellet of paper which the prisoner had tossed upon the table. It was the note with which Holmes had decoyed Slaney.

"See if you can read it, Watson," said he, with a smile.

It contained no word, but this little line of dancing men:

"If you use the code which I have explained," said Holmes, "you will find that it simply means 'Come here at once.' I was convinced that it was an invitation which he could not refuse, since he could never imagine that it could come from any one but the lady. And so, my dear Watson, we have ended by turning the dancing men to good when they have so often been the agents of evil, and I think that I have fulfilled my promise of giving you something unusual for your notebook. Three-forty is our train, and we should be back in Baker Street for dinner."

Only one word of epilogue. The American, Abe Slaney, was condemned to death at the winter assizes at Norwich, but his penalty was changed to penal servitude in consideration of mitigating circumstances, and the certainty that Hilton Cubitt had fired the first shot. Of Mrs. Hilton Cubitt I only know that I have heard she recovered entirely, and that she still remains a widow, devoting her life to the care of the poor and to administering her husband's estate.

The Pit and the Pendulum

by Edgar Allan Poe

Impia tortorum longas hic turba furores
Sanguinis innocui, non satiata, aluit.
Sospite nunc patria, fracto nunc funeris antro,
Mors ubi dira fuit vita salusque patent.*

> *Quatrain composed for the gates of a market to be erected upon the site of the Jacobin Club House at Paris.*

I was sick—sick unto death with that long agony; and when they at length unbound me, and I was permitted to sit, I felt that my senses were leaving me. The sentence—the dread sentence of death—was the last of distinct accentuation which reached my ears. After that, the sound of the inquisitorial voices seemed merged in one dreamy indeterminate hum. It conveyed to my soul the idea of *revolution,* perhaps from its association in fancy with the burr of a mill-wheel. This only for a brief period; for presently I heard no more. Yet, for a while, I saw; but with how terrible an exaggeration! I saw the lips of the black-robed judges. They appeared to me white, whiter than the sheet upon which I trace these words, and thin even to grotesqueness; thin with the intensity of their expression of firmness—of im-

---

* Latin. "Here the impious clamor of the torturers, insatiate, fed long its rage for innocent blood. Now happy is the land, destroyed the pit of horror; and where grim death stalked, life and health are revealed." Jacobin Club: a society of French revolutionists who with Robespierre as leader were in power during the Reign of Terror.

movable resolution, of stern contempt of human torture. I saw that the decrees of what to me was Fate were still issuing from those lips. I saw them writhe with a deadly locution. I saw them fashion the syllables of my name; and I shuddered because no sound succeeded. I saw, too, for a few moments of delirious horror, the soft and nearly imperceptible waving of the sable draperies which enwrapped the walls of the apartment. And then my vision fell upon the seven tall candles upon the table. At first they wore the aspect of charity, and seemed white slender angels who would save me; but then, all at once, there came a most deadly nausea over my spirit, and I felt every fibre in my frame thrill as if I had touched the wire of a galvanic battery, while the angel forms became meaningless spectres, with heads of flame, and I saw that from them there would be no help. And then there stole into my fancy, like a rich musical note, the thought of what sweet rest there must be in the grave. The thought came gently and stealthily, and it seemed long before it attained full appreciation; but just as my spirit came at length properly to feel and entertain it, the figures of the judges vanished, as if magically, from before me; the tall candles sank into nothingness; their flames went out utterly; the blackness of darkness supervened; all sensations appeared swallowed up in a mad rushing descent as of the soul into Hades. Then silence, and stillness, and night were the universe.

I had swooned; but still will not say that all of consciousness was lost. What of it there remained I will not attempt to define, or even to describe; yet all was not lost. In the deepest slumber—no! In delirium—no! In a swoon—no! In death—no! even in the grave all is not lost. Else there is no immortality for man. Arousing from the most profound of slumbers, we break the gossamer web of *some* dream. Yet in a second afterward (so frail may that web have been) we remember not that we have dreamed. In the return to life from the swoon there are two stages; first, that of the sense of

The Pit and the Pendulum

mental or spiritual, secondly, that of the sense of physical, existence. It seems probable that if, upon reaching the second stage, we could recall the impressions of the first, we should find these impressions eloquent in memories of the gulf beyond. And that gulf is—what? How at least shall we distinguish its shadows from those of the tomb? But if the impressions of what I have termed the first stage are not at will recalled, yet, after a long interval, do they not come unbidden, while we marvel whence they come? He who has never swooned is not he who finds strange palaces and wildly familiar faces in coals that glow; is not he who beholds floating in mid-air the sad visions that the many may not view; is not he who ponders over the perfume of some novel flower; is not he whose brain grows bewildered with the meaning of some musical cadence which has never before arrested his attention.

Amid frequent and thoughtful endeavors to remember, amid earnest struggles to regather some token of the state of seeming nothingness into which my soul had lapsed, there have been moments when I have dreamed of success; there have been brief, very brief periods when I have conjured up remembrances which the lucid reason of a later epoch assures me could have had reference only to that condition of seeming unconsciousness. These shadows of memory tell, instinctively, of tall figures that lifted and bore me in silence down—down—still down—till a hideous dizziness oppressed me at the mere idea of the interminableness of the descent. They tell also of a vague horror at my heart, on account of that heart's unnatural stillness. Then comes a sense of sudden motionlessness throughout all things; as if those who bore me (a ghastly train!) had outrun in their descent the limits of the limitless, and paused from the wearisomeness of their toil. After this I call to mind flatness and dampness; and then all is *madness*— the madness of a memory which busies itself among forbidden things.

Very suddenly there came back to my soul motion

and sound—the tumultuous motion of the heart and, in my ears, the sound of its beating. Then a pause in which all is blank. Then again sound, and motion, and touch—a tingling sensation pervading my frame. Then the mere consciousness of existence, without thought— a condition which lasted long. Then, very suddenly, *thought,* and shuddering terror, and earnest endeavor to comprehend my true state. Then a strong desire to lapse into insensibility. Then a rushing revival of soul and a successful effort to move. And now a full memory of the trial, of the judges, of the sable draperies, of the sentence, of the sickness, of the swoon. Then entire forgetfulness of all that followed; of all that a later day and much earnestness of endeavor have enabled me vaguely to recall.

So far, I had not opened my eyes. I felt that I lay upon my back, unbound. I reached out my hand, and it fell heavily upon something damp and hard. There I suffered it to remain for many minutes, while I strove to imagine where and *what* I could be. I longed yet dared not to employ my vision. I dreaded the first glance at objects around me. It was not that I feared to look upon things horrible, but that I grew aghast lest there should be *nothing* to see. At length, with a wild desperation at heart, I quickly unclosed my eyes. My worst thoughts, then, were confirmed. The blackness of eternal night encompassed me. I struggled for breath. The intensity of the darkness seemed to oppress and stifle me. The atmosphere was intolerably close. I still lay quietly, and made effort to exercise my reason. I brought to mind the inquisitorial proceedings, and attempted from that point to deduce my real condition. The sentence had passed; and it appeared to me that a very long interval of time had since elapsed. Yet not for a moment did I suppose myself actually dead. Such a supposition, notwithstanding what we read in fiction, is altogether inconsistent with real existence—but where and in what state was I? The condemned to death, I knew, perished usually at the *autos-da-fé,* and one of these had been held on the very night of the day of my trial. Had I been remanded to my dungeon to await the next sacrifice, which would not take place for many months? This I at once saw could not be. Victims had been in immediate demand. Moreover, my dungeon, as well as all the condemned cells at Toledo, had a stone floor, and light was not altogether excluded.

A fearful idea now suddenly drove the blood in torrents upon my heart, and for a brief period I once more relapsed into insensibility. Upon recovering, I at once started to my feet, trembling convulsively in every fibre. I thrust my arms wildly above and around me in all directions. I felt nothing; yet dreaded to move a step, lest I should be impeded by the walls of a *tomb*. Perspiration burst from every pore, and stood in cold, big beads upon my forehead. The agony of suspense grew at length intolerable, and I cautiously moved forward, with my arms extended, and my eyes straining from their sockets, in the hope of catching some faint ray of light. I proceeded for many paces; but still all was blackness and vacancy. I breathed more freely. It seemed evident that mine was not, at least, the most hideous of fates.

And now, as I still continued to step cautiously onward, there came thronging upon my recollection a thousand vague rumors of the horrors of Toledo. Of the dungeons there had been strange things narrated—fables I had always deemed them—but yet strange, and too ghastly to repeat, save in a whisper. Was I left to perish of starvation in this subterranean world of darkness; or what fate, perhaps even more fearful, awaited me? That the result would be death, and a death of more than customary bitterness, I knew too well the character of my judges to doubt. The mode and the hour were all that occupied or distracted me.

My outstretched hands at length encountered some solid obstruction. It was a wall, seemingly of stone masonry—very smooth, slimy, and cold. I followed it up; stepping with all the careful distrust with which certain antique narratives had inspired me. This process, however, afforded me no means of ascertaining the dimensions of my dungeon; as I might make its circuit, and return to the point whence I set out, without being aware of the fact, so perfectly uniform seemed the wall. I therefore sought the knife which had been in my pocket when led into the inquisitorial chamber; but it was gone; my clothes had been exchanged for a wrapper of coarse serge. I had thought of forcing the blade in some minute crevice of the masonry, so as to identify my point of departure. The difficulty, nevertheless, was but trivial; although, in the disorder of my fancy, it seemed at first insuperable. I tore a part of the hem from the robe and placed the fragment at full length, and at right angles to the wall. In groping my way around the prison I could not fail to encounter this rag upon completing the circuit. So, at least, I thought; but I had not counted upon the extent of the dungeon, or upon my own weakness. The ground was moist and slippery. I staggered onward for some time, when I stumbled and fell. My excessive fatigue induced me to remain prostrate; and sleep soon overtook me as I lay.

Upon awaking, and stretching forth an arm, I found beside me a loaf and a pitcher with water. I was too much exhausted to reflect upon this circumstance, but ate and drank with avidity. Shortly afterward, I resumed my tour around the prison, and with much toil came at last upon the fragment of the serge. Up to the period when I fell, I had counted fifty-two paces, and, upon resuming my walk, I had counted forty-eight more—when I arrived at the rag. There were in all, then, a hundred paces; and, admitting two paces to the yard, I presumed the dungeon to be fifty yards in circuit. I had met, however, with many angles in the wall, and thus I could form no guess at the shape of the vault; for vault I could not help supposing it to be.

I had little object—certainly no hope—in these re-

The Pit and the Pendulum

searches; but a vague curiosity prompted me to continue them. Quitting the wall, I resolved to cross the area of the enclosure. At first, I proceeded with extreme caution, for the floor, although seemingly of solid material, was treacherous with slime. At length, however, I took courage, and did not hesitate to step firmly—endeavoring to cross in as direct a line as possible. I had advanced some ten or twelve paces in this manner, when the remnant of the torn hem of my robe became entangled between my legs. I stepped on it and fell violently on my face.

In the confusion attending my fall, I did not immediately apprehend a somewhat startling circumstance, which yet, in a few seconds afterwards, and while I still lay prostrate, arrested my attention. It was this: my chin rested upon the floor of the prison, but my lips and the upper portion of my head, although seemingly at a less elevation than the chin, touched nothing. At the same time, my forehead seemed bathed in a clammy vapor, and the peculiar smell of decayed fungus arose to my nostrils. I put forward my arm, and shuddered to find that I had fallen at the brink of a circular pit, whose extent, of course, I had no means of ascertaining at the moment. Groping about the masonry just below the margin, I succeeded in dislodging a small fragment, and let it fall into the abyss. For many seconds I hearkened to its reverberations as it dashed against the sides of the chasm in its descent; at length there was a sullen plunge into water, succeeded by loud echoes. At the same moment there came a sound resembling the quick opening and as rapid closing of a door overhead, while a faint gleam of light flashed suddenly through the gloom, and as suddenly faded away.

I saw clearly the doom which had been prepared for me, and congratulated myself upon the timely accident by which I had escaped. Another step before my fall, and the world had seen me no more. And the death just avoided was of that very character which I had regarded as fabulous and frivolous in the tales respecting the Inquisition. To the victims of its tyranny there was the choice of death with its direst physical agonies, or death with its most hideous moral horrors. I had been reserved for the latter. By long suffering my nerves had been unstrung, until I trembled at the sound of my own voice, and had become in every respect a fitting subject for the species of torture which awaited me.

Shaking in every limb, I groped my way back to the wall—resolving there to perish rather than risk the terrors of the wells, of which my imagination now pictured many in various positions about the dungeon. In other conditions of mind, I might have had courage to end my misery at once, by a plunge into one of these abysses; but now I was the veriest of cowards. Neither could I forget what I had read of these pits—that the *sudden* extinction of life formed no part of their most horrible plan.

Agitation of spirit kept me awake for many long hours; but at length I again slumbered. Upon arousing, I found by my side, as before, a loaf and a pitcher of water. A burning thirst consumed me, and I emptied the vessel at a draught. It must have been drugged—for scarcely had I drunk, before I became irresistibly drowsy. A deep sleep fell upon me—a sleep like that of death. How long it lasted, of course, I know not; but, when once again I unclosed my eyes, the objects around me were visible. By a wild, sulphurous luster, the origin of which I could not at first determine, I was enabled to see the extent and aspect of the prison.

In its size I had been greatly mistaken. The whole circuit of its walls did not exceed twenty-five yards. For some minutes this fact occasioned me a world of vain trouble; vain indeed—for what could be of less importance, under the terrible circumstances which environed me, than the mere dimensions of my dungeon? But my soul took a wild interest in trifles, and I busied myself in endeavors to account for the error I had committed in my measurement. The truth at

The Pit and the Pendulum

length flashed upon me. In my first attempt at exploration I had counted fifty-two paces, up to the period when I fell: I must then have been within a pace or two of the fragment of serge; in fact, I had nearly performed the circuit of the vault. I then slept—and, upon waking, I must have returned upon my steps, thus supposing the circuit nearly double what it actually was. My confusion of mind prevented me from observing that I began my tour with the wall to the left, and ended it with the wall to the right.

I had been deceived, too, in respect to the shape of the enclosure. In feeling my way, I had found many angles, and thus deduced an idea of great irregularity; so potent is the effect of total darkness upon one arousing from lethargy or sleep! The angles were simply those of a few slight depressions, or niches, at odd intervals. The general shape of the prison was square. What I had taken for masonry, seemed now to be iron, or some other metal, in huge plates, whose sutures or joints occasioned the depression. The entire surface of this metallic enclosure was rudely daubed in all the hideous and repulsive devices to which the charnel superstition of the monks has given rise. The figures of fiends in aspects of menace, with skeleton forms, and other more really fearful images, overspread and disfigured the walls. I observed that the outlines of these monstrosities were sufficiently distinct, but that the colors seemed faded and blurred, as if from the effects of a damp atmosphere. I now noticed the floor, too, which was of stone. In the center yawned the circular pit from whose jaws I had escaped; but it was the only one in the dungeon.

All this I saw distinctly and by much effort, for my personal condition had been greatly changed during slumber. I now lay upon my back, and at full length, on a species of low framework of wood. To this I was securely bound by a long strap resembling a surcingle. It passed in many convolutions about my limbs and body, leaving at liberty only my head, and my left arm to such extent that I could, by dint of much exertion, supply myself with food from an earthen dish which lay by my side on the floor. I saw, to my horror, that the pitcher had been removed. I say, to my horror—for I was consumed with intolerable thirst. This thirst it appeared to be the design of my persecutors to stimulate, for the food in the dish was meat pungently seasoned.

Looking upward, I surveyed the ceiling of my prison. It was some thirty or forty feet overhead, and constructed much as the side walls. In one of its panels a very singular figure riveted my whole attention. It was the painted figure of Time as he is commonly represented, save that, in lieu of a scythe, he held what, at a casual glance, I supposed to be the pictured image of a huge pendulum, such as we see on antique clocks. There was something, however, in the appearance of this machine which caused me to regard it more attentively. While I gazed directly upward at it (for its position was immediately over my own), I fancied that I saw it in motion. In an instant afterward the fancy was confirmed. Its sweep was brief, and of course slow. I watched it for some minutes, somewhat in fear, but more in wonder. Wearied at length with observing its dull movement, I turned my eyes upon the other objects in the cell.

A slight noise attracted my notice, and, looking to the floor, I saw several enormous rats traversing it. They had issued from the well, which lay just within view to my right. Even then, while I gazed, they came up in troops, hurriedly, with ravenous eyes, allured by the scent of the meat. From this it required much effort and attention to scare them away.

It might have been half an hour, perhaps even an hour (for I could take but imperfect note of time) before I again cast my eyes upward. What I then saw, confounded and amazed me. The sweep of the pendulum had increased in extent by nearly a yard. As a natural consequence, its velocity was also much greater. But

The Pit and the Pendulum 163

what mainly disturbed me, was the idea that it had perceptibly *descended*. I now observed—with what horror it is needless to say—that its nether extremity was formed of a crescent of glittering steel, about a foot in length from horn to horn; the horns upward, and the under edge evidently as keen as that of a razor. Like a razor also, it seemed massy and heavy, tapering from the edge into a solid and broad structure above. It was appended to a weighty rod of brass, and the whole *hissed* as it swung through the air.

I could no longer doubt the doom prepared for me by monkish ingenuity in torture. My cognizance of the pit had become known to the inquisitorial agents—*the pit,* whose horrors had been destined for so bold a recusant as myself—*the pit,* typical of hell, and regarded by rumor as the Ultima Thule of all their punishments. The plunge into this pit I had avoided by the merest of accidents, and I knew that surprise, or entrapment into torment, formed an important portion of all the grotesquerie of these dungeon deaths. Having failed to fall, it was no part of the demon plan to hurl me into the abyss; and thus (there being no alternative), a different and a milder destruction awaited me. Milder! I half smiled in my agony as I thought of such application of such a term.

What boots it to tell of the long, long hours of horror more than mortal, during which I counted the rushing oscillations of the steel! Inch by inch—line by line—with a descent only appreciable at intervals that seemed ages—down and still down it came! Days passed—it might have been that many days passed—ere it swept so closely over me as to fan me with its acrid breath. The odor of the sharp steel forced itself into my nostrils. I prayed—I wearied heaven with my prayer for its more speedy descent. I grew frantically mad, and struggled to force myself upward against the sweep of the fearful scimitar. And then I fell suddenly calm, and lay smiling at the glittering death, as a child at some rare bauble.

There was another interval of utter insensibility; it

was brief; for, again lapsing into life, there had been no perceptible descent in the pendulum. But it might have been long; for I knew there were demons who took note of my swoon, and who could have arrested the vibration at pleasure. Upon my recovery, too, I felt very—oh, inexpressibly—sick and weak, as if through long inanition. Even amid the agonies of that period the human nature craved food. With painful effort, I outstretched my left arm as far as my bonds permitted, and took possession of the small remnant which had been spared my by the rats. As I put a portion of it within my lips, there rushed to my mind a half-formed thought of joy—of hope. Yet what business had *I* with hope? It was, as I say, a half-formed thought: man has many such, which are never completed. I felt that it was of joy—of hope; but I felt also that it had perished in its formation. In vain I struggled to perfect—to regain it. Long suffering had nearly annihilated all my ordinary powers of mind. I was an imbecile—an idiot.

The vibration of the pendulum was at right angles to my length. I saw that the crescent was designed to cross the region of the heart. It would fray the serge of my robe—it would return and repeat its operations—again—and again. Notwithstanding its terrifically wide sweep (some thirty feet or more), and the hissing vigor of its descent, sufficient to sunder these very walls of iron, still the fraying of my robe would be all that, for several minutes, it would accomplish. And at this thought I paused. I dared not go farther than this reflection. I dwelt upon it with a pertinacity of attention—as if in so dwelling, I could arrest *here* the descent of the steel. I forced myself to ponder upon the sound of the crescent as it should pass across the garment—upon the peculiar thrilling sensation which the friction of cloth produces on the nerves. I pondered upon all this frivolity until my teeth were on edge.

Down—steadily down it crept. I took a frenzied pleasure in contrasting its downward with its lateral velocity. To the right—to the left—far and wide—with the shriek of a damned spirit! to my heart, with the stealthy pace of the tiger! I alternately laughed and howled, as the one or the other idea grew predominant.

Down—certainly, relentlessly down! It vibrated within three inches of my bosom! I struggled violently—furiously—to free my left arm. This was free only from the elbow to the hand. I could reach the latter from the platter beside me to my mouth, with great effort, but no farther. Could I have broken the fastenings above the elbow, I would have seized and attempted to arrest the pendulum. I might as well have attempted to arrest an avalanche!

Down—still unceasingly—still inevitably down! I gasped and struggled at each vibration. I shrank convulsively at its every sweep. My eyes followed its outward or upward whirls with the eagerness of the most unmeaning despair; they closed themselves spasmodically at the descent, although death would have been a relief, oh, how unspeakable! Still I quivered in every nerve to think how slight a sinking of the machinery would precipitate that keen, glistening axe upon my bosom. It was *hope* that prompted the nerve to quiver—the frame to shrink. It was *hope*—the hope that triumphs on the rack—that whispers to the death-condemned even in the dungeons of the Inquisition.

I saw that some ten or twelve vibrations would bring the steel in actual contact with my robe; and with this observation there suddenly came over my spirit all the keen, collected calmness of despair. For the first time during many hours—or perhaps days—I *thought*. It now occurred to me, that the bandage, or surcingle, which enveloped me, was unique. I was tied by no separate cord. The first stroke of the razor-like crescent athwart any portion of the band would so detach it that it might be unwound from my person by means of my left hand. But how fearful, in that case, the proximity of the steel! The result of the slightest struggle, how deadly! Was it likely, moreover, that the minions of the torturer had not foreseen and provided for this possibility? Was it probable that the bandage crossed my bosom in the track of the pendulum? Dreading to find my faint, and as it seemed, my last hope frustrated, I so far elevated my head as to obtain a distinct view of my breast. The surcingle enveloped my limbs and body close in all directions—*save in the path of the destroying crescent.*

Scarcely had I dropped my head back into its original position, when there flashed upon my mind what I cannot better describe than as the unformed half of that idea of deliverance to which I have previously alluded, and of which a moiety only floated indeterminately through my brain when I raised food to my burning lips. The whole thought was now present—feeble, scarcely sane, scarcely definite—but still entire. I proceeded at once, with the nervous energy of despair, to attempt its execution.

For many hours the immediate vicinity of the low framework upon which I lay had been literally swarming with rats. They were wild, bold, ravenous—their red eyes glaring upon me as if they waited but for motionlessness on my part to make me their prey. "To what food," I thought, "have they been accustomed in the well?"

They had devoured, in spite of all my efforts to prevent them, all but a small remnant of the contents of the dish. I had fallen into an habitual see-saw, or wave of the hand about the platter; and, at length, the unconscious uniformity of the movement deprived it of effect. In their voracity the vermin frequently fastened their sharp fangs in my fingers. With the particles of the oily and spicy viand which now remained I thoroughly rubbed the bandage wherever I could reach it; then, raising my hand from the floor, I lay breathlessly still.

At first, the ravenous animals were startled and terrified at the change—the cessation of movement. They shrank alarmedly back; many sought the well. But this was only for a moment. I had not counted in vain upon their voracity. Observing that I remained without motion, one or two of the boldest leaped upon the framework, and smelt at the surcingle. This seemed the signal for a general rush. Forth from the well they hurried in fresh troops. They clung to the wood—they overran it, and leaped in hundreds upon my person. The measured movement of the pendulum disturbed them not at all. Avoiding its strokes, they busied themselves with the anointed bandage. They pressed—they swarmed upon me in ever-accumulating heaps. They writhed upon my throat; their cold lips sought my own; I was half stifled by their thronging pressure; disgust, for which the world has no name, swelled my bosom, and chilled, with a heavy clamminess, my heart. Yet one minute, and I felt that the struggle would be over. Plainly I perceived the loosening of the bandage. I knew that in more than one place it must be already severed. With a more than human resolution I lay still.

Nor had I erred in my calculations—nor had I endured in vain. I at length felt that I was *free*. The surcingle hung in ribbons from my body. But the stroke of the pendulum already pressed upon my bosom. It had divided the serge of the robe. It had cut through the linen beneath. Twice again it swung, and a sharp sense of pain shot through every nerve. But the moment of escape had arrived. At a wave of my hand my deliverers hurried tumultuously away. With a steady movement—cautious, sidelong, shrinking, and slow—I slid from the embrace of the bandage and beyond the reach of the scimitar. For the moment, at least, *I was free*.

Free!—and in the grasp of the Inquisition! I had scarcely stepped from my wooden bed of horror upon the stone floor of the prison, when the motion of the hellish machine ceased, and I beheld it drawn up, by some invisible force, through the ceiling. This was a lesson which I took desperately to heart. My every motion was undoubtedly watched. Free!—I had but escaped death in one form of agony to be delivered unto worse than death in some other. With that thought I rolled my eyes nervously around on the barriers of iron that hemmed me in. Something unusual—some change which, at first, I could not appreciate distinctly—it was obvious, had taken place in the apartment. For many minutes of a dreamy and trembling abstraction I busied myself in vain, unconnected conjecture. During this period, I became aware, for the first time, of the origin of the sulphurous light which illumined the cell. It proceeded from a fissure, about half an inch in width, extending entirely around the prison at the base of the walls, which thus appeared completely separated from the floor. I endeavored, but of course in vain, to look through the aperture.

As I arose from the attempt, the mystery of the alteration in the chamber broke at once upon my understanding. I have observed that, although the outlines of the figures upon the walls were sufficiently distinct, yet the colors seemed blurred and indefinite. These colors had now assumed, and were momentarily assuming, a startling and most intense brilliancy, that gave to the spectral and fiendish portraitures an aspect that might have thrilled even firmer nerves than my own. Demon eyes, of a wild and ghastly vivacity, glared upon me in a thousand directions, where none had been visible before, and gleamed with the lurid lustre of a fire that I could not force my imagination to regard as unreal.

Unreal!—even while I breathed there came to my nostrils the breath of the vapor of heated iron! A suffocating odor pervaded the prison. A deeper glow settled each moment in the eyes that glared at my agonies! A richer tint of crimson diffused itself over the pictured horrors of blood. I panted! I gasped for breath! There could be no doubt of the design of my tormentors—oh, most unrelenting! oh, most demoniac of men! I shrank from the glowing metal to the centre of the cell. Amid the thought of the fiery destruction that impended, the idea of the coolness of the well came over my soul like balm. I rushed to its deadly

The Pit and the Pendulum

brink. I threw my straining vision below. The glare from the enkindled roof illuminated its inmost recesses. Yet, for a wild moment, did my spirit refuse to comprehend the meaning of what I saw. At length it forced —it wrestled its way into my soul—it burned itself in upon my shuddering reason. Oh, for a voice to speak!— oh, horror!—oh, any horror but this! With a shriek, I rushed from the margin, and buried my face in my hands—weeping bitterly.

The heat rapidly increased, and once again I looked up, shuddering as with a fit of the ague. There had been a second change in the cell—and now the change was obviously in the *form*. As before, it was in vain that I at first endeavored to appreciate or understand what was taking place. But not long was I left in doubt. The inquisitorial vengeance had been hurried by my twofold escape, and there was to be no more dallying with the King of Terrors. The room had been square. I saw that two of its iron angles were now acute—two, consequently, obtuse. The fearful difference quickly increased with a low rumbling or moaning sound. In an instant the apartment had shifted its form into that of a lozenge. But the alteration stopped not here—I neither hoped nor desired it to stop. I could have clasped the red walls to my bosom as a garment of eternal peace. "Death," I said, "any death but that of the pit!" Fool! might I not have known that *into the pit* it was the object of the burning iron to urge me? Could I resist its glow? or if even that, could I withstand its pressure? And now, flatter and flatter grew the lozenge, with a rapidity that left me no time for contemplation. Its centre, and, of course, its greatest width, came just over the yawning gulf. I shrank back—but the closing walls pressed me resistlessly onward. At length for my seared and writhing body there was no longer an inch of foothold on the firm floor of the prison. I struggled no more, but the agony of my soul found vent in one loud, long, and final scream of despair. I felt that I tottered upon the brink—I averted my eyes—

There was a discordant hum of human voices! There was a loud blast as of many trumpets! There was a harsh grating as of a thousand thunders! The fiery walls rushed back! An outstretched arm caught my own as I fell, fainting, into the abyss. It was that of General Lasalle. The French army had entered Toledo. The Inquisition was in the hands of its enemies.

Rescue Party

by Arthur C. Clarke

Who was to blame? For three days Alveron's thoughts had come back to that question, and still he had found no answer. A creature of a less civilized or a less sensitive race would never have let it torture his mind, and would have satisfied himself with the assurance that no one could be responsible for the working of fate. But Alveron and his kind had been lords of the Universe since the dawn of history, since that far distant age when the Time Barrier had been folded round the cosmos by the unknown powers that lay beyond the Beginning. To them had been given all knowledge—and with infinite knowledge went infinite responsibility. If there were mistakes and errors in the administration of the galaxy, the fault lay on the heads of Alvernon and his people. And this was no mere mistake: it was one of the greatest tragedies in history.

The crew still knew nothing. Even Rugon, his closest friend and the ship's deputy captain, had been told only part of the truth. But now the doomed worlds lay less than a billion miles ahead. In a few hours, they would be landing on the third planet.

Once again Alveron read the message from Base; then, with a flick of a tentacle that no human eye could have followed, he pressed the "General Attention" button. Throughout the mile-long cylinder that was the Galactic Survey Ship S9000, creatures of many races laid down their work to listen to the words of their captain.

"I know you have all been wondering," began Alveron, "why we were ordered to abandon our survey and to proceed at such an acceleration to this region of space. Some of you may realize what this acceleration means. Our ship is on its last voyage: the generators have already been running for sixty hours at Ultimate Overload. We will be very lucky if we return to Base under our own power.

"We are approaching a sun which is about to become a Nova. Detonation will occur in seven hours, with an uncertainty of one hour, leaving us a maximum of only four hours for exploration. There are ten planets in the system about to be destroyed—and there is a civilization on the third. That fact was discovered only a few days ago. It is our tragic mission to contact that doomed race and if possible to save some of its members. I know that there is little we can do in so short a time with this single ship. No other machine can possibly reach the system before detonation occurs."

There was a long pause during which there could have been no sound or movement in the whole of the mighty ship as it sped silently toward the worlds ahead. Alveron knew what his companions were thinking and he tried to answer their unspoken question.

"You will wonder how such a disaster, the greatest of which we have any record, has been allowed to occur. On one point I can reassure you. The fault does not lie with the Survey.

"As you know, with our present fleet of under twelve thousand ships, it is possible to re-examine each of the eight thousand million solar systems in the Galaxy at intervals of about a million years. Most worlds change very little in so short a time as that.

"Less than four hundred thousand years ago, the survey ship S5060 examined the planets of the system we are approaching. It found intelligence on none of them, though the third planet was teeming with animal life and two other worlds had once been inhabited. The usual report was submitted and the system is due for its next examination in six hundred thousand years.

"It now appears that in the incredibly short period since the last survey, intelligent life has appeared in the system. The first intimation of this occurred when unknown radio signals were detected on the planet Kulath in the system X29.35, Y34.76, Z27.93. Bearings were taken on them; they were coming from the system ahead.

"Kulath is two hundred light-years from here, so those radio waves had been on their way for two centuries. Thus for at least that period of time a civilization has existed on one of these worlds—a civilization that can generate electromagnetic waves and all that that implies.

"An immediate telescopic examination of the system was made and it was then found that the sun was in the unstable pre-nova stage. Detonation might occur at any moment, and indeed might have done so while the light waves were on their way to Kulath.

"There was a slight delay while the supervelocity scanners on Kulath II were focused on to the system. They showed that the explosion had not yet occurred but was only a few hours away. If Kulath had been a fraction of a light-year further from this sun, we should never have known of its civilization until it had ceased to exist.

"The Adminstrator of Kulath contacted Sector Base immediately, and I was ordered to proceed to the system at once. Our object is to save what members we can of the doomed race, if indeed there are any left. But we have assumed that a civilization possessing radio could have protected itself against any rise of temperature that may have already occurred.

"This ship and the two tenders will each explore a section of the planet. Commander Torkalee will take Number One, Commander Orostron Number Two. They will have just under four hours in which to explore this world. At the end of that time, they must be back in the ship. It will be leaving then, with or without them. I will give the two commanders detailed instructions in the control room immediately.

"That is all. We enter atmosphere in two hours."

On the world once known as Earth the fires were dying out: there was nothing left to burn. The great forests that had swept across the planet like a tidal wave with the passing of the cities were now no more than glowing charcoal and the smoke of their funeral pyres still stained the sky. But the last hours were still to come, for the surface rocks had not yet begun to flow. The continents were dimly visible through the haze, but their outlines meant nothing to the watchers in the approaching ship. The charts they possessed were out of date by a dozen Ice Ages and more deluges than one.

The S9000 had driven past Jupiter and seen at once that no life could exist in those half-gaseous oceans of compressed hydrocarbons, now erupting furiously under the sun's abnormal heat. Mars and the outer planets they had missed, and Alveron realized that the worlds nearer the sun than Earth would be already melting. It was more than likely, he thought sadly, that the tragedy of this unknown race was already finished. Deep in his heart, he thought it might be better so. The ship could only have carried a few hundred survivors, and the problem of selection had been haunting his mind.

Rugon, Chief of Communications and Deputy Captain, came into the control room. For the last hour he had been striving to detect radiation from Earth, but in vain.

"We're too late," he announced gloomily. "I've monitored the whole spectrum and the ether's dead except for our own stations and some two-hundred-year-old programs from Kulath. Nothing in this system is radiating any more."

He moved toward the giant vision screen with a

graceful flowing motion that no mere biped could ever hope to imitate. Alveron said nothing; he had been expecting this news.

One entire wall of the control room was taken up by the screen, a great black rectangle that gave an impression of almost infinite depth. Three of Rugon's slender control tentacles, useless for heavy work but incredibly swift at all manipulation, flickered over the selector dials and the screen lit up with a thousand points of light. The star field flowed swiftly past as Rugon adjusted the controls, bringing the projector to bear upon the sun itself.

No man of Earth would have recognized the monstrous shape that filled the screen. The sun's light was white no longer: great violet-blue clouds covered half its surface and from them long streamers of flame were erupting into space. At one point an enormous prominence had reared itself out of the photosphere, far out even into the flickering veils of the corona. It was as though a tree of fire had taken root in the surface of the sun—a tree that stood half a million miles high and whose branches were rivers of flame sweeping through space at hundreds of miles a second.

"I suppose," said Rugon presently, "that you are quite satisfied about the astronomers' calculations. After all—"

"Oh, we're perfectly safe," said Alveron confidently. "I've spoken to Kulath Observatory and they have been making some additional checks through our own instruments. That uncertainty of an hour includes a private safety margin which they won't tell me in case I feel tempted to stay any longer."

He glanced at the instrument board.

"The pilot should have brought us to the atmosphere now. Switch the screen back to the planet, please. Ah, there they go!"

There was a sudden tremor underfoot and a raucous clanging of alarms, instantly stilled. Across the vision screen two slim projectiles dived toward the looming mass of Earth. For a few miles they traveled together, then they separated, one vanishing abruptly as it entered the shadow of the planet.

Slowly the huge mother ship, with its thousand times greater mass, descended after them into the raging storms that already were tearing down the deserted cities of Man.

It was night in the hemisphere over which Orostron drove his tiny command. Like Torkalee, his mission was to photograph and record, and to report progress to the mother ship. The little scout had no room for specimens or passengers. If contact was made with the inhabitants of this world, the S9000 would come at once. There would be no time for parleying. If there was any trouble the rescue would be by force and the explanations could come later.

The ruined land beneath was bathed with an eerie, flickering light, for a great auroral display was raging over half the world. But the image on the vision screen was independent of external light, and it showed clearly a waste of barren rock that seemed never to have known any form of life. Presumably this desert land must come to an end somewhere. Orostron increased his speed to the highest value he dared risk in so dense an atmosphere.

The machine fled on through the storm, and presently the desert of rock began to climb toward the sky. A great mountain range lay ahead, its peaks lost in the smoke-laden clouds. Orostron directed the scanners toward the horizon, and on the vision screen the line of mountains seemed suddenly very close and menacing. He started to climb rapidly. It was difficult to imagine a more unpromising land in which to find civilization and he wondered if it would be wise to change course. He decided against it. Five minutes later, he had his reward.

Miles below lay a decapitated mountain, the whole of its summit sheared away by some tremendous feat of engineering. Rising out of the rock and straddling the artificial plateau was an intricate structure of metal girders, supporting masses of machinery. Orostron brought his ship to a halt and spiraled down toward the mountain.

The slight Doppler blur had now vanished, and the picture on the screen was clear-cut. The latticework was supporting some scores of great metal mirrors, pointing skyward at an angle of forty-five degrees to the horizontal. They were slightly concave, and each had some complicated mechanism at its focus. There seemed something impressive and purposeful about the great array; every mirror was aimed at precisely the same spot in the sky—or beyond.

Orostron turned to his colleagues.

"It looks like some kind of observatory to me," he said. "Have you ever seen anything like it before?"

Klarten, a multitentacled, tripedal creature from a globular cluster at the edge of the Milky Way, had a different theory.

"That's communication equipment. Those reflectors are for focusing electromagnetic beams. I've seen the same kind of installation on a hundred worlds before. It may even be the station that Kulath picked up— though that's rather unlikely, for the beams would be very narrow from mirrors that size."

"That would explain why Rugon could detect no radiation before we landed," added Hansur II, one of the twin beings from the planet Thargon.

Orostron did not agree at all.

"If that is a radio station, it must be built for interplanetary communication. Look at the way the mirrors are pointed. I don't believe that a race which has only had radio for two centuries can have crossed space. It took my people six thousand years to do it."

"We managed it in three," said Hansur II mildly, speaking a few seconds ahead of his twin. Before the inevitable argument could develop, Klarten began to wave his tentacles with excitement. While the others had been talking, he had started the automatic monitor.

"Here it is! Listen!"

He threw a switch, and the little room was filled with a raucous whining sound, continually changing in pitch but nevertheless retaining certain characteristics that were difficult to define.

The four explorers listened intently for a minute; then Orostron said, "Surely that can't be any form of speech! No creature could produce sounds as quickly as that!"

Hansur 1 had come to the same conclusion. "That's a television program. Don't you think so, Klarten?"

The other agreed.

"Yes, and each of those mirrors seems to be radiating a different program. I wonder where they're going? If I'm correct, one of the other planets in the system must lie along those beams. We can soon check that."

Orostron called the S9000 and reported the discovery. Both Rugon and Alveron were greatly excited, and made a quick check of the astronomical records.

The result was surprising—and disappointing. None of the other nine planets lay anywhere near the line of transmission. The great mirrors appeared to be pointing blindly into space.

There seemed only one conclusion to be drawn, and Klarten was the first to voice it.

"They had interplanetary communication," he said. "But the station must be deserted now, and the transmitters no longer controlled. They haven't been switched off, and are just pointing where they were left."

"Well, we'll soon find out," said Orostron. "I'm going to land."

He brought the machine slowly down to the level of the great metal mirrors, and past them until it came to rest on the mountain rock. A hundred yards away, a white building crouched beneath the maze of steel girders. It was windowless, but there were several doors in the wall facing them.

Orostron watched his companions climb into their protective suits and wished he could follow. But someone had to stay in the machine to keep in touch with the mother ship. Those were Alveron's instructions, and they were very wise. One never knew what would happen on a world that was being explored for the first time, especially under conditions such as these.

Very cautiously, the three explorers stepped out of the airlock and adjusted the antigravity field of their suits. Then, each with the mode of locomotion peculiar to his race, the little party went toward the building, the Hansur twins leading and Klarten following close behind. His gravity control was apparently giving trouble, for he suddenly fell to the ground, rather to the amusement of his colleagues. Orostron saw them pause for a moment at the nearest door—then it opened slowly and they disappeared from sight.

So Orostron waited, with what patience he could, while the storm rose around him and the light of the aurora grew even brighter in the sky. At the agreed times he called the mother ship and received brief acknowledgments from Rugon. He wondered how Torkalee was faring, halfway round the planet, but he could not contact him through the crash and thunder of solar interference.

It did not take Klarten and the Hansurs long to discover that their theories were largely correct. The building was a radio station, and it was utterly deserted. It consisted of one tremendous room with a few small offices leading from it. In the main chamber, row after row of electrical equipment stretched into the distance; lights flickered and winked on hundreds of control panels, and a dull glow came from the elements in a great avenue of vacuum tubes.

But Klarten was not impressed. The first radio sets his race had built were now fossilized in strata a thousand million years old. Man, who had possessed electrical machines for only a few centuries, could not compete with those who had known them for half the lifetime of the Earth.

Nevertheless, the party kept their recorders running as they explored the building. There was still one problem to be solved. The deserted station was broadcasting programs, but where were they coming from? The central switchboard had been quickly located. It was designed to handle scores of programs simultaneously, but the source of those programs was lost in a maze of cables that vanished underground. Back in the S9000, Rugon was trying to analyze the broadcasts and perhaps his researches would reveal their origin. It was impossible to trace cables that might lead across continents.

The party wasted little time at the deserted station. There was nothing they could learn from it, and they were seeking life rather than scientific information. A few minutes later the little ship rose swiftly from the plateau and headed toward the plains that must lie beyond the mountains. Less than three hours were still left to them.

As the array of enigmatic mirrors dropped out of sight, Orostron was struck by a sudden thought. Was it imagination, or had they all moved through a small angle while he had been waiting, as if they were still compensating for the rotation of the Earth? He could not be sure, and he dismissed the matter as unimportant. It would only mean that the directing mechanism was still working, after a fashion.

They discovered the city fifteen minutes later. It was a great, sprawling metropolis, built around a river that had disappeared leaving an ugly scar winding its way among the great buildings and beneath bridges that looked very incongruous now.

Even from the air, the city looked deserted. But only two and a half hours were left—there was no time for further exploration. Orostron made his decision, and landed near the largest structure he could see. It seemed reasonable to suppose that some creatures would have sought shelter in the strongest buildings, where they would be safe until the very end.

The deepest caves—the heart of the planet itself—would give no protection when the final cataclysm came. Even if this race had reached the outer planets, its doom would only be delayed by the few hours it would take for the ravening wavefronts to cross the Solar System.

Orostron could not know that the city had been deserted not for a few days or weeks, but for over a century. For the culture of cities, which had outlasted so many civilizations had been doomed at last when the helicopter brought universal transportation. Within a few generations the great masses of mankind, knowing that they could reach any part of the globe in a matter of hours, had gone back to the fields and forests for which they had always longed. The new civilization had machines and resources of which earlier ages had never dreamed, but it was essentially rural and no longer bound to the steel and concrete warrens that had dominated the centuries before. Such cities as still remained were specialized centers of research, administration or entertainment; the others had been allowed to decay, where it was too much trouble to destroy them. The dozen or so greatest of all cities, and the ancient university towns, had scarcely changed and would have lasted for many generations to come. But the cities that had been founded on steam and iron and surface transportation had passed with the industries that had nourished them.

And so while Orostron waited in the tender, his colleagues raced through endless empty corridors and deserted halls, taking innumerable photographs but learning nothing of the creatures who had used these buildings. There were libraries, meeting places, council rooms, thousands of offices—all were empty and deep with dust. If they had not seen the radio station on its mountain eyrie, the explorers could well have believed that this world had known no life for centuries.

Through the long minutes of waiting, Orostron tried to imagine where this race could have vanished. Perhaps they had killed themselves knowing that escape was impossible; perhaps they had built great shelters in the bowels of the planet, and even now were cowering in their millions beneath his feet, waiting for the end. He began to fear that he would never know.

It was almost a relief when at last he had to give the order for the return. Soon he would know if Torkalee's party had been more fortunate. And he was anxious to get back to the mother ship, for as the minutes passed the suspense had become more and more acute. There had always been the thought in his mind: What if the astronomers of Kulath have made a mistake? He would begin to feel happy when the walls of the S9000 were around him. He would be happier still when they were out in space and this ominous sun was shrinking far astern.

As soon as his colleagues had entered the airlock, Orostron hurled his tiny machine into the sky and set the controls to home on the S9000. Then he turned to his friends.

"Well, what have you found?" he asked.

Klarten produced a large roll of canvas and spread it out on the floor.

"This is what they were like," he said quietly. "Bipeds, with only two arms. They seem to have managed well, in spite of that handicap. Only two eyes as well, unless there are others in the back. We were lucky to find this; it's about the only thing they left behind."

The ancient oil paintings stared stonily back at the three creatures regarding it so intently. By the irony of fate, its complete worthlessness had saved it from oblivion. When the city had been evacuated, no one had bothered to move Alderman John Richards, 1909–1974. For a century and a half he had been gathering dust while far away from the old cities the new civilization had been rising to heights no earlier culture had ever known.

"That was almost all we found," said Klarten. "The city must have been deserted for years. I'm afraid our expedition has been a failure. If there are any living beings on this world, they've hidden themselves too well for us to find them."

His commander was forced to agree.

"It was an almost impossible task," he said. "If we'd had weeks instead of hours we might have succeeded. For all we know, they may even have built shelters under the sea. No one seems to have thought of that."

He glanced quickly at the indicators and corrected the course.

"We'll be there in five minutes. Alveron seems to be moving rather quickly. I wonder if Torkalee has found anything."

The S9000 was hanging a few miles above the seaboard of a blazing continent when Orostron homed upon it. The danger line was thirty minutes away and there was no time to lose. Skillfully, he maneuvered the little ship into its launching tube and the party stepped out of the airlock.

There was a small crowd waiting for them. That was to be expected, but Orostron could see at once that something more than curiosity had brought his friends here. Even before a word was spoken, he knew that something was wrong.

"Torkalee hasn't returned. He's lost his party and we're going to the rescue. Come along to the control room at once."

From the beginning, Torkalee had been luckier than Orostron. He had followed the zone of twilight, keeping away from the intolerable glare of the sun, until he came to the shores of an inland sea. It was a very recent sea, one of the latest of Man's works, for the land it covered had been desert less than a century before. In a few hours it would be desert again, for the water was boiling and clouds of steam were rising to the skies. But they could not veil the loveliness of the great white city that overlooked the tideless sea.

Flying machines were still parked neatly round the square in which Torkalee landed. They were disappointingly primitive, though beautifully finished, and depended on rotating airfoils for support. Nowhere was there any sign of life, but the place gave the impression that its inhabitants were not very far away. Lights were still shining from some of the windows.

Torkalee's three companions lost no time in leaving the machine. Leader of the party, by seniority of rank and race was T'sinadree, who like Alveron himself had been born on one of the ancient planets of the Central Suns. Next came Alarkane, from a race which was one of the youngest in the Universe and took a perverse pride in the fact. Last came one of the strange beings from the system of Palador. It was nameless, like all its kind, for it possessed no identity of its own, being merely a mobile but still dependent cell in the consciousness of its race. Though it and its fellows had long been scattered over the galaxy in the exploration of countless worlds, some unknown link still bound them together as inexorably as the living cells in a human body.

When a creature of Palador spoke, the pronoun it used was always "We." There was not, nor could there ever be, any first person singular in the language of Palador.

The great doors of the splendid building baffled the explorers, though any human child would have known their secret. T'sinadree wasted no time on them but called Torkalee on his personal transmitter. Then the three hurried aside while their commander maneuvered his machine into the best position. There was a brief burst of intolerable flame; the massive steelwork flickered once at the edge of the visible spectrum and was gone. The stones were still glowing when the eager

Rescue Party

party hurried into the building, the beams of their light projectors fanning before them.

The torches were not needed. Before them lay a great hall, glowing with light from lines of tubes along the ceiling. On either side, the hall opened out into long corridors, while straight ahead a massive stairway swept majestically toward the upper floors.

For a moment T'sinadree hesitated. Then, since one way was as good as another, he led his companions down the first corridor.

The feeling that life was near had now become very strong. At any moment, it seemed, they might be confronted by the creatures of this world. If they showed hostility—and they could scarcely be blamed if they did—the paralyzers would be used at once.

The tension was very great as the party entered the first room, and only relaxed when they saw that it held nothing but machines—row after row of them, now stilled and silent. Lining the enormous room were thousands of metal filing cabinets, forming a continuous wall as far as the eye could reach. And that was all; there was no furniture, nothing but the cabinets and the mysterious machines.

Alarkane, always the quickest of the three, was already examining the cabinets. Each held many thousand sheets of tough, thin material, perforated with innumerable holes and slots. The Paladorian appropriated one of the cards and Alarkane recorded the scene together with some close-ups of the machines. Then they left. The great room, which had been one of the marvels of the world, meant nothing to them. No living eye would ever again see that wonderful battery of almost human Hollerith analyzers and the five thousand million punched cards holding all that could be recorded of each man, woman and child on the planet.

It was clear that this building had been used very recently. With growing excitement, the explorers hurried on to the next room. This they found to be an enormous library, for millions of books lay all around them on miles and miles of shelving. Here, though the explorers could not know it, were the records of all the laws that Man had ever passed, and all the speeches that had ever been made in his council chambers.

T'sinadree was deciding his plan of action, when Alarkane drew his attention to one of the racks a hundred yards away. It was half empty, unlike all the others. Around it books lay in a tumbled heap on the floor, as if knocked down by someone in frantic haste. The signs were unmistakable. Not long ago, other creatures had been this way. Faint wheel marks were clearly visible on the floor to the acute sense of Alarkane, though the others could see nothing. Alarkane could even detect footprints, but knowing nothing of the creatures that had formed them he could not say which way they led.

The sense of nearness was stronger than ever now, but it was nearness in time, not in space. Alarkane voiced the thoughts of the party.

"Those books must have been valuable, and someone has come to rescue them—rather as an afterthought, I should say. That means there must be a place of refuge, possibly not very far away. Perhaps we may be able to find some other clues that will lead us to it."

T'sinadree agreed; the Paladorian wasn't enthusiastic.

"That may be so," it said, "but the refuge may be anywhere on the planet, and we have just two hours left. Let us waste no more time if we hope to rescue these people."

The party hurried forward once more, pausing only to collect a few books that might be useful to the scientists at Base—though it was doubtful if they could ever be translated. They soon found that the great building was composed largely of small rooms, all showing signs of recent occupation. Most of them were in a neat and tidy condition, but one or two were very much the reverse. The explorers were particularly puzzled by one room—clearly an office of some kind—that appeared to have been completely wrecked. The floor was littered with papers, the furniture had been smashed, and smoke was pouring through the broken windows from the fires outside.

T'sinadree was rather alarmed.

"Surely no dangerous animal could have got into a place like this!" he exclaimed, fingering his paralyzer nervously.

Alarkane did not answer. He began to make that annoying sound which his race called "laughter." It was several minutes before he would explain what had amused him.

"I don't think any animal has done it," he said. "In fact, the explanation is very simple. Suppose *you* had been working all your life in this room, dealing with endless papers, year after year. And suddenly, you are told that you will never see it again, that your work is finished, and that you can leave it forever. More than that—no one will come after you. Everything is finished. How would you make your exit, T'sinadree?"

The other thought for a moment.

"Well, I suppose I'd just tidy things up and leave. That's what seems to have happened in all the other rooms."

Alarkane laughed again.

"I'm quite sure you would. But some individuals have a different psychology. I think I should have liked the creature that used this room."

He did not explain himself further, and his two colleagues puzzled over his words for quite a while before they gave it up.

It came as something of a shock when Torkalee gave the order to return. They had gathered a great deal of information, but had found no clue that might lead them to the missing inhabitants of this world. That problem was as baffling as ever, and now it seemed that it would never be solved. There were only forty minutes left before the S9000 would be departing.

They were halfway back to the tender when they saw the semicircular passage leading down into the depths of the building. Its architectural style was quite different from that used elsewhere, and the gently sloping floor was an irresistible attraction to creatures whose many legs had grown weary of the marble staircases which only bipeds could have built in such profusion. T'sinadree had been the worst sufferer, for he normally employed twelve legs and could use twenty when he was in a hurry, though no one had ever seen him perform this feat.

The party stopped dead and looked down the passageway with a single thought. A tunnel, leading down into the depths of Earth! At its end, they might yet find the people of this world and rescue some of them from their fate. For there was still time to call the mother ship if the need arose.

T'sinadree signaled to his commander and Torkalee brought the little machine immediately overhead. There might not be time for the party to retrace its footsteps through the maze of passages, so meticulously recorded in the Paladorian mind that there was no possibility of going astray. If speed was necessary, Torkalee could blast his way through the dozen floors above their head. In any case, it should not take long to find what lay at the end of the passage.

It took only thirty seconds. The tunnel ended quite abruptly in a very curious cylindrical room with magnificently padded seats along the walls. There was no way out save that by which they had come and it was several seconds before the purpose of the chamber dawned on Alarkane's mind. It was a pity, he thought, that they would never have time to use this. The thought was suddenly interrupted by a cry from T'sinadree. Alarkane wheeled around, and saw that the entrance had closed silently behind them.

Even in that first moment of panic, Alarkane found himself thinking with some admiration: Whoever they were, they knew how to build automatic machinery!

Rescue Party

The Paladorian was the first to speak. It waved one of its tenacles toward the seats.

"We think it would be best to be seated," it said. The multiplex mind of Palador had already analyzed the situation and knew what was coming.

They did not have long to wait before a low-pitched hum came from a grill overhead, and for the very last time in history a human, even if lifeless, voice was heard on Earth. The words were meaningless, though the trapped explorers could guess their message clearly enough.

"Choose your stations, please, and be seated."

Simultaneously, a wall panel at one end of the compartment glowed with light. On it was a simple map, consisting of a series of a dozen circles connected by a line. Each of the circles had writing alongside it, and beside the writing were two buttons of different colors.

Alarkane looked questioningly at his leader.

"Don't touch them," said T'sinadree. "If we leave the controls alone, the doors may open again."

He was wrong. The engineers who had designed the automatic subway had assumed that anyone who entered it would naturally wish to go somewhere. If they selected no intermediate station, their destination could only be the end of the line.

There was another pause while the relays and thyratrons waited for their orders. In those thirty seconds, if they had known what to do, the party could have opened the doors and left the subway. But they did not know, and the machines geared to a human psychology acted for them.

The surge of acceleration was not very great; the lavish upholstery was a luxury, not a necessity. Only an almost imperceptible vibration told of the speed at which they were traveling through the bowels of the earth, on a journey the duration of which they could not even guess. And in thirty minutes, the S9000 would be leaving the Solar System.

There was a long silence in the speeding machine.

T'sinadree and Alarkane were thinking rapidly. So was the Paladorian, though in a different fashion. The conception of personal death was meaningless to it, for the destruction of a single unit meant no more to the group mind than the loss of a nail-paring to a man. But it could, though with great difficulty, appreciate the plight of individual intelligences such as Alarkane and T'sinadree, and it was anxious to help them if it could.

Alarkane had managed to contact Torkalee with his personal transmitter, though the signal was very weak and seemed to be fading quickly. Rapidly he explained the situation, and almost at once the signals became clearer. Torkalee was following the path of the machine, flying above the ground under which they were speeding to their unknown destination. That was the first indication they had of the fact that they were traveling at nearly a thousand miles an hour, and very soon after that Torkalee was able to give the still more disturbing news that they were rapidly approaching the sea. While they were beneath the land, there was a hope, though a slender one, that they might stop the machine and escape. But under the ocean—not all the brains and the machinery in the great mother ship could save them. No one could have devised a more perfect trap.

T'sinadree had been examining the wall map with great attention. Its meaning was obvious, and along the line connecting the circles a tiny spot of light was crawling. It was already halfway to the first of the stations marked.

"I'm going to press one of those buttons," said T'sinadree at last. "It won't do any harm, and we may learn something."

"I agree. Which will you try first?"

"There are only two kinds, and it won't matter if we try the wrong one first. I suppose one is to start the machine and the other is to stop it."

Alarkane was not very hopeful.

"It started without any button pressing," he said. "I

think it's completely automatic and we can't control it from here at all."

T'sinadree could not agree.

"These buttons are clearly associated with the stations, and there's no point in having them unless you can use them to stop yourself. The only question is, which is the right one?"

His analysis was perfectly correct. The machine could be stopped at any intermediate station. They had only been on their way ten minutes, and if they could leave now, no harm would have been done. It was just bad luck that T'sinadree's first choice was the wrong button.

The little light on the map crawled slowly through the illuminated circle without checking its speed. And at the same time Torkalee called from the ship overhead.

"You have just passed underneath a city and are heading out to sea. There cannot be another stop for nearly a thousand miles."

Alveron had given up all hope of finding life on this world. The S9000 had roamed over half the planet, never staying long in one place, descending ever and again in an effort to attract attention. There had been no response; Earth seemed utterly dead. If any of its inhabitants were still alive, thought Alveron, they must have hidden themselves in its depths where no help could reach them, though their doom would be nonetheless certain.

Rugon brought news of the disaster. The great ship ceased its fruitless searching and fled back through the storm to the ocean above which Torkalee's little tender was still following the track of the buried machine.

The scene was truly terrifying. Not since the days when Earth was born had there been such seas as this. Mountains of water were racing before the storm which had now reached velocities of many hundred miles an hour. Even at this distance from the mainland the air was full of flying debris—trees, fragments of houses, sheets of metal, anything that had not been anchored to the ground. No airborne machine could have lived for a moment in such a gale. And ever and again even the roar of the wind was drowned as the vast watermountains met head-on with a crash that seemed to shake the sky.

Fortunately, there had been no serious earthquakes yet. Far beneath the bed of the ocean, the wonderful piece of engineering which had been the World President's private vacuum-subway was still working perfectly, unaffected by the tumult and destruction above. It would continue to work until the last minute of the Earth's existence, which, if the astronomers were right, was not much more than fifteen minutes away—though precisely how much more Alveron would have given a great deal to know. It would be nearly an hour before the trapped party could reach land and even the slightest hope of rescue.

Alveron's instructions had been precise, though even without them he would never have dreamed of taking any risks with the great machine that had been entrusted to his care. Had he been human, the decision to abandon the trapped members of his crew would have been desperately hard to make. But he came of a race far more sensitive than Man, a race that so loved the things of the spirit that long ago, and with infinite reluctance, it had taken over control of the Universe since only thus could it be sure that justice was being done. Alveron would need all his superhuman gifts to carry him through the next few hours.

Meanwhile, a mile below the bed of the ocean Alarkane and T'sinadree were very busy indeed with their private communicators. Fifteen minutes is not a long time in which to wind up the affairs of a lifetime. It is indeed scarcely long enough to dictate more than a few of those farewell messages which at such moments are so much more important than all other matters.

All the while the Paladorian had remained silent and

motionless, saying not a word. The other two, resigned to their fate and engrossed in their personal affairs, had given it no thought. They were startled when suddenly it began to address them in its peculiarly passionless voice.

"We perceive that you are making certain arrangements concerning your anticipated destruction. That will probably be unnecessary. Captain Alveron hopes to rescue us if we can stop this machine when we reach land again."

Both T'sinadree and Alarkane were too surprised to say anything for a moment. Then the latter gasped, "How do you know?"

It was a foolish question, for he remembered at once that there were several Paladorians—if one could use the phrase—in the S9000, and consequently their companion knew everything that was happening in the mother ship. So he did not wait for an answer but continued, "Alveron can't do that! He daren't take such a risk!"

"There will be no risk," said the Paladorian. "We have told him what to do. It is really very simple."

Alarkane and T'sinadree looked at their companion with something approaching awe, realizing now what must have happened. In moments of crisis, the single units comprising the Paladorian mind could link together in an organization no less close than that of any physical brain. At such moments they formed an intellect more powerful than any other in the Universe. All ordinary problems could be solved by a few hundred or thousand units. Very rarely, millions would be needed, and on two historic occasions the billions of cells of the entire Paladorian consciousness had been welded together to deal with emergencies that threatened the race. The mind of Palador was one of the greatest mental resources of the Universe; its full force was seldom required, but the knowledge that it was available was supremely comforting to other races. Alarkane wondered how many cells had co-ordinated to deal with this particular emergency. He also wondered how so trivial an incident had ever come to its attention.

To that question he was never to know the answer, though he might have guessed it had he known that the chillingly remote Paladorian mind possessed an almost human streak of vanity. Long ago, Alarkane had written a book trying to prove that eventually all intelligent races would sacrifice individual consciousness and that one day only group-minds would remain in the Universe. Palador, he had said, was the first of those ultimate intellects, and the vast, dispersed mind had not been displeased.

They had no time to ask any further questions before Alveron himself began to speak through their communicators.

"Alveron calling! We're staying on this planet until the detonation waves reach it, so we may be able to rescue you. You're heading toward a city on the coast which you'll reach in forty minutes at your present speed. If you cannot stop yourselves then, we're going to blast the tunnel behind and ahead of you to cut off your power. Then we'll sink a shaft to get you out—the chief engineer says he can do it in five minutes with the main projectors. So you should be safe within an hour, unless the sun blows up before."

"And if that happens, you'll be destroyed as well! You mustn't take such a risk!"

"Don't let that worry you; we're perfectly safe. When the sun detonates, the explosion wave will take several minutes to rise to its maximum. But apart from that, we're on the night side of the planet, behind an eight-thousand-mile screen of rock. When the first warning of the explosion comes, we will accelerate out of the Solar System, keeping in the shadow of the planet. Under our maximum drive, we will reach the velocity of light before leaving the cone of shadow, and the sun cannot harm us then."

Rescue Party

T'sinadree was still afraid to hope. Another objection came at once into his mind.

"Yes, but how will you get any warning, here on the night side of the planet?"

"Very easily," replied Alveron. "This world has a moon which is now visible from this hemisphere. We have telescopes trained on it. If it shows any sudden increase in brilliance, our main drive goes on automatically and we'll be thrown out of the system."

The logic was flawless. Alveron, cautious as ever, was taking no chances. It would be many minutes before the eight-thousand-mile shield of rock and metal could be destroyed by the fires of the exploding sun. In that time, the S9000 could have reached the safety of the velocity of light.

Alarkane pressed the second button when they were still several miles from the coast. He did not expect anything to happen then, assuming that the machine could not stop between stations. It seemed too good to be true when, a few minutes later, the machine's slight vibration died away and they came to a halt.

The doors slid silently apart. Even before they were fully open, the three had left the compartment. They were taking no more chances. Before them a long tunnel stretched into the distance, rising slowly out of sight. They were starting along it when suddenly Alveron's voice called from the communicators.

"Stay where you are! We're going to blast!"

The ground shuddered once, and far ahead there came the rumble of falling rock. Again the earth shook—and a hundred yards ahead the passageway vanished abruptly. A tremendous vertical shaft had been cut clean through it.

The party hurried forward again until they came to the end of the corridor and stood waiting on its lip. The shaft in which it ended was a full thousand feet across and descended into the earth as far as the torches could throw their beams. Overhead, the storm clouds fled beneath a moon that no man would have recognized, so luridly brilliant was its disk. And, most glorious of all sights, the S9000 floated high above, the great projectors that had drilled this enormous pit still glowing cherry red.

A dark shape detached itself from the mother ship and dropped swiftly toward the ground. Torkalee was returning to collect his friends. A little later, Alveron greeted them in the control room. He waved to the great vision screen and said quietly, "See, we were barely in time."

The continent below them was slowly settling beneath the mile-high waves that were attacking its coasts. The last that anyone was ever to see of Earth was a great plain, bathed with the silver light of the abnormally brilliant moon. Across its face the waters were pouring in a glittering flood toward a distant range of mountains. The sea had won its final victory, but its triumph would be short-lived for soon sea and land would be no more. Even as the silent party in the control room watched the destruction below, the infinitely greater catastrophe to which this was only the prelude came swiftly upon them.

It was as though dawn had broken suddenly over this moonlit landscape. But it was not dawn: it was only the moon, shining with the brilliance of a second sun. For perhaps thirty seconds that awesome, unnatural light burnt fiercely on the doomed land beneath. Then there came a sudden flashing of indicator lights across the control board. The main drive was on. For a second Alveron glanced at the indicators and checked their information. When he looked again at the screen, Earth was gone.

The magnificent, desperately overstrained generators quietly died when the S9000 was passing the orbit of Persephone. It did not matter, the sun could never harm them now, and although the ship was speeding helplessly out into the lonely night of interstellar space, it would only be a matter of days before rescue came.

There was irony in that. A day ago, they had been the rescuers, going to the aid of a race that now no longer existed. Not for the first time Alveron wondered about the world that had just perished. He tried, in vain, to picture it as it had been in its glory, the streets of its cities thronged with life. Primitive though its people had been, they might have offered much to the Universe. If only they could have made contact! Regret was useless; long before their coming, the people of this world must have buried themselves in its iron heart. And now they and their civilization would remain a mystery for the rest of time.

Alveron was glad when his thoughts were interrupted by Rugon's entrance. The chief of communications had been very busy ever since the take-off, trying to analyze the programs radiated by the transmitter Orostron had discovered. The problem was not a difficult one, but it demanded the construction of special equipment, and that had taken time.

"Well, what have you found?" asked Alveron.

"Quite a lot," replied his friend. "There's something mysterious here, and I don't understand it.

"It didn't take long to find how the vision transmissions were built up, and we've been able to convert them to suit our own equipment. It seems that there were cameras all over the planet, surveying points of interest. Some of them were apparently in cities, on the tops of very high buildings. The cameras were rotating continually to give panoramic views. In the programs we've recorded there are about twenty different scenes.

"In addition, there are a number of transmissions of a different kind, neither sound nor vision. They seem to be purely scientific—possibly instrument readings or something of that sort. All these programs were going out simultaneously on different frequency bands.

"Now there must be a reason for all this. Orostron still thinks that the station simply wasn't switched off when it was deserted. But these aren't the sort of programs such a station would normally radiate at all. It was certainly used for interplanetary relaying—Klarten was quite right there. So these people must have crossed space, since none of the other planets had any life at the time of the last survey. Don't you agree?"

Alveron was following intently.

"Yes, that seems reasonable enough. But it's also certain that the beam was pointing to none of the other planets. I checked that myself."

"I know," said Rugon. "What I want to discover is why a giant interplanetary relay station is busily transmitting pictures of a world about to be destroyed— pictures that would be of immense interest to scientists and astronomers. Someone had gone to a lot of trouble to arrange all those panoramic cameras. I am convinced that those beams were going somewhere."

Alveron started up.

"Do you imagine that there might be an outer planet that hasn't been reported?" he asked. "If so, your theory's certainly wrong. The beam wasn't even pointing in the plane of the Solar System. And even if it were—just look at this."

He switched on the vision screen and adjusted the controls. Against the velvet curtain of space was hanging a blue-white sphere, apparently composed of many concentric shells of incandescent gas. Even though its immense distance made all movement invisible, it was clearly expanding at an enormous rate. At its center was a blinding point of light—the white dwarf star that the sun had now become.

"You probably don't realize just how big that sphere is," said Alveron. "Look at this."

He increased the magnification until only the center portion of the nova was visible. Close to its heart were two minute condensations, one on either side of the nucleus.

"Those are the two giant planets of the system. They have still managed to retain their existence— after a fashion. And they were several hundred million miles from the sun. The nova is still expanding—but it's already twice the size of the Solar System."

Rugon was silent for a moment.

"Perhaps you're right," he said, rather grudgingly. "You've disposed of my first theory. But you still haven't satisfied me."

He made several swift circuits of the room before speaking again. Alveron waited patiently. He knew the almost intuitive powers of his friend, who could often solve a problem when mere logic seemed insufficient.

Then, rather slowly, Rugon began to speak again.

"What do you think of this?" he said. "Suppose we've completely underestimated this people? Orostron did it once—he thought they could never have crossed space, since they'd only known radio for two centuries. Hansur II told me that. Well, Orostron was quite wrong. Perhaps we're all wrong. I've had a look at the material that Klarten brought back from the transmitter. He wasn't impressed by what he found, but it's a marvelous achievement for so short a time. There were devices in that station that belonged to civilizations thousands of years older. Alveron, can we follow that beam to see where it leads?"

Alveron said nothing for a full minute. He had been more than half expecting the question, but it was not an easy one to answer. The main generators had gone completely. There was no point in trying to repair them. But there was still power available, and while there was power, anything could be done in time. It would mean a lot of improvisation, and some difficult maneuvers, for the ship still had its enormous initial velocity. Yes, it could be done, and the activity would keep the crew from becoming further depressed, now that the reaction caused by the mission's failure had started to set in. The news that the nearest heavy repair ship could not reach them for three weeks had also caused a slump of morale.

The engineers, as usual, made a tremendous fuss.

Again as usual, they did the job in half the time they had dismissed as being absolutely impossible. Very slowly, over many hours, the great ship began to discard the speed its main drive had given it in as many minutes. In a tremendous curve, millions of miles in radius, the S9000 changed its course and the star fields shifted round it.

The maneuver took three days, but at the end of that time the ship was limping along a course parallel to the beam that had once come from Earth. They were heading out into emptiness, the blazing sphere that had been the sun dwindling slowly behind them. By the standards of interstellar flight, they were almost stationary.

For hours Rugon strained over his instruments, driving his detector beams far ahead into space. There were certainly no planets within many light-years; there was no doubt of that. From time to time Alveron came to see him and always he had to give the same reply: "Nothing to report." About a fifth of the time Rugon's intuition let him down badly; he began to wonder if this was such an occasion.

Not until a week later did the needles of the mass-detectors quiver feebly at the ends of their scales. But Rugon said nothing, not even to his captain. He waited until he was sure, and he went on waiting until even the short-range scanners began to react, and to build up the first faint pictures on the vision screen. Still he waited patiently until he could interpret the images. Then, when he knew that his wildest fancy was even less than the truth, he called his colleagues into the control room.

The picture on the vision screen was the familiar one of endless star fields, sun beyond sun to the very limits of the Universe. Near the center of the screen a distant nebula made a patch of haze that was difficult for the eye to grasp.

Rugon increased the magnification. The stars flowed

out of the field; the little nebula expanded until it filled the screen and then—it was a nebula no longer. A simultaneous gasp of amazement came from all the company at the sight that lay before them.

Lying across league after league of space, ranged in a vast three-dimensional array of rows and columns with the precision of a marching army, were thousands of tiny pencils of light. They were moving swiftly; the whole immense lattice holding its shape as a single unit. Even as Alveron and his comrades watched, the formation began to drift off the screen and Rugon had to recenter the controls.

After a long pause, Rugon started to speak.

"This is the race," he said softly, "that has known radio for only two centuries—the race that we believed had crept to die in the heart of its planet. I have examined those images under the highest possible magnification.

"That is the greatest fleet of which there has ever been a record. Each of those points of light represents a ship larger than our own. Of course, they are very primitive—what you see on the screen are the jets of their rockets. Yes, they dared to use rockets to bridge interstellar space! You realize what that means. It would take them centuries to reach the nearest star. The whole race must have embarked on this journey in the hope that its descendants would complete it, generations later.

"To measure the extent of their accomplishment, think of the ages it took us to conquer space, and the longer ages still before we attempted to reach the stars. Even if we were threatened with annihilation, could we have done so much in so short a time? Remember, this is the youngest civilization in the Universe. Four hundred thousand years ago it did not even exist. What will it be a million years from now?"

An hour later, Orostron left the crippled mother ship to make contact with the great fleet ahead. As the little torpedo disappeared among the stars, Alveron turned to his friend and made a remark that Rugon was often to remember in the years ahead.

"I wonder what they'll be like?" he mused. "Will they be nothing but wonderful engineers, with no art or philosophy? They're going to have such a surprise when Orostron reaches them—I expect it will be rather a blow to their pride. It's funny how all isolated races think they're the only people in the Universe. But they should be grateful to us; we're going to save them a good many hundred years of travel."

Alveron glanced at the Milky Way, lying like a veil of silver mist across the vision screen. He waved toward it with a sweep of a tentacle that embraced the whole circle of the galaxy, from the Central Planets to the lonely suns of the Rim.

"You know," he said to Rugon, "I feel rather afraid of these people. Suppose they don't like our little Federation?" He waved once more toward the starclouds that lay massed across the screen, glowing with the light of their countless suns.

"Something tells me they'll be very determined people," he added. "We had better be polite to them. After all, we only outnumber them about a thousand million to one."

Rugon laughed at his captain's little joke.

Twenty years afterward, the remark didn't seem funny.

August Heat

by William Fryer Harvey

PHENISTONE ROAD, CLAPHAM,

August 20th, 190—. I have had what I believe to be the most remarkable day in my life, and while the events are still fresh in my mind, I wish to put them down on paper as clearly as possible.

Let me say at the outset that my name is James Clarence Withencroft.

I am forty years old, in perfect health, never having known a day's illness.

By profession I am an artist, not a very successful one, but I earn enough money by my black-and-white work to satisfy my necessary wants.

My only near relative, a sister, died five years ago, so that I am independent.

I breakfasted this morning at nine, and after glancing through the morning paper I lighted my pipe and proceeded to let my mind wander in the hope that I might chance upon some subject for my pencil.

The room, though door and windows were open, was oppressively hot, and I had just made up my mind that the coolest and most comfortable place in the neighborhood would be the deep end of the public swimming bath, when the idea came.

I began to draw. So intent was I on my work that I left my lunch untouched, only stopping work when the clock of St. Jude's struck four.

The final result, for a hurried sketch, was, I felt sure, the best thing I had done.

It showed a criminal in the dock immediately after

the judge had pronounced sentence. The man was fat—enormously fat. The flesh hung in rolls about his chin; it creased his huge, stumpy neck. He was clean shaven (perhaps I should say a few days before he must have been clean shaven) and almost bald. He stood in the dock, his short, stumpy fingers clasping the rail, looking straight in front of him. The feeling that his expression conveyed was not so much one of horror as of utter, absolute collapse.

There seemed nothing in the man strong enough to sustain that mountain of flesh.

I rolled up the sketch, and without quite knowing why, placed it in my pocket. Then with the rare sense of happiness which the knowledge of a good thing well done gives, I left the house.

I believe that I set out with the idea of calling upon Trenton, for I remember walking along Lytton Street and turning to the right along Gilchrist Road at the bottom of the hill where the men were at work on the new tram lines.

From there onward I have only the vaguest recollections of where I went. The one thing of which I was fully conscious was the awful heat, that came up from the dusty asphalt pavement as an almost palpable wave. I longed for the thunder promised by the great banks of copper-colored cloud that hung low over the western sky.

I must have walked five or six miles, when a small boy roused me from my reverie by asking the time.

It was twenty minutes to seven.

When he left me I began to take stock of my bearings. I found myself standing before a gate that led into a yard bordered by a strip of thirsty earth, where there were flowers, purple stock and scarlet geranium. Above the entrance was a board with the inscription—

CHAS. ATKINSON
MONUMENTAL MASON
WORKER IN ENGLISH AND ITALIAN MARBLES

From the yard itself came a cheery whistle, the noise of hammer blows, and the cold sound of steel meeting stone.

A sudden impulse made me enter.

A man was sitting with his back toward me, busy at work on a slab of curiously veined marble. He turned round as he heard my steps and stopped short.

It was the man I had been drawing, whose portrait lay in my pocket.

He sat there, huge and elephantine, the sweat pouring from his scalp, which he wiped with a red silk handkerchief. But though the face was the same, the expression was absolutely different.

He greeted me smiling, as if we were old friends, and shook my hand.

I apologized for my intrusion.

"Everything is hot and glary outside," I said. "This seems an oasis in the wilderness."

"I don't know about the oasis," he replied, "but it certainly is hot, as hot as hell. Take a seat, sir!"

He pointed to the end of the gravestone on which he was at work, and I sat down.

"That's a beautiful piece of stone you've got hold of," I said.

He shook his head. "In a way it is," he answered; "the surface here is as fine as anything you could wish, but there's a big flaw at the back, though I don't expect you'd ever notice it. I could never make really a good job of a bit of marble like that. It would be all right in the summer like this; it wouldn't mind the blasted heat. But wait till the winter comes. There's nothing like frost to find out the weak points in stone."

"Then what's it for?" I asked.

The man burst out laughing.

"You'd hardly believe me if I was to tell you it's for an exhibition, but it's the truth. Artists have exhibitions: so do grocers and butchers; we have them too. All the latest little things in headstones, you know."

He went on to talk of marbles, which sort best withstood wind and rain, and which were easiest to work; then of his garden and a new sort of carnation he had bought. At the end of every other minute he would drop his tools, wipe his shining head, and curse the heat.

I said little, for I felt uneasy. There was something unnatural, uncanny, in meeting this man.

I tried at first to persuade myself that I had seen him before, that his face, unknown to me, had found a place in some out-of-the-way corner of my memory, but I knew that I was practicing little more than a plausible piece of self-deception.

Mr. Atkinson finished his work, spat on the ground, and got up with a sigh of relief.

"There! What do you think of that?" he said, with an air of evident pride.

The inscription which I read for the first time was this—

SACRED TO THE MEMORY
OF
JAMES CLARENCE WITHENCROFT.
BORN JAN. 18TH, 1860.
HE PASSED AWAY VERY SUDDENLY
ON AUGUST 20TH, 190–

"In the midst of life we are in death."

For some time I sat in silence. Then a cold shudder ran down my spine. I asked him where he had seen the name.

"Oh, I didn't see it anywhere," replied Mr. Atkinson. "I wanted some name, and I put down the first that came into my head. Why do you want to know?"

"It's a strange coincidence, but it happens to be mine."

He gave a long, low whistle.

"And the dates?"

"I can only answer for one of them, and that's correct."

August Heat

"It's a rum go!" he said.

But he knew less than I did. I told him of my morning's work. I took the sketch from my pocket and showed it to him. As he looked, the expression of his face altered until it became more and more like that of the man I had drawn.

"And it was only the day before yesterday," he said, "that I told Maria there were no such things as ghosts!"

Neither of us had seen a ghost, but I knew what he meant.

"You probably heard my name," I said.

"And you must have seen me somewhere and have forgotten it! Were you at Clacton-on-Sea last July?"

I had never been to Clacton in my life. We were silent for some time. We were both looking at the same thing, the two dates on the gravestone, and one was right.

"Come inside and have some supper," said Mr. Atkinson.

His wife is a cheerful little woman, with the flaky red cheeks of the country-bred. Her husband introduced me as a friend of his who was an artist. The result was unfortunate, for after the sardines and watercress had been removed, she brought me out a Doré Bible, and I had to sit and express my admiration for nearly half an hour.

I went outside, and found Atkinson sitting on the gravestone smoking.

We resumed the conversation at the point we had left off.

"You must excuse my asking," I said, "but do you know of anything you've done for which you could be put on trial?"

He shook his head.

"I'm not a bankrupt, the business is prosperous enough. Three years ago I gave turkeys to some of the guardians at Christmas, but that's all I can think of. And they were small ones, too," he added as an afterthought.

He got up, fetched a can from the porch, and began to water the flowers. "Twice a day regular in the hot weather," he said, "and then the heat sometimes gets the better of the delicate ones. And ferns, good Lord! they could never stand it. Where do you live?"

I told him my address. It would take an hour's quick walk to get back home.

"It's like this," he said. "We'll look at the matter straight. If you go back home to-night, you take your chance of accidents. A cart may run over you, and there's always banana skins and orange peel, to say nothing of fallen ladders."

He spoke of the improbable with an intense seriousness that would have been laughable six hours before. But I did not laugh.

"The best thing we can do," he continued, "is for you to stay here till twelve o'clock. We'll go upstairs and smoke; it may be cooler inside."

To my surprise I agreed.

We are sitting in a long, low room beneath the eaves. Atkinson has sent his wife to bed. He himself is busy sharpening some tools at a little oilstone, smoking one of my cigars the while.

The air seems charged with thunder. I am writing this at a shaky table before the open window. The leg is cracked, and Atkinson, who seems a handy man with his tools, is going to mend it as soon as he has finished putting an edge on his chisel.

It is after eleven now. I shall be gone in less than an hour.

But the heat is stifling.

It is enough to send a man mad.

To Build a Fire

by Jack London

Day had broken cold and gray, exceedingly cold and gray, when the man turned aside from the main Yukon trail and climbed the high earth-bank, where a dim and little-traveled trail led eastward through the fat spruce timberland. It was a steep bank, and he paused for breath at the top, excusing the act to himself by looking at his watch. It was nine o'clock. There was no sun nor hint of sun, though there was not a cloud in the sky. It was a clear day, and yet there seemed an intangible pall over the face of things, a subtle gloom that made the day dark, and that was due to the absence of sun. This fact did not worry the man. He was used to the lack of sun. It had been days since he had seen the sun, and he knew that a few more days must pass before that cheerful orb, due south, would just peep above the sky-line and dip immediately from view.

The man flung a look back along the way he had come. The Yukon lay a mile wide and hidden under three feet of ice. On top of this ice were as many feet of snow. It was all pure white, rolling in gentle undulations where the ice-jams of the freeze-up had formed. North and south, as far as his eye could see, it was unbroken white, save for a dark hair-line that curved and twisted from around the spruce-covered island to the south, and that curved and twisted away into the north, where it disappeared behind another spruce-covered island. This dark hair-line was the trail—the main trail—that led south five hundred miles to the Chilcoot Pass, Dyea, and salt water; and that led north seventy miles to Dawson, and still on to the north a thousand miles to Nulato, and finally to St. Michael on Bering Sea, a thousand miles and half a thousand more.

But all this—the mysterious, far-reaching hair-line trail, the absence of sun from the sky, the tremendous cold, and the strangeness and weirdness of it all—made no impression on the man. It was not because he was long used to it. He was a newcomer in the land, a *chechaquo*, and this was his first winter. The trouble with him was that he was without imagination. He was quick and alert in the things of life, but only in the things, and not in the significances. Fifty degrees below zero meant eighty-odd degrees of frost. Such fact impressed him as being cold and uncomfortable, and that was all. It did not lead him to meditate upon his frailty as a creature of temperature, and upon man's frailty in general, able only to live within certain narrow limits of heat and cold; and from there on it did not lead him to the conjectural field of immortality and man's place in the universe. Fifty degrees below zero stood for a bite of frost that hurt and that must be guarded against by the use of mittens, earflaps, warm moccasins and thick socks. Fifty degrees below zero was to him just precisely fifty degrees below zero. That there should be anything more to it than that was a thought that never entered his head.

As he turned to go on, he spat speculatively. There was a sharp, explosive crackle that startled him. He spat again. And again, in the air, before it could fall to the snow, the spittle crackled. He knew that at fifty below spittle crackled on the snow, but this spittle had crackled in the air. Undoubtedly it was colder than fifty below—how much colder he did not know. But the temperature did not matter. He was bound for the old claim on the left fork of Henderson Creek, where the boys were already. They had come over across the divide from the Indian Creek country, while he had come the roundabout way to take a look at the possibilities of getting out logs in the spring from the islands in the Yukon. He would be in to camp by six o'clock; a bit after dark, it was true, but the boys would be there, a fire would be going, and a hot supper would be ready. As for lunch, he pressed his hand against the protruding bundle under his jacket. It was also under his shirt, wrapped up in a handkerchief and lying against the naked skin. It was the only way to keep the biscuits from freezing. He smiled agreeably to himself as he thought of those biscuits, each cut open and sopped in bacon grease, and each enclosing a generous slice of fried bacon.

He plunged in among the big spruce trees. The trail was faint. A foot of snow had fallen since the last sled had passed over, and he was glad he was without a sled, traveling light. In fact, he carried nothing but the lunch wrapped in the handkerchief. He was surprised, however, at the cold. It certainly was cold, he concluded, as he rubbed his numb nose and cheekbones with his mittened hand. He was a warm-whiskered man, but the hair on his face did not protect the high cheek-bones and the eager nose that thrust itself aggressively into the frosty air.

At the man's heels trotted a dog, a big native husky, the proper wolf-dog, gray-coated and without any visible or temperamental difference from its brother, the wild wolf. The animal was depressed by the tremendous cold. It knew that it was no time for traveling. Its instinct told it a truer tale than was told to the man by the man's judgment. In reality, it was not merely colder than fifty below zero; it was colder than sixty below, than seventy below. It was seventy-five below zero. Since the freezing-point is thirty-two above zero, it meant that one hundred and seven degrees of frost obtained. The dog did not know anything about thermometers. Possibly in its brain there was no sharp consciousness of a condition of very cold such as was in the man's brain. But the brute had its instinct. It experienced a vague but menacing apprehension that subdued it and made it slink along at the man's heels, and that made it question eagerly every unwonted movement of the man as if expecting him to go into camp or to seek shelter somewhere and build a fire. The dog had learned fire, and it wanted fire, or else to burrow under the snow and cuddle its warmth away from the air.

The frozen moisture of its breathing had settled on its fur in a fine powder of frost, and especially were its jowls, muzzle, and eyelashes whitened by its crystaled breath. The man's red beard and mustache were likewise frosted, but more solidly, the deposit taking the form of ice and increasing with every warm, moist breath he exhaled. Also, the man was chewing tobacco, and the muzzle of ice held his lips so rigidly that he was unable to clear his chin when he expelled the juice. The result was that a crystal beard of the color and solidity of amber was increasing its length on his chin. If he fell down it would shatter itself, like glass, into brittle fragments. But he did not mind the appendage. It was the penalty all tobacco-chewers paid in that country, and he had been out before in two cold snaps. They had not been so cold as this, he knew, but by the spirit thermometer at Sixty Mile he knew they had been registered at fifty below and at fifty-five.

He held on through the level stretch of woods for several miles, crossed a wide flat of niggerheads, and dropped down a bank to the frozen bed of a small stream. This was Henderson Creek, and he knew he was ten miles from the forks. He looked at his watch. It was ten o'clock. He was making four miles an hour, and he calculated that he would arrive at the forks at half-past twelve. He decided to celebrate that event by eating his lunch there.

The dog dropped in again at his heels, with a tail drooping discouragement, as the man swung along the creek-bed. The furrow of the old sled-trail was plainly visible, but a dozen inches of snow covered the marks of the last runners. In a month no man had come up or

To Build a Fire

down that silent creek. The man held steadily on. He was not much given to thinking, and just then particularly he had nothing to think about save that he would eat lunch at the forks and that at six o'clock he would be in camp with the boys. There was nobody to talk to; and, had there been, speech would have been impossible because of the ice-muzzle on his mouth. So he continued monotonously to chew tobacco and to increase the length of his amber beard.

Once in a while the thought reiterated itself that it was very cold and that he had never experienced such cold. As he walked along he rubbed his cheek-bones and nose with the back of his mittened hand. He did this automatically, now and again changing hands. But rub as he would, the instant he stopped his cheek-bones went numb, and the following instant the end of his nose went numb. He was sure to frost his cheeks; he knew that, and experienced a pang of regret that he had not devised a nose-strap of that sort Bud wore in cold snaps. Such a strap passed across the cheeks, as well, and saved them. But it didn't matter much, after all. What were frosted cheeks? A bit painful, that was all; they were never serious.

Empty as the man's mind was of thoughts, he was keenly observant, and he noticed the changes in the creek, and curves and bends and timber-jams, and always he sharply noted where he placed his feet. Once, coming around a bend, he shied abruptly, like a startled horse, curved away from the place where he had been walking, and retreated several paces back along the trail. The creek he knew was frozen clear to the bottom—no creek could contain water in that arctic winter—but he knew also that there were springs that bubbled out from the hillsides and ran along under the snow and on top of the ice of the creek. He knew that the coldest snaps never froze these springs, and he knew likewise their danger. They were traps. They hid pools of water under the snow that might be three inches deep, or three feet. Sometimes a skin of ice half an inch thick covered them, and in turn was covered by the snow. Sometimes there were alternate layers of water and ice-skin, so that when one broke through he kept on breaking through for a while, sometimes wetting himself almost to the waist.

That was why he had shied in such panic. He had felt the give under his feet and heard the crackle of a snow-hidden ice-skin. And to get his feet wet in such a temperature meant trouble and danger. At the very least it meant delay, for he would be forced to stop and build a fire, and under its protection to bare his feet while he dried his socks and moccasins. He stood and studied the creek-bed and its banks, and decided that the flow of water came from the right. He reflected awhile, rubbing his nose and cheeks, then skirted to the left, stepping gingerly and testing the footing for each step. Once clear of the danger, he took a fresh chew of tobacco and swung along at his four-mile gait.

In the course of the next two hours he came upon several similar traps. Usually the snow above the hidden pools had a sunken, candied appearance that advertised the danger. Once again, however, he had a close call; and once, suspecting danger, he compelled the dog to go on in front. The dog did not want to go. It hung back until the man shoved it forward, and then it went quickly across the white, unbroken surface. Suddenly it broke through, floundered to one side, and got away to firmer footing. It had wet its forefeet and legs, and almost immediately the water that clung to it turned to ice. It made quick efforts to lick the ice off its legs, then dropped down in the snow and began to bite out the ice that had formed between the toes. This was a matter of instinct. To permit the ice to remain would mean sore feet. It did not know this. It merely obeyed the mysterious prompting that arose from the deep crypts of its being. But the man knew, having achieved a judgment on the subject, and he removed the mitten from his right hand and helped tear out the ice-particles. He did not expose his fingers more than a minute, and was astonished at the swift numbness that smote them. It certainly was cold. He pulled on the mitten hastily, and beat the hand savagely across his chest.

At twelve o'clock the day was at its brightest. Yet the sun was too far south on its winter journey to clear the horizon. The bulge of the earth intervened between it and Henderson Creek, where the man walked under a clear sky at noon and cast no shadow. At half-past twelve, to the minute, he arrived at the forks of the creek. He was pleased at the speed he had made. If he kept it up, he would certainly be with the boys by six. He unbuttoned his jacket and shirt and drew forth his lunch. The action consumed no more than a quarter of a minute, yet in that brief moment the numbness laid hold of the exposed fingers. He did not put the mitten on, but, instead, struck the fingers a dozen sharp smashes against his leg. Then he sat down on a snow-covered log to eat. The sting that followed upon the striking of his fingers against his leg ceased so quickly that he was startled. He had had no chance to take a bite of biscuit. He struck the fingers repeatedly and returned them to the mitten, baring the other hand for the purpose of eating. He tried to take a mouthful, but the ice-muzzle prevented. He had forgotten to build a fire and thaw out. He chuckled at his foolishness, and as he chuckled he noted the numbness creeping into the exposed fingers. Also, he noted that the stinging which had first come to his toes when he sat down was already passing away. He wondered whether his toes were warm or numb. He moved them inside the moccasins and decided that they were numb.

He pulled the mitten on hurriedly and stood up. He was a bit frightened. He stamped up and down until the stinging returned into the feet. It certainly was cold, was his thought. That man from Sulphur Creek had spoken the truth when telling how cold it sometimes got in the country. And he had laughed at him at the time! That showed one must not be too sure of things.

There was no mistake about it, it *was* cold. He strode up and down, stamping his feet and threshing his arms, until reassured by the returning warmth. Then he got out matches and proceeded to make a fire. From the undergrowth, where high water of the previous spring had lodged a supply of seasoned twigs, he got his firewood. Working carefully from a small beginning, he soon had a roaring fire, over which he thawed the ice from his face and in the protection of which he ate his biscuits. For the moment the cold of space was outwitted. The dog took satisfaction in the fire, stretching out close enough for warmth and far enough away to to escape being singed.

When the man had finished, he filled his pipe and took his comfortable time over a smoke. Then he pulled on his mittens, settled the earflaps of his cap firmly about his ears, and took the creek trail up the left fork. The dog was disappointed and yearned back toward the fire. This man did not know cold. Possibly all the generations of his ancestry had been ignorant of cold, of real cold, of cold one hundred and seven degrees below freezing-point. But the dog knew; all its ancestry knew, and it had inherited the knowledge. And it knew that it was not good to walk abroad in such fearful cold. It was the time to lie snug in a hole in the snow and wait for a curtain of cloud to be drawn across the face of outer space whence this cold came. On the other hand, there was no keen intimacy between the dog and the man. The one was the toil-slave of the other, and the only caress it had ever received were the caresses of the whip-lash and of harsh and menacing throat-sounds that threatened the whip-lash. So the dog made no effort to communicate its apprehension to the man. It was not concerned in the welfare of the man; it was for its own sake that it yearned back toward the fire. But the man whistled, and spoke to it with the sound of whip-lashes, and the dog swung in at the man's heels and followed after.

The man took a chew of tobacco and proceeded to

To Build a Fire

start a new amber beard. Also, his moist breath quickly powdered with white his mustache, eyebrows, and lashes. There did not seem to be so many springs on the left fork of the Henderson, and for half an hour the man saw no signs of any. And then it happened. At a place where there were no signs, where the soft, unbroken snow seemed to advertise solidity beneath, the man broke through. It was not deep. He wet himself half way to the knees before he floundered out to the firm crust.

He was angry, and cursed his luck aloud. He had hoped to get into camp with the boys at six o'clock, and this would delay him an hour, for he would have to build a fire and dry out his footgear. This was imperative at that low temperature—he knew that much; and he turned aside to the bank, which he climbed. On top, tangled in the underbrush about the trunks of several small spruce trees, was a high-water deposit of dry fire-wood—sticks and twigs, principally, but also larger portions of seasoned branches and fine, dry, last year's grasses. He threw down several large pieces on top of the snow. This served for a foundation and prevented the young flame from drowning itself in the snow it otherwise would melt. The flame he got by touching a match to a small shred of birch-bark that he took from his pocket. This burned even more readily than paper. Placing it on the foundation, he fed the young flame with wisps of dry grass and with the tiniest dry twigs.

He worked slowly and carefully, keenly aware of his danger. Gradually, as the flame grew stronger, he increased the size of the twigs with which he fed it. He squatted in the snow, pulling the twigs out from their entanglement in the brush and feeding directly to the flame. He knew there must be no failure. When it is seventy-five below zero, a man must not fail in his first attempt to build a fire—that is, if his feet are wet. If his feet are dry, and he fails, he can run along the trail for half a mile and restore his circulation. But the circulation of wet and freezing feet cannot be restored by running when it is seventy-five below. No matter how fast he runs, the wet feet will freeze the harder.

All this the man knew. The oldtimer on Sulphur Creek had told him about it the previous fall, and now he was appreciating the advice. Already all sensation had gone out of his feet. To build the fire he had been forced to remove his mittens, and the fingers had quickly gone numb. His pace of four miles an hour had kept his heart pumping blood to the surface of his body and to all the extremities. But the instant he stopped, the action of the pump eased down. The cold of space smote the unprotected tip of the planet, and he, being on that unprotected tip, received the full force of the blow. The blood of his body recoiled before it. The blood was alive, like the dog, and like the dog it wanted to hide away and cover itself up from the fearful cold. So long as he walked four miles an hour, he pumped that blood, willy-nilly, to the surface; but now it ebbed away and sank down into the recesses of his body. The extremities were the first to feel its absence. His wet feet froze the faster, and his exposed fingers numbed the faster, though they had not yet begun to freeze. Nose and cheeks were already freezing, while the skin of all his body chilled as it lost its blood.

But he was safe. Toes and nose and cheeks would be only touched by the frost, for the fire was beginning to burn with strength. He was feeding it with twigs the size of his finger. In another minute he would be able to feed it with branches the size of his wrist, and then he could remove his wet foot-gear, and, while it dried, he could keep his naked feet warm by the fire, rubbing them at first, of course, with snow. The fire was a success. He was safe. He remembered the advice of the oldtimer on Sulphur Creek, and smiled. The oldtimer had been very serious in laying down the law that no man must travel alone in the Klondike after fifty below. Well, here he was; he had had the accident; he was alone; and he had saved himself. Those oldtimers were rather womanish, some of them, he thought. All a man had to do was keep his head, and he was all right. Any man who was a man could travel alone. But it was surprising, the rapidity with which his cheeks and nose were freezing. And he had not thought his fingers could go lifeless in so short a time. Lifeless they were, for he could scarcely make them move together to grip a twig, and they seemed remote from his body and from him. When he touched a twig, he had to look and see whether or not he had hold of it. The wires were pretty well down between him and his finger-ends.

All of which counted for little. There was the fire, snapping and crackling and promising life with every dancing flame. He started to untie his moccasins. They were coated with ice; the thick German socks were like sheaths of iron halfway to the knees; and the moccasin strings were like rods of steel all twisted and knotted as by some conflagration. For a moment he tugged with his numb fingers, then, realizing the folly of trying to work with that lifeless flesh, he drew his sheath-knife.

But before he could cut the strings, it happened. It was his own fault or, rather, his mistake. He should not have built the fire under the spruce tree. He should have built it in the open. But it had been easier to pull the twigs from the brush and drop them directly on the fire. Now the tree under which he had done this carried a weight of snow on its boughs. No wind had blown for weeks, and each bough was fully freighted. Each time he had pulled a twig he had communicated a slight agitation to the tree—an imperceptible agitation, so far as he was concerned, but an agitation sufficient to bring about the disaster. High up in the tree one bough capsized its load of snow. This fell on the boughs beneath, capsizing them. This process continued, spreading out and involving the whole tree. It grew like an avalanche, and it descended without warning upon the man and the fire, and the fire was blotted out! Where it had burned there was now spread a mantle of fresh and disordered snow.

The man was shocked. It was as though he had just heard his own sentence of death. For a moment he sat and stared at the spot where the fire had been. Then he grew very calm. Perhaps the oldtimer on Sulphur Creek was right. If he had only had a trail-mate he would have been in no danger now. The trail-mate could have built the fire. Well, it was up to him to build the fire over again, and this second time there must be no failure. Even if he succeeded, he would most likely lose some toes. His feet must be badly frozen by now, and there would be some time before the second fire was ready.

Such were his thoughts, but he did not sit and think them. He was busy all the time they were passing through his mind. He made a new foundation for a fire, this time in the open, where no treacherous tree could blot it out. Next, he gathered dry grasses and tiny twigs from the high-water flotsam. He could not bring his fingers together to pull them out, but he was able to gather them by the handful. In this way he got many rotten twigs and bits of green moss that were undesirable, but it was the best he could do. He worked methodically, even collecting an armful of the larger branches to be used later when the fire gathered strength. And all the while the dog sat and watched him, a certain yearning wistfulness in its eyes, for it looked upon him as the fire-provider, and the fire was slow in coming.

When all was ready, the man reached in his pocket for a second piece of birch-bark. He knew the bark was there, and though he could not feel it with his fingers, he could hear its crisp rustling as he fumbled for it. Try as he would, he could not clutch hold of it. And all the time, in his consciousness, was the knowledge that each instant his feet were freezing. This thought tended to put him in a panic, but he fought against it and kept calm. He pulled up his mittens with his teeth, and threshed his arms back and forth, beating his hands with all his might against his sides. He did this sitting down, and he stood up to do it; and all the while the dog sat in the snow, its wolf-brush of a tail curled around warmly over its forefeet, its sharp wolf-ears pricked forward intently as it watched the man. And the man, as he beat and threshed with his arms and hands, felt a great surge of envy as he regarded the creature that was warm and secure in its natural covering.

After a time he was aware of the first far-away signals of sensation in his beaten fingers. The faint tingling grew stronger till it evolved into a stinging ache that was excruciating, but which the man hailed with satisfaction. He stripped the mitten from his right hand and fetched forth the birch-bark. The exposed fingers were quickly going numb again. Next he brought out his bunch of sulphur matches. But the tremendous cold had already driven the life out of his fingers. In his effort to separate one match from the others, the whole bunch fell in the snow. He tried to pick it out of the snow, but failed. The dead fingers could neither touch nor clutch. He was very careful. He drove the thought of his freezing feet, and nose, and cheeks, out of his mind, devoting his whole soul to the matches. He watched, using the sense of vision in place of that of touch, and when he saw his fingers on each side of the bunch, he closed them—that is, he willed to close them, for the wires were down, and the fingers did not obey. He pulled the mitten on the right hand, and beat it fiercely against his knee. Then, with both mittened hands, he scooped the bunch of matches, along with much snow, into his lap. Yet he was no better off.

After some manipulation he managed to get the bunch between the heels of his mittened hands. In this fashion he carried it to his mouth. The ice crackled and snapped when by a violent effort he opened his mouth. He drew the lower jaw in, curled the upper lip out of the way, and scraped the bunch with his upper teeth in order to separate a match. He succeeded in getting one, which he dropped on his lap. He was no better off. He could not pick it up. Then he devised a way. He picked it up in his teeth and scratched it on his leg. Twenty times he scratched it before he succeeded in lighting it. As it flamed he held it with his teeth to the birch-bark. But the burning brimstone went up his nostrils and into his lungs, causing him to cough spasmodically. The match fell into the snow and went out.

The oldtimer on Sulphur Creek was right, he thought in the moment of controlled despair that ensued: after fifty below, a man should travel with a partner. He beat his hands, but failed in exciting any sensation. Suddenly he bared both hands, removing the mittens with his teeth. He caught the whole bunch between the heels of his hands. His arm-muscles not being frozen enabled him to press the hand-heels tightly against the matches. Then he scratched the bunch along his leg. It flared into flame, seventy sulphur matches at once! There was no wind to blow them out. He kept his head to one side to escape the strangling fumes, and held the blazing bunch to the birch-bark. As he so held it, he became aware of sensation in his hand. His flesh was burning. He could smell it. Deep down below the surface he could feel it. The sensation developed into pain that grew acute. And still he endured it, holding the flame of the matches clumsily to the bark that would not light readily because his own burning hands were in the way, absorbing most of the flame.

At last, when he could endure no more, he jerked his hands apart. The blazing matches fell sizzling into the snow, but the birch-bark was alight. He began laying dry grasses and the tiniest twigs on the flame. He could not pick and choose, for he had to lift the fuel between the heels of his hands. Small pieces of rotten wood and green moss clung to the twigs, and he bit them off as well as he could with his teeth. He cherished the flame carefully and awkwardly. It meant life, and it must not perish. The withdrawal of blood from the surface

To Build a Fire

of his body now made him begin to shiver, and he grew more awkward. A large piece of green moss fell squarely on the little fire. He tried to poke it out with his fingers, but his shivering frame made him poke too far, and he disrupted the nucleus of the little fire, the burning grasses and tiny twigs separating and scattering. He tried to poke them together again, but in spite of the tenseness of the effort, his shivering got away from him, and the twigs were hopelessly scattered. Each twig gushed a puff of smoke and went out. The fire-provider had failed. As he looked apathetically about him, his eyes chanced on the dog, sitting across the ruins of the fire from him, in the snow, making restless, hunching movements, slightly lifting one forefoot and then the other, shifting its weight back and forth on them with wistful eagerness and eyeing the fire-provider expectantly.

The sight of the dog put a wild idea into his head. He remembered the tale of the man, caught in a blizzard, who killed a steer, and crawled inside the carcass, and so was saved. He would kill the dog and bury his hands in the warm body until the numbness went out of them. Then he could build another fire. He spoke to the dog, calling it to him; but in his voice was a strange note of fear that frightened the animal, who had never known the man to speak in such a way before. Something was the matter, and its suspicious nature sensed danger—it knew not what danger, but somewhere, somehow, in its brain arose an apprehension of the man. It flattened its ears down at the sound of the man's voice, and its restless, hunching movements and the liftings and shiftings of its forefeet became more pronounced; but it would not come to the man. He got on his hands and knees and crawled toward the dog. This unusual posture again excited suspicion, and the animal sidled mincingly away.

The man sat up in the snow for a moment and struggled for calmness. Then he pulled on his mittens, by means of his teeth, and got upon his feet. He glanced down at first in order to assure himself that he was really standing up, for the absence of sensation in his feet left him unrelated to the earth. His erect position in itself started to drive the webs of suspicion from the dog's mind; and when he spoke peremptorily, with the sound of whip-lashes in his voice, the dog rendered its customary allegiance and came to him. As it came within reaching distance, the man lost his control. His arms flashed out to the dog, and he experienced genuine surprise when he discovered that his hands could not clutch, that there was neither bend nor feeling in the fingers. He had forgotten for the moment that they were frozen and that they were freezing more and more. All this happened quickly, and before the animal could get away, he encircled its body with his arms. He sat down in the snow, and in this fashion held the dog, while it snarled and whined and struggled.

But it was all he could do, hold its body encircled in his arms and sit there. He realized that he could not kill the dog. There was no way to do it. With his helpless hands he could neither draw nor hold his sheath-knife nor throttle the animal. He released it, and it plunged wildly away, with tail between its legs, and still snarling. It halted forty feet away and surveyed him curiously, with ears sharply pricked forward. The man looked down at his hands in order to locate them, and found them hanging on the ends of his arms. It struck him as curious that one should have to use his eyes in order to find out where his hands were. He began threshing his arms back and forth, beating the mittened hands against his sides. He did this for five minutes, violently, and his heart pumped enough blood up to the surface to put a stop to his shivering. But no sensation was aroused in the hands. He had an impression that they hung like weights on the ends of his arms, but when he tried to run the impression down, he could not find it.

A certain fear of death, dull and oppressive, came to him. This fear quickly became poignant as he realized

To Build a Fire

that it was no longer a mere matter of freezing his fingers and toes, or of losing his hands and feet, but that it was a matter of life and death, with the chances against him. This threw him into a panic, and he turned and ran up the creek-bed along the old, dim trail. The dog joined in behind and kept up with him. He ran blindly, without intention, in fear such as he had never known in his life. Slowly, as he ploughed and floundered through the snow, he began to see things again—the banks of the creek, the old timber-jams, the leafless aspens, and the sky. The running made him feel better. He did not shiver. Maybe, if he ran on, his feet would thaw out; and, anyway, if he ran far enough, he would reach camp and the boys. Without doubt he would lose some fingers and toes and some of his face; but the boys would take care of him, and save the rest of him when he got there. And at the same time there was another thought in his mind that said he would never get to the camp and the boys; that it was too many miles away, that the freezing had too great a start on him, and that he would soon be stiff and dead. This thought he kept in the background and refused to consider. Sometimes it pushed itself forward and demanded to be heard, but he thrust it back and strove to think of other things.

It struck him as curious that he could run at all on feet so frozen that he could not feel them when they struck the earth and took the weight of his body. He seemed to himself to skim along above the surface, and to have no connection with the earth. Somewhere he had once seen a winged Mercury, and he wondered if Mercury felt as he felt when skimming over the earth.

His theory of running until he reached camp and the boys had one flaw in it: he lacked the endurance. Several times he stumbled, and finally he tottered, crumpled up, and fell. When he tried to rise, he failed. He must sit and rest, he decided, and next time he would merely walk and keep on going. As he sat and regained his breath, he noted that he was feeling quite warm and comfortable. He was not shivering, and it even seemed that a warm glow had come to his chest and trunk. And yet, when he touched his nose or cheeks, there was no sensation. Running would not thaw them out. Nor would it thaw out his hands and feet. Then the thought came to him that the frozen portions of his body must be extending. He tried to keep this thought down, to forget it, to think of something else; he was aware of the panicky feeling that it caused, and he was afraid of the panic. But the thought asserted itself, and persisted, until it produced a vision of his body totally frozen. This was too much, and he made another wild run along the trail. Once he slowed down to a walk, but the thought of the freezing extending itself made him run again.

And all the time the dog ran with him, at his heels. When he fell down a second time, it curled its tail over its forefeet and sat in front of him, facing him, curiously eager and intent. The warmth and security of the animal angered him, and he cursed it till it flattened down its ears appeasingly. This time the shivering came more quickly upon the man. He was losing in his battle with the frost. It was creeping into his body from all sides. The thought of it drove him on, but he ran no more than a hundred feet, when he staggered and pitched headlong. It was his last panic. When he had recovered his breath and control, he sat up and entertained in his mind the conception of meeting death with dignity. However, the conception did not come to him in such terms. His idea of it was that he had been making a fool of himself, running around like a chicken with its head cut off—such was the simile that occurred to him. Well, he was bound to freeze anyway, and he might as well take it decently. With this new-found peace of mind came the first glimmerings of drowsiness. A good idea, he thought, to sleep off to death. It was like taking an anaesthetic. Freezing was

To Build a Fire

not so bad as people thought. There were lots worse ways to die.

He pictured the boys finding his body the next day. Suddenly he found himself with them, coming along the trail and looking for himself. And, still with them, he came around a turn in the trail and found himself lying in the snow. He did not belong with himself any more, for even then he was out of himself, standing with the boys and looking at himself in the snow. It certainly was cold, was his thought. When he got back to the States he could tell the folks what real cold was. He drifted on from this to a vision of the oldtimer on Sulphur Creek. He could see him quite clearly, warm and comfortable.

"You were right, old hoss; you were right," the man mumbled to the oldtimer of Sulphur Creek.

Then the man drowsed off into what seemed to him the most comfortable and satisfying sleep he had ever known. The dog sat facing him and waiting. The brief day drew to a close in a long, slow twilight. There were no signs of a fire to be made, and, besides, never in the dog's experience had it known a man to sit like that in the snow and make no fire. As the twilight drew on, its eager yearning for the fire mastered it, with a great lifting and shifting of forefeet, it whined softly, then flattened its ears down in anticipation of being chidden by the man. But the man remained silent. Later, the dog whined loudly. And still later it crept close to the man and caught the scent of death. This made the animal bristle and back away. A little longer it delayed, howling under the stars that leaped and danced and shone brightly in the cold sky. Then it turned and trotted up the trail in the direction of the camp it knew, where were the other food-providers and fire-providers.

Action

by C. E. Montague

When Christopher Bell was just fifty-two he woke up, one September morning, to feel a slight numbness all down his right side. Some of the numbness was in his right arm; a good deal of it in his right thigh, along its outside, rather less in his right foot; and just a little in his head—all over the hinterland of his right ear.

It seemed a big percentage of a man to "go to sleep" at one time. He lay still for a minute, to let it pass off. But it didn't. So he began to speculate. When he got up, would he be able to stand? And to walk straight? Would his head go on working all right, with that bit of it stiff? Just how hard a punch would it turn out to be, that some god or devil had given him in the night?

He tried. Yes, he could stand, walk, dress, and shave. No portion of him was absolutely on strike. But the numbness went on. And somehow he couldn't feel sure that some part of the right flank of his body or brain would not give way, without notice, and give him a cropper. You never know how deliciously sure you have been of yourself, of every scrap of yourself, all the days of your health, till some small gadget inside you is put out of action: Bell made this deep reflection while going downstairs to his solitary breakfast. He kept one hand on the banisters.

II

Christopher Bell was the reigning sovereign of a respectable dynasty of "merchant princes" in Manchester. For several generations his clan had embraced the higher civilization so far as English public schools and universities lead to such embraces. He had read with understanding and relish, and he had travelled with open eyes. He could value the great things in the arts and in science—indeed, in the whole ampler life of the race. And always, till now, his blood had pretty well bubbled with health. He had rowed, run, swum, and ridden well. To his body, at forty years old, the war had brought a second boyhood of happy absorption in efforts merely physical.

Halfway through the war, the wife he had loved in every tissue of body and soul had died of something brought on by too passionate overwork for the cause. The news came to Bell in a hospital where he had just begun to grow a new skin on a face and hands well flayed and charred by chemical warfare. He could not see at the time, so a nurse read the telegram out. His face was buried deep in a canary-coloured mask of wadding stained with picric acid, so the nurse could not see how he took it—only knew that he thanked her very civilly through the little blowhole left for his mouth. I fancy Bell was hanging on hard to the thought that he still had two children, a boy and a girl, both in their teens. Soldiers, even educated ones, are apt to grow sentimental, especially when wounded. Bell, the war widower, lay, week by week, behind his fancy-dress mask, staying his mind on an ingenious vision of an improved world, to come after the war. He saw it as a young man and a young woman standing in summer twilight, under the stars, with their eyes all a-shine at the loveliness of the life which it had taken so much pain and shame to make possible for them.

Many soldiers hugged these quaint fancies, in their

bad times. They helped, for the moment. It was afterward that they had to be paid for. In the foul enervatory air that filled England and Europe just after the war, Bell's boy and girl drifted feebly into failure. Both were married lovelessly now, each to another small waste product of that waste-producing time. Somewhere out of Bell's sight these forfeited objects of his pride and joy were shuffling punily through life. He gathered that they were rather ashamed of him as an old slow-coach provincial.

Bell was not given to wallowing in self-pity. Still, as you see, he had had his losses, like another.

III

Your merchant prince, in these days, is prone to lose heart, get himself up as an owner of land and beeves, and melt weakly into the common herd of squires who know not, poor fellows, what it is to go on 'Change. Bell was different. He had pride. He stuck, as his father had done, to his post among the garrison of the smutty city that had done well by them. He lived where he could hear the Town Hall clock strike twelve when the traffic was quiet at night, and a northwind blowing. He liked the sound, he was so oddly civic a person.

To this old-fashioned hobby Bell added some cheap habits less rare in rich men. He stood on guard against his wealth, lest it should cut him off from the sight and sound of ordinary and unprincely men, for whom his regard had been redoubled by four years of living with them in the war. Because of this fad he nearly always went in to the city by tram. This morning he walked the three hundred yards from his house to the tram's stopping place with deliberate caution. He could not be sure of that sleepy right leg. He was still distrusting it temperately when he had taken his seat and was tendering his fare to town.

The conductor rejected the tender, at sight. "We doan't taäke boottons," he said with civil composure.

Bell examined the bright disk that he had offered as a sixpence.

Behold! a silvery trouser button. Last night it had come off and he had slipped it into a pocket. He put his finger tips ruefully up to his eyes. "I'm sorry," he said to the man, as he gave the right coin.

"It's aal reet, sir," the conductor said quietly. Once he saw that no pulling of legs had been intended, his tact and sympathy were perfect.

He passed on to collect other fares. But a new care remained in Bell's mind. Sight, too? Was that going? Sight, touch, the whole sensory business, losing precision, entering on the long slope to decay—the silver cord going loose and the golden bowl cracking? When a man who has known how to read feels the first clap of the hand of Time on his shoulder, he has plenty of ready prompters to ruefulness; so many excellent poets have found handsome words for the mists and mellow poignancy of man's autumn, the lapse from old vigour and vision into mere drug-takers' dreams while we are led down the avenue lined with overblown roses, to lie in the dust at its end.

Bell kept his head. But his memory was beginning to bulge with lovely quotations not conducive to high spirits—"Bare ruined choirs where late the sweet birds sang," and all that lot.

IV

The morning's office work did him good, while it lasted. He had more than most men of the gift of forgetting himself in the excitement of getting a job to come right—any old job, the dictating of letters, anything. And just now the affairs of his firm were of quite stirring interest. Like many others it had been making large losses for several years. Bell's game was to keep these losses as low as he could without stopping the work and wages of a moorland villageful of people who spun and wove cotton for Bell to sell for less than it cost to make it. This unacquisitive practice brought Bell into great infamy. Most of his fellow employers wanted to close all the factories down, or half close them down, and leave the work-people to live on their fat. So Bell was an arrant traitor to them. Still, he was an employer: and so, to ardent Socialist eyes, he was a sucker of blood, ex officio. This lively crossfire of censures braced Bell. If it had to be woe unto you when all men spoke well of you, it might be safer when everyone slated you hard. Anyhow it livened you up, like a good stinging wind that has blown across snow. While he schemed to find some not quite ruinous sale for the stuff that piled itself up at the mills, Bell could forget the thing that had clawed him in its clutch during the night.

But the clouds return after the rain: luncheon time set his mind free to worry, the way your sore tongue returns and returns to the amusement of hurting itself on the sharp point of a tooth lately broken. He lunched at the club; and twice in the one hour it took him, his mind accused younger members of paying him the pestilential kind of unarguing deference which is really the civil refusal of youth to keep its communications open with age. Could they have noticed the way he walked down the stairs—a canny way, like a horse's when it is afraid on a slippery slope? One younger man opened the door of the billiard room for him. Damn these good manners that ain't good at all.

Going home at twilight, in the tram, Bell thought over all this so absorbedly that he kept his legs crossed the whole way. So, when he stood up, to get off, his right leg had gone clean asleep. It was only asleep in the common and blameless way. Still, he couldn't know that, at first. For all he could tell, a second stroke might have fallen, and this time a real knockout. Of course he kept his fears dark; still, he stepped off the car with such unconcealable care that the conductor slipped a friendly hand under his arm and led him slowly to the safety of the foot path, like a blind man or a drunk.

Action

When Bell had walked a few yards by himself the extra numbness was gone. But the other numbness remained. And so did the feel of that patiently guarding hand under his arm. Of course he had not needed it. Still, perhaps he would, presently, "Mene, mene, etc."—every wall seemed to be covered with sinister shreds of writing. An object for everybody's protection, a call on everyone's forbearance—that was the kind of pest that he might become. Soon, too, perhaps. This kind of plague crept on and on. It never turned back. Five years might bring an invalid chair and a male nurse to put him to bed and to see that he was carted securely about from place to place, to sprawl in the sun—Mentone, the Canaries, Egypt, all the places to which the passé butterflies of our commonwealth were brought to lie out and doze in the warmth when too much eating and idling had brought them back all the way to the status of larvæ. Disgusting!

V

Bell gazed steadily into this smiling future, while eating his dinner alone. From the table he went straight, like a man who knew what he needed, to that shelf in his study on which there were all his pet Alpine books. No other sport had ever so wholly ravished his soul as mountaineering. On the high snows it seemed as if magical fires were lit in your blood; the flame of life burned amazingly; something was added unto a man as divine as whatever it is that makes its way into the vapid juice of a fruit and turns it to wine. Nowhere else in the world was the taste of success so wholly and indefeasibly sweet as it was on the tip of some spire of granite and ice that had all but turned you back in despair by the Daphnean rigour of its resistance. There, uplifted on the swell of the round earth, you could see how men had come to dream Gardens of Eden and Ages of Gold.

He took from the shelf a great climber's narratives of

his greatest adventures. Two of these, in especial, could always entrance Bell as soon as he had read a few lines: their vividness gave him an almost physical sense of what they described. Each was a case of cutting steps up a long and extremely steep slope of ice. And in each case the slope had, at one point, ceased even to slope. For just a few feet of its height it had become as vertical as the wall of a house: each man of the party had had to hold himself in to the perpendicular wall, by sheer strength and good hand-hold, against gravitation.

In each case the party had come safely through. But with how big a margin of safety, as engineers say? Bell wondered. A pretty big one, he fancied. Few good climbers slipped in really difficult places; all their faculties were bent up too intently for that, with danger about; they were above their own everyday form. But what if such a party were to try paring and paring away at that pretty wide margin? Something like an experiment, that! To what untold heights of achievement might not the party attain before all the margin was gone! And of course the party might be a party of one.

Bell had once had a holiday dream of climbing a crag that grew steeper and steeper till it was vertical first, and then overhung, more and more, but still he climbed on and on because the crag beetled out over a warm summer sea, so that, when he lost hold in the end, he would only fall from one pleasure into another, out of the mountaineer's paradise into a swimmer's. Cut out the old fear of death in that way, or some other, and—why, you could do anything.

As he sat back with the open book on his knees, a light wind stirred the trees in the garden. It may have been this that called up another old notion of his. This one had visited him in a wood close to Arras, in 1916. During some dark windless weeks of that autumn the unfallen leaves had been fading inertly from green to a dull rusty red, and so down to a dead russet brown;

the whole burning heart of the year was collapsing into shabby ashes. Then a night of frost came and then a gale on a day of broken sunshine thrown wildly about between clouds. As the gale stripped the trees it had seemed almost to blow them aflame; sparks of brave yellow flew in the air; the dun beech leaves took light and fell lustrously. Somehow the sight had filled Bell, at the time, with a wish that, when he had to go, he might do it like that—all a-stir and a-glow, by one of the "violent" deaths, as most of the easy ones seemed to be called. Anything but to lie on a bed in a hushed room, with the lights low and life's jolly noises shut out, and people whispering among the shadows. One wrench for the undecayed body, and then unbreakable sleep—what end could equal it?

Now, almost suddenly, these several notions ran into one, as raindrops do on a newly wet window. Here was the moment to put into practice that old and sound choice of his between the long decrepitude of the flesh and the one clean cut and summary pang that saved you it all. Suicide? Oh! no. But just to carry on, right to the end, the piquant experiment of paring and paring away that limiting and restraining margin of safety which mountaineers, even the boldest, keep in reserve. Had not all things conspired to free him from too much love of remaining alive—bereavement and baulked hope and now this first lick of fire from heaven, soon to blast the whole of him by degrees? Why, fate had brought him the fulfilment of his old dream. No precipice in the world would now have an abhorred death waiting at its foot—merely a warm, quiet sea of painless forgetfulness.

Only—he must be quick, before the accursed thing that was setting to work on him could pith so much of the vigour out of his body that he could not make his own way to a place—already he had a good place in his mind—where he might try the thing out.

VI

At the end of September a savoursome blend of jollity and melancholy pervades the little Val d'Anniviers. The summer hotels of Zinal, at the head of the valley, are closing. Down the bridle path, through forests of fir, the hotel staffs stream along joyously, laden with the year's vintage of tips, to their snug winter homes in the Rhone Valley below. Reconverted, after four months of restraint and disguise, into young, natural Swiss men and women, they caper like Alpine cows let out in the spring. Shouting, chaffing, and singing, they seem to flout with their merriment Nature's yearly menace to marmots and men. And Nature answers them back. Almost hour by hour the new snow creeps down the forested slopes of the valley and grizzles more of its firs; the morning dew lies late, and even at noon the weakening sun hangs lazily low above the main chain of the Alps. You feel, all about you, a big closing-in, the rustle of a heavy curtain falling upon a good time that is played out at last.

As Bell walked the six miles up from Cissoye to Zinal, he breasted that jovial current of waiters and chambermaids thawed and rehumanized. Jove! they were good to see and to hear, with their jokes and catches and bold, friendly, unobsequious looks at any man and brother they met. But everything was good in this place. Even the smell of Vissoye and its pigs, as he passed, had been the smell of the best holiday of his boyhood. How he had liked life—every bit of it, coloured or plain, the high lights and the low! Even the jars had been part of the makings of the incomparable adventure. He wondered whether the mere feel of things—common things, all sorts of things—could ever have given anyone else such raptures of secret contentment as they had given to him.

He had made sure of a room at Zinal. He dined by the light of one lamp in a corner of the hotel's dining room, now empty and shadowy. An elderly woman waited upon him; everyone else in the house had gone down the valley; she had been left for a week or two more, to cook, wait, make a bed, and draw out a bill for anyone mad enough to turn up so belatedly. Bell had known her for thirty years—ever since her marriage to an old guide of his, recently killed on the Meije. She told him how their son Pierre was now a guide too, rather to her alarm. She seemed amazingly glad to see Bell, as if he were a bit of some good old world that had been slipping away. And he—? she asked. Was he making a *grande course*, as always? Surely not, at this time of year?

He fenced with her apt, friendly questions. He felt like a liar. Indeed, he was one, pretty well; for he fully meant to deceive. He would go for a walk by himself, he said, after breakfast to-morrow—perhaps to the Arpitetta Alp only, perhaps, rather farther.

She looked at him sadly, with peasant directness. "All alone now!" she said simply. "And once it was you and Madame—and Gaspard and me. Ah! the good times." She had all humanity's fate in her face, like an old woman drawn by Rembrandt—hopes and happy love and then the dust of the day, dimming the roses, and then great loneliness and unconsolable tears. Would Monsieur have coffee? she asked.

Bell could face her no longer. It was too treacherous. No, he said, he would want nothing more. Let her go to bed early, like all the good marmots. So would he, too, when he had smoked a little end of tobacco.

When she was gone, he sat by a fire of log she had lit for him in the small smoking room. To his surprise he found he had nothing to do. There could be no saying good-bye, no specious last letter to write, no will to be made, no manifesto of any sort to be left. People do not do such things just before unforeseen accidents— for the wood must look raw at the break. A real good tip for the widow of Gaspard would have to be left in an obvious place: that was all.

It went beyond having nothing to do. There was nothing to think. He had no fear of post-mortem torture to busy his brain, for the God of his faith was no fiend. He was equally void of covetous hopes of a sensational "good time" when the breath should be out of his body. So far he might have expected his mind to be free. The strange thing was to find how much of one's usual matter for thought is taken away if, in twenty hours or so, one will have nothing whatever to fix up or to see to, no house or business to run, no social beat to patrol, no arts or letters to care for, nor "public duties" to mind. It was a release. But it was a queer one—a kind of vacuous and disquieting freedom, such as a man might attain who was suddenly let off the pressure of gravitation, so that he needn't keep his feet down to the earth any more—in fact, couldn't press on it hard if he tried, and so couldn't get any purchase for putting forth his strength upon anything at all. Bell's released mind did its best to think firmly of what he was going to do the next day. But no firmness came: the levers of thought could not find any fulcrum; they worked at a loss feebly and fumblingly.

He brought over the lamp to review the Inn's tiny library—two shelves freakishly peopled with the printed leavings of guests lettered, half-lettered, unlettered, conventional, independent, and odd. There was the common aphrodisiac novel of commerce; there was *The Vicar of Wakefield,* all golden sunshine and wit; there were Nat Gould and the wise, humane book of the great William James on the incessant endeavour of men to find or to imagine some larger life on which to rest the frail and soon-tired figure of their own. Yes, that was it: something to lean against; something sure not to give when you put your whole weight on it, in any state of yourself; that was where peace and strength were to be had; nowhere else. So he fancied, at least; he could not be sure; he was still in that vacuum where his thoughts had no pivot to work on; the wheels did not bite on the road; the cogs would not engage; he thought and he felt, but gropingly, not with the sure and eager drive of a mind and heart that have found themselves by forgetting themselves.

VII

The place that Bell had picked for his purpose was on the west side of the Schallijoch. The Schallijoch, as you may know, is a dip in the ridge that joins the Weisshorn to the Schallihorn. Even the lowest point of the dip is more than 12,000 feet high. The last part of the rise to the ridge from the west is up one of the steepest slopes of ice that are climbed. That is, if you mount it where it is least steep. At some other points it is steeper than any slope that is climbed, or thought to be climbable. The surface of this wall of ice undulates like a sheet of hammered copper—here a concave patch and there a convex one. Though the wall, at its steepest, leans back from the straight, as a whole, it has parts—the upper halves of these hollows and lower of these bulges—at which it is vertical for some feet at a time; and at two or three parts it even overhangs slightly. These last, avoided by climbers happily wedded to life, were what Bell had in mind. He would start up the wall at the steepest part he could find; as he went on, he would make, at each stage, for the point where there seemed to be most an overhang. He would do the thing honestly—try all that was in him to bring the climb off, reach the ridge and prove that, in this small matter, man could do more than he knew. With careful timing he would be up, if up at all, about dusk. In that unlikely event he would carry the test a step further and try to come down his ice ladder by feel, in the dark, instead of descending the gentle snow slopes on the eastern side of the pass.

He worked out a time-table. Three hours' work up to the Arpitetta Alp from Zinal. Three more up from the Alp to the foot of the final ice wall. Half an hour for eating; another half hour for sundries. Four for the ultimate work on the wall. Eleven hours in all. Tomorrow's evening dusk would be over by seven. He would push off at eight in the morning.

VIII

Probably you would have thought him rather a pleasant sight as he quitted Zinal—the outward figure of a hale, fit mountaineer; just a little stricken with years, but vigorous; brindled but not at all bald; leanly and brownly good-looking, turning out by himself, with his ax under his arm and a little luncheon in his pocket, for a walk among the feet of sporting old friends like the Weisshorn and Rothhorn. How can you tell by the looks of a man that he would not feel the point of a pin if you ran it into his thigh, or that this exemption from pain is causing any disturbance of his spirits?

Nobody was to be seen at the emerald Alp of Arpitetta. Like the almost deserted Zinal, like yesterday's valley path streaming with walkers carrying bundles, the empty hovels on the Alp recalled the sight of a whole countryside in flight before the army of an invader. The ashes left from the cheese-maker's fire were wet with drippings from the roof; the rough wooden crane used for swinging the cauldron over the flames flapped in a draught from the door. Outside, the intoxicant beauty of gentian and orchis was over for the year; the rich grass had spread back over the trodden mud of the milking place; but snow was lying a few hundred feet higher up. The invader was near.

Bell's legs were liking the work. The numb one was numb, but it did not give out; it would not let him down. By one o'clock he had reached the tail end—some would call it the snout—of the big Weisshorn Glacier, eaten his rations, and set a first foot on the rough convex swell of honeycombed ice with water flushing out its millions of cells; for the sun was on it. He pawed the stuff tenderly with his ax. Perdition catch his soul but

Action

he did love it—strong as iron, carvable as cheese: what genius could have conceived so delicious a union of opposites if, by some disaster, no glaciers had been made.

By three o'clock he was through the freak shapes of the ice fall, across the snowfield above it, and close to the wall that he sought. Yes, its great width and height had the wavy surface that he remembered. It showed like a vast relief map of some low-rolling downland, modelled in ice and then set up to stand on its edge. Off to his right, as he looked up, the general angle was easiest. That was the regular way—very steep but quite practicable. That was of no use for his purpose. Far away to his left the slope looked ferocious enough. But down it an almost continuous fall of stones of all sizes, broken away from the sun-warmed rocks of the Weisshorn, came sliding and hissing, or bounding and smashing explosively. That was no use either. That way would be suicide, not experiment.

He soon saw what he wanted—almost directly above him. There, nearly all the way up to the ridge, the ice was steep and bare and blue, and the face of it waved more at this place than anywhere else. Several broad bosses of rocks must have underlain the smooth surface. Over these the close-fitting ice swelled like a stocking upon a bent knee. Up to the centre of each of these bosses it bulged out overhangingly; just above each centre it would recede at a more merciful angle; but nowhere in the whole thousand feet of ascent would a man have a foothold to stand on, unless he made it.

Bell conscientiously tightened each boot lace and puttee string. Then he set off for the point where he had descried the best overhangs. It was halfway, as he judged, to the top of the wall. If he should conquer that one, then he would look for another, more bulgy.

He cut his steps with almost fanatical care. He had a disagreeable sense of doing something furtive: he couldn't help asking himself, against his own will,

"What if somebody saw?" Damn somebody, another part of him said. Still, he cut every step as if he defied the whole solar system to say that it was not the work of a good craftsman bent upon keeping alive. So, he rose slowly. It took a good two hours' work to mount a third of the way to the ridge. But then he was close to what mattered more—the great bulge that he was making for.

The bulge stood out like a gigantic blister upon the face of the ice. It must have been forty feet in diameter and it jutted so much that a stone dropped from its outermost point would only have touched the slope again some fifty feet lower. So the climax had come. To reach that outermost point he would have to climb for about twenty feet as you climb up the under side of a ladder that leans against a wall. And he would have to make the ladder, rung by rung, as he climbed it—fashion each rung out of the ice with his ax, held in one hand, while with the other hand and both feet he clung to three of the rungs made already, and held up the body against the drag of its weight. Every rung would have to be made like a letter box in a door, big enough for the toe of a boot to go in, but so shaped that, when a hand entered, the fingers could bend down inside and grip as you grip the top of a fence. The grand, the crucial question was how long one hand and one arm could hold the body in to the projecting ice wall. For what part of the two hours or so that the other labouring hand might require to cut that fantastical staircase? Of course, if his ax should slip out of his hand, or if one step should break, that would end the affair. But away with the thought of any such bungling.

The moment the overhang started Bell discovered the theory of gravitation to be exceedingly true. The work was amazingly hard. When he had carved five letter boxes, and used them, an hour had gone. He carved five more and observed that daylight was failing. Behind his back an unsensational sunset was going on at its ease. His left hand was chilled almost dead with all the ice it had gripped; his right wrist was swollen and sore with the intensity of the ax work; his right knee had begun to shake as uncontrollably as chattering teeth; he heard his breath as if it were somebody else's: it made a dry rustling noise, like a bird struggling silently in the hand.

The centre of the boss was now, he reckoned, some eight feet above his head. Beyond it he could see nothing as yet but a tranquil sky with a rose-coloured flush dying out of it. Five letter boxes more, he thought, might take him up to the nipple of this frozen breast and bring the receding slope of its upper half into his sight. It was just at this point that it struck him as a clear, sober matter of fact that he could not get up those eight feet. His strength was running out fast: one more good letter box was all that he could conceive himself able to make. He made it, hacking away with slow, painful strokes, his ax handle slippery with his sweat. He reached up his left hand to grab the new hold and dragged a foot up to its new place below. Then, just to go down fighting, he went through the movements of starting to chip out yet another step. Second by second the effort held out; his strokes were the taps of a child; his wrist felt like breaking; yet somehow he finished the hole and forced his left hand to rise up to it; then he even hauled up in its turn a right foot of infinite weight; the poor quivering knee had to straighten out next, and did it, after a long, doubtful struggle. But that was the end, he felt, of all possible effort.

By this time all his senses had the morbid exultation that will sometimes come of fierce physical effort. His mind was at leisure, after a fashion. He was fully aware of the sunset; he did not miss the charm of its sabbatical calm; the majesty and mystery of mountains were still there, all right. A verse he had liked as a boy came into his head, as beautiful things that have built themselves into your mind are apt to do at a crisis—as people who once went to church will cry out "Oh! God" when a smash comes.

> "And here indeed might death be fair
> If death be dying into air
> And souls evanished mix with the
> Illumined sky, eternal sea."

But no pretty dying for him, if death could be still headed off. He started desperately to try again, sweating and straining. No good: the feeble strokes of his ax scarcely scratched the bare ice; his left hand was frostbitten now, past feeling anything. Only five feet to relative safety, but five more than any spur worn by his will could drive the spent body. "I'm done," he said, and ceased to struggle upward.

IX

Some innate impulse to take the thing well and not let human dignity down at a pinch kept him resolved to hold on, foot and hand, to the last moment possible.
While he clung so, the sun left him. A high Alpine sunset is sudden, like tropical ones. A cold, sharp-edged shadow raced up from the valley, chasing the sunlight before it. Pursuer and fugitive scudded up over the tops of the firs and across the bright green of the Alp Bell had passed, and then up the ice fall and on up the wall till the shadow came down like a great frigid hand on the sweaty back of his neck. Next moment the last warmth and light fleeted up out of sight, over the bulge. As his gaze followed, his cheeks felt the sting of a few falling granules of ice; little chips of it, rather; even a few rather big ones. A trickle of ice scraps seemed to be sliding down the upper half of the bulge, to dive into space on reaching its centre —most of them clear of his back.

Queer! Was an ice avalanche coming? No need to

suppose it, though. Glaciers, crushed and huddled things, always heaving and cracking, played curious tricks and ground out all sorts of freak rubbish. Oh! let the ice do what it liked, all his business with it was done; all that he could now attend to was a kind of dream noise, big, muted and almost asleep, that the torrent was making, enormously far off, down in the blackening trench of the valley—that and a kind of emotional dream of himself, the dying man doing his best to take leave as was meet—a figure at which he could look, as it were, from outside, and dreamily feel it to be rather touching.

Into this semidream there managed to enter, also, a sound more abrupt—a little noise like the low startled cry that some women give when they see a horse fall or a big window is smashed. The cry worked itself into his dream, but also it roused him. "Getting light-headed," he thought. But he wasn't. Almost as quick as that thought, a new sound, a light hissing rub, rushed down to his ears and an ice ax slid over the bulge overhead and out into the air: it whizzed past the back of his head.

To anyone versed in high mountains an ice ax loose and falling in any such place is a portent of horror, like a child's pony galloping riderless home or a boat adrift, bottom uppermost, in a Thames lasher. It means that somebody may have just lost the power to move, without help, at a place where a man unable to move will soon be unable to live. Suddenly Bell's mind took eyes to itself; it saw a party of some sort above him, trying to cut its way down the ice wall, straight toward the deadly bulge that now beetled over himself. At this hour! And by such a route! They must be mad; so he thought—forgetting himself. And now one of them was disabled—perhaps had disabled the whole of his party —tethered it to the ice wall. The idea was frightful to Bell.

Another sound came. From somewhere not far overhead there broke, like an explosion, the singular cry that Swiss peasants and some mountaineers employ as a long-distance hail. No other noise of purely human production will carry so far. Harsh, wild, and long, it starts, as the noise of a rocket does, at its maximum loudness, and then wails itself out in a dying fall that has an effect of collapse into despair. Though commonly uttered on quite cheerful occasions, it might be the passionate scream of some wretched animal terrified by the solitude of a desolate place and trying to empty, into one impetuous lamentation, all its burden of loneliness and desire.

Bell held his breath as the sinking shriek thinned away into silence. Then he counted off the seconds half aloud, by guesswork, as bomb throwers learned how to do in the war. The count ran to seven—eight—nine—and, just as Bell was muttering "Ten," the great yell smashed into the silence again. Yes: he had expected that. Someone above was in the last extremity of danger—was trying the last shift of all, the most all-but-hopeless of all—was sending out the Alpine signal of distress into this stone and snow desert where autumn and night had joined to make it utterly certain that no answer could come. It was like praying to God, for dear life, that a well of fresh water might open itself in the dry middle of the Sahara.

X

Up to that point of time, as you have seen, Bell had been the kind of dual creature that most of us are for nearly the whole of our days. Part of him had toiled, sweated, and ached, and another part of him had been sorry for that one. But, from the moment the second yell came, this twofold arrangement was somehow abolished. All craving or need for any part of himself to be troubled about any other was over; now there was nothing at all to work out any more, no next move to be consciously planned, nor hesitant will to be coaxed or hustled, nor any plaguey choice to be made.

Action

All of the man was one unit at last, and it lived intently and intensely, moved by some force which it had no more desire to question than flames have to ask, "Why burn upward?"

The next mystery was that out of the mind so suddenly lightened there seemed, as it were, to overflow lightness into Bell's body of lead. Strangely empowered, his left foot was rising already to thrust itself into the next letter box; almost gaily his right arm, freed from its preoccupation with pain, was beginning to hack a new hand hold above. How long it took him to make he could not have told, then or after. For time, too, was abolished; long trains of executive, practical thought could run on to their end instantaneously; courses, whole courses, of study of relevant things—of the state of the ice, minute changes of gradient, the swift regelation following sundown—were carried out without any sense of duration. One of the revelatory trances had come, in which even a plain man sees for once that an eternity need not be long and that in a single moment he may have everlasting life.

A minor, but still a piquant, discovery was that he had never really known till now what it was to cut a good sizable strip off that old margin of safety which he had imagined himself to have all but used up. His new letter boxes were marvels of sketchy adequacy; they were high art in the skimpiness of the means that they took to their end; triumphs of confident "cheek" to Nature, they bluffed that august power quite wittily. Almost before the vocalist overhead had completed the long S O S of the mountains—it takes three minutes in all—Bell had his chest up to the dead centre of the bulge and saw what he had come for.

Some thirty feet higher up, a woman in mountain kit, with no ax and no hold for hand or foot, was dangling at a long rope's end. Her body revolved a little as it hung against the steep ice, but she was making no voluntary movement. The rope constricting her chest was held with one straining hand by a man perched eighty feet higher up. He was clearly unable to move, hand or foot, without being dragged off his stance by the weight of the woman. He stood on one foot—his right: it seemed to be firmly placed on a tiny step; and a little above his hand he had the pick of his ax driven well into the ice. To the steel bracket thus formed by the ax head the man was holding on stoutly with his right hand.

The sorry sight explained itself. The woman must have been cutting steps down the slope; she must have slipped from a step, and dropped her ax with the shock. The man had checked her fall well, but both were hung up as immovably as a couple of stoats nailed to a gamekeeper's door. And now the rope must be slowly killing the woman. Just as Bell's head topped the bulge she called out in a strangled voice to the man: "Can you cut the rope, Teddy? I'm done, anyhow. Think of the kiddies. You *must*." The man held on.

Bell gave tongue as loud as the dry brown fur lining his mouth would allow. "Well held, sir," he roared. "It's all right, I'm coming."

Not once in a long and respectable Alpine career had Bell thought he would ever entrust his person to ledges quite so narrow as those on which he made the rest of his way up to that pendant woman. And yet he had never, in any hard place, felt such absolute freedom from any uneasiness. As he romped up, he sang out, at intervals: "There in three minutes," "Just two minutes more," "Only one minute more," "Half a shake—I'm just there." Then he arrived. He cut a big step close to where the woman's feet hung, planted his own firmly on it, and then stooping and straightening up again, took the weight of her, sitting, on his right shoulder. Lest she be fainting he put up his right hand behind her, to hold her in place.

She was no fainter, though she was white, yellow, greenish—all the bad colours that beauty itself may have to put on in bad times. "She's a good 'un," Bell thought, as she sat quiet, panting.

"*You're* a great sportsman," she gasped, when she had breath enough.

Feeling all the weight off the rope of a sudden, the man above shouted down thickly, "Sure you have got her, sir?"

"Right as rain," she called up from her perch.

Bell added: "Leave the rope slack, and dig in. We'll come up when you're comfy."

The man gave a tuneless yodel of joy and was plying his ax the same instant; chips and wedges of ice came pelting down from the great step that he must be cutting, from which to make the whole caravan fast. In five minutes he ceased hacking, braced himself, drew in the slack of the rope and announced that now he could hold up a cow for a day.

Bell let the woman cannily down till her feet found a trim ledge that he had managed to scratch out while holding her up. But some four or five feet of smooth ledgeless ice intervened between this and the lowest step the woman had cut, coming down, before she slipped off. Some new ones had to be made. "Care to cut 'em?" Bell asked. "Or shall I?"

She ruefully opened the hands in which no ax was now held. "I dropped it," she said, "like a mug. I feel sick with shame."

"Have mine," he said, holding it out.

Her open boy face shone with joyous relief, as if at a a gift of free absolution from sin. Even now their lives hung on this ax that he was entrusting to her, the convicted ax dropper. She took it. "You are a very generous person," she said. "Now I'll unrope, and go up by myself, and you shall tie on."

He shook his hear firmly. "You mustn't unrope."

Her eyes broke out in a quick sparkle of anger. "You've *got* to rope up," she said, flushing. "I know that I've done a dud thing and can't preach. But what about you? Climbing alone! coming up out of nowhere, almost at night. Up a worse slope than this beast! Think it bears looking into? Eh? Well, do you mean to rope up, or shall both of us climb in this way that you seem to think right?"

Bell fairly funked the scrutiny of the young woman's spirited simplicity. When once simplicity sets out to inquire, what else is so penetrating? "Well, you tie on in the middle," he said, "and I at the end."

"That's fair," she agreed. A few feet of spare rope were let down by her husband. In two or three minutes, at most, the man who would have shuffled off the mortal coil was securely girt with the most delectable of its loops, the cheerfullest symbol of human determination not to withdraw from the banquet of life—only to salt a dish now and then with a few little hazards.

XI

The last daylight was gone when the three stood safe on the level roof of the ridge, scrunching its gritty granular snow somewhat shyly, though partly kept in countenance by the dark, which is itself a shy, friendly thing. Bell, now a mere dual creature again, had been wondering, all the way up the last flight of ice stairs, how he should give these married lovers a chance to reassert their lately threatened right to possession of each other's lips. Best, he thought, just to turn his back on them when he got up, and try to look busy, coiling the rope.

But they also seemed to have some sort of plan. The man was waiting above the last step, to shake Bell by the hand—really to shake him—and mumbling something which Bell did not desire to make out more clearly. The cup of his consternation was filled when the lady raised his disengaged hand to her lips, a gesture for which he had not been prepared by her vivacity lower down.

Then, with one silent consent, they all stampeded away from the key of emotion. "You travel light, sir," said Bell, just to say something trivial. The other two seemed to carry not so much as a prune or a biscuit between them.

"Well—" said the man, and then Bell imagined the man must be having a quiet laugh in the dark.

"Oh! I know I can't talk," Bell admitted. "The fact is I didn't expect to be coming right over the Pass."

"Same here," said the man. "We just walked up from Randa—meant to go only as far as the hut for the Wiesshorn, eat our sandwiches there, and go back to dinner. Then—it *was* rather mad, but the snow was so toppingly good—we thought we might just rush the Schallijoch before dark, sleep at Zinal, and come back tomorrow."

"Gosh, it was rash!" exclaimed Bell, off his guard. He felt sure, the next instant, the man was quite seeing the humour of such a rebuke from such a sinner. Hastily trying to cover the slip, Bell made another. He asked, "How on earth did you miss the way down?"

The man didn't exactly say, "How did *you* miss the way up?" but he did say, "Yes, it was stupid, but—well, you know how it isn't so easy to see a way down from above as it is from below?"

"Hadn't we better push off?" said Bell rather hurriedly. "We'll be getting friz, up here." But it was not the cold that he minded. It was the heat. It felt as if he couldn't move his tongue without burning his fingers.

The three truants had luck. Just such a full moon as they needed, not having a lantern, was on the point of rising from behind the snowy mass of the Mischabel, beyond the forest glen of the Visp. The mounting light could no longer contain itself. Its bright animation was pulsing up the dark violet of the sky in tremulous waves. It would be easy, by such a light as was coming, to follow the downward track left by the couple, on their way up, almost to the door of the old Weisshorn hut, a refuge squat, squalid, flea-haunted and cramped, but divinely rich in raw materials for manufacturing heat, against a long night of hard frost.

At any time it is rather exciting to walk in the dark, and in silence, with anyone whom you like but don't yet know very well. What is he thinking about? You? And, if so, in what way? Barring you? Liking you? Wanting to throw down the conventional fence and talk frankly? An hour or two of this blindfold contact between mind and mind may so work on them both that when their eyes meet under a lamp at the end of the walk it may feel as if they had had a long and intimate conversation, leaving each of them just slightly anxious to know that the other has taken nothing amiss. Even thus, with friendly and deprecatory looks, did Bell and the strangers regard each other by candle-light two hours later, among the strong shadows and smells of the hut.

In ten minutes more the man's wife, who had walked like a true Joan of Arc, was exercising the blessed privilege of healthy and tired young people of thirty or so. While she slept like a prosperous babe, her man and Bell smoked as they lay in the hay at the big sleeping shelf's other end. Smoking helps to keep talk good. A man can puff at his pipe between each thing he really wants to say and the next. No gap-filling rubble is required.

Bell ascertained first that the man's name was Gollen and that he was a doctor—the Harley Street species of doctor. Bell gave in return his own name and description. Then they enjoyed one of those unembarrassing pauses. Then Bell said, somewhat brusquely, "There's one thing we have to get straight."

"Go it," said Gollen.

"You seem to imagine you're under some sort of obligation to me."

"Well, you see, we're alive. And, before you appeared, our number was up."

"So was mine."

"Oh! everyone's is, in a sense. 'All condemned to death,' doesn't somebody say, 'with an indefinite reprieve.' But ours wasn't indefinite. We were booked to go West in five minutes."

"I was to do it in one. In less. I should have dropped off my holds in ten seconds if you people hadn't blown in."

"Hullo?"

"Sure thing. I was done. I had never known until then how far doneness could go. That's how it felt, anyhow. Then your wife's ax came along. That by itself held me on for a jiffy or two. And then you hollered— gad! you *can* holler—and everything changed. There was something new in me, or round me, at work on me somehow. Every bit of soreness and worry and funk was taken right off me—nothing was left in the world but one energy—just an enveloping, mastering sort of a push. It went up like a flame and it took me along —it made everything easy and light. And it wasn't only a thing in the mind. Old brother body himself was roped into the movement: some of the waft of this impulse seemed to get itself into my muscles. D'you follow these ravings?"

"Rather. Physicians aren't the fools that they were. We don't go on missing out what the mind—or the soul, if you like—has to say to all the dynamic affairs of the body."

Bell puffed his pipe for a while. Then he said, "See? That's how you two preserved me. So if thanking is what we're about, thanky kindly."

Gollen, too, smoked in silence for the next minute or two, before asking, "The ice overhung where you were when I first caterwauled?"

"Can't tell you the angle. Hadn't got a clinometer thing. Of course it wasn't a motoring road."

Gollen laughed. Bell liked Gollen's face when he laughed, so far as it could be seen among the tangle of wry shadows thrown about the hut by a small flame that still leapt in the stove. Gollen's face made Bell think of a trade term—"good ordinary." He had blunt goodish features, strong and good tempered. A straight, friendly man, you would say, and easily amused; a good man to be in a hole with. Bell enjoyed such men. They made the world go round. As he was thinking so, Gollen suddenly asked, "I say—why did you do it?"

As Bell did not answer at once, Gollen added, "Of course, it's cheek—asking. Tell me to go to hell, if you like, and I'll warmly approve. Only, well—I'm a doctor."

Bell cut the thing short. He answered at once what Gollen might go on to ask in another few minutes. "Yes—the spring's running dry. The salt losing its savour, you know—the wine going flat. And worse coming."

Again Gollen did the bold thing. "Any particular evil?" he said.

Bell liked the man. And when two men would both have been dead a few hours ago if either had failed at a pinch, they may soon get on terms. Bell avowed the whole business—his symptoms, his surmises and disgusts, and his specious experiment.

Gollen listened, as wise doctors do. "Did that numbness cramp you to-day?" he asked at the end.

"No. But it was there all the day—except just the time—ten minutes or so, I suppose—when—" Bell hesitated for a moment.

"When you were in action?" said Gollen.

"Action?"

"Oh! I don't mean just doing violent things out of doors—pressing triggers or lassoing cows. I mean getting every Jack fibre there is in your nature alive and utterly turned on to something outside you—absorbed in it, lost in it—every bit of your consciousness taken up into some ecstasy of endeavour that's passion and peace."

Bell nodded, and Gollen went on: "I guess the great artists—all sorts of 'em—know how to bring the fit on, or it comes when they're at the top of their form—they seem to get further and further above 'emselves—hold the note out in a way that we can't—bring every tissue they have in their being to bear on the effort to get a wee touch to come right. Saints, too, I suppose—the pukka ones, like Francis, the man at Assisi: they have the knack too: they can get more alive; they've found how to exist at a sort of top pressure. I fancy all of us get just a glimpse of the thing now and then—of what living might be, you know—at a great turn in a game, or when we're in love, or if some beautiful thing in a book bowls us over. Only, we can't hold the note, or we can't do it yet: the pitch is too high for our reach; so we flop back into flatness. But we shall get there. I do believe that. What we've done since we started as jelly-fish is to get more and more of ourselves into action, and we shall go on until we are as much more in action —real true action—than now, as we are now than when we were jellyfish. Why, in a few thousand years we may all be able to live half our time as you lived to-day for ten minutes."

"Something in that," Bell assented.

Gollen apologized meekly. "Sorry to verge upon 'uplift.' Still, one can't always bother about the convention that talk has got to be pessimist piffle."

Bell nodded. Reigning conventions had few less dutiful followers than he.

They smoked again for a while. Presently Gollen said, "How goes the weather?" He rose and opened the door of the hut very quietly. Bell followed him out to the hut's tiny terrace.

Nothing at all was wrong with that night. Beyond the queenly white shape of Mont Rose the moon rode gloriously high, burnished and flashing with frost, above sleeping Lombardy. Gowned in new snow and bejewelled with sparkles of light the Weisshorn, the greatest great lady in nature, looked as lovely to Bell as when the first sight of that pale supreme grace had taken his breath away in his youth. At the height where they stood the frost had silenced every trickle of water, leaving all space to be filled with subtler challenges to the ear. The air almost crackled with crispness: it was alive with the massed animation of millions of infinitesimal crystallizations. The Schalliberg Glacier, a little away to their right, had its own living whisper, the sum of the innumerable tiny creaks and fractures of its jostling molecules of ice. Up here, where the quiet of night was suffused with this audible stir of the forces fashioning the earth, it felt as if some murmurous joint voice of all existence were abroad and life itself were trying to make its high urgency felt.

"Pretty good!" Gollen said presently.

"Yes, it's all right," answered Bell.

Gollen waited a minute or two. Then he asked, "Is it all right—enough?"

"Oh! yes," said Bell. "I'm sticking on."